THIS IS WHO I AM

OTHER HARPER BLISS NOVELS

Our Secret Summer
Nothing Heals Me Like You Do
I Hope That I Don't Fall in Love With You
Still the One
The Love We Make
A Family Affair
The Duet
And Then She Kissed Me
That Woman Next Door
About That Kiss
At Your Most Beautiful
A Breathless Place
If You Kiss Me Like That
Two Hearts Trilogy
Next in Line for Love
A Lesson in Love
Life in Bits (with T.B. Markinson)
A Swing at Love (with Caroline Bliss)
Once Upon a Princess (with Clare Lydon)
In the Distance There Is Light
The Road to You
Far from the World We Know
Seasons of Love
Release the Stars
At the Water's Edge
High Rise (The Complete Collection)

THE PINK BEAN SERIES

THE FRENCH KISSING SERIES

THIS IS WHO I AM

HARPER BLISS

Published by Ladylit Publishing – an imprint of First Page V.O.F., Belgium
ISBN-13 9789464339574
D/2025/15201/05
Edited by Cheyenne Blue
Proofread by Claire Jarrett
Cover design by Bailey McGinn

For Sophie Lennox, my long-time beta reader.
This one's for you, friendo.

CHAPTER 1
CASS

"Not again," I mutter under my breath as I try to stop the inevitable. It's like trying to stop the tide outside. A hot flash doesn't wait for an opportune moment. Or as my late mother always said: "Menopause is nature's way of letting you know you're not the boss of anything—especially your own body."

I move away from the stove and shout for Kelly. She doesn't need me to say anything. She's used to it by now.

"Step out for a moment, Boss," she says. "I'll take over."

"Thanks," I manage to say as a heat wave crashes over me from the inside, drenching me, instantly, in a layer of sweat. I stumble out of the back door of the restaurant but, as I make my way outside, bump my hip against the edge of a shelf in the pantry.

"Fucking fuck." Another bruise. Another way for my crumbling body to let me down.

I pull my chef's whites away from my chest to let some of the cool ocean breeze waft over my skin—not that it helps.

I know it's not true—highly irrational even—but for a few seconds I let myself believe that this particularly nasty and highly inconvenient flash is caused by Sarah's presence in the restaurant. That she somehow controls my menopausal fate, which is bullshit—it's just why she left me.

I try to control my breathing and repeat the mantra Suzy taught me. *It's just for now and now is already over.*

Although always annoying and embarrassing and making me feel that my life as I always knew it is well and truly over, it's also true that my hot flashes recede as swiftly and abruptly as they arrive. But the long minutes that they last are plenty to ruin a perfectly good evening.

I remove my chef's hat and wave it in my face, trying to produce airflow. Why do I still have an open kitchen? I will find a way to close it off from the dining room for as long as menopause lasts. Not only is it highly unappetizing for customers to see me like this, but it's also humiliating—despite what Suzy says. She keeps repeating that I'm a woman in her fifties and this is completely normal and natural. That it's only our patriarchal society which has ingrained in me that this automatically renders me disgusting and over-the-hill. Someone who needs to hide in the shadows, especially when overcome by another fucking hot flash.

The patriarchy be damned, but right now I feel more like a sweaty mess than the owner and acclaimed head chef of Savor. The two don't go together. It's impossible to swagger into the kitchen feeling like this. Like I'm someone else—a far lesser version of who I used to be.

The heat drains from my body. It's a chilly spring evening in Clearwater Bay with a crisp wind coming off the Pacific. I'll get cold if I don't make my way inside again soon. I don my hat, take another breath, and pretend I'm a chef in complete control of her kitchen.

My hip stings and my ego is a little bruised as well—I'm not sure if I'm ready for the jibes that will surely follow from my staff. While humor might soften the awkwardness for others, I can't find the funny side of this yet.

"Are you good?" Kelly, my trusty sous-chef, asks.

"Yeah," I say, which is a lie and the truth at the same time. I'm good for now; good to finish tonight's service, but I'm not good in general.

I resume my place behind the stove and try not to look into the dining room. Sarah and I broke up three years ago. I'm over it—have been for a long time. But it's what she stands for. It's how she reminds me of all the things I'm not or couldn't be for her.

We're civil enough—her dining here with her new wife proves that—but we'll never be those lesbian exes who become best friends. I never actually banned her, but it was an unspoken rule that, after we broke up, she would no longer frequent my business. It went without saying. It was the only respectful outcome. But time does heal most wounds and if not heal, at least makes them easier to live with. I can live with it—with all the things I'm not.

"Did you see?" Kelly whispers in my ear. "She's here again, scribbling away in her notebook."

"It's Friday evening, so yeah." My gaze is drawn to the Black woman sitting alone at a table by the window. She couldn't look more serious, more studious if she tried. She never looks like she's here to have a good time, although she keeps coming back, so she must enjoy my food.

"What the hell is she writing?" Kelly muses. "My money is still on her being a restaurant critic."

"A critic who comes back every Friday night for three weeks in a row?" I shake my head. "That's just too weird."

"Or maybe things just change."

"Coming through," a gruff voice warns us from behind. It's Johnny, my pastry chef. He looks like a boxer who goes a few rounds every week, but he makes the most delicate desserts I've ever tasted.

"Soufflé for table fifteen," he says.

"Shall I ring it?" Kelly asks.

"You know what?" I examine the soufflé. It looks perfect but it can't stay on the pass for too long. "I'll take it over myself. Look that possible critic straight in the eye."

"Ooh. Go, Boss," Kelly coos. "Investigate the hell out of the sitch."

I make my way into the dining room. The sound of forks against plates creates a familiar symphony, the kind that used to make me feel invincible.

As usual, heads turn. Up to a few years ago, I actually enjoyed the sensation of parading through the front of house, gorging on the admiring gaze from the people eating my food, but my body isn't the same anymore. As my hips have grown in size, my self-esteem has shrunk accordingly. But still, despite the grueling hot flash, and my ex having a romantic dinner with her wife in front of my eyes, I grab the plate with the soufflé and saunter over to the stranger with the notepad.

CHAPTER 2
ESTELLE

"Here you go." A perky female voice pulls me from my calculations. "Our Black Forest soufflé. Enjoy." The aroma of dark chocolate and cherry drifts up, making my mouth water even as my mind tries to cling to the half-formed equation I'd been working on.

I glance up and look into the face of Savor's one and only head chef.

"What a treat," I say. "A gorgeous dessert and a chat with the chef." I keep coming back to this restaurant, securing a booking for the next week as soon as I get home after another delicious meal.

"I hope the food was to your liking?" The chef's smile seems forced, a hint of unease beneath it. Her professional mask is perfect, polished by years of practice, but I recognize armor when I see it.

"It was divine, as usual. I'm a big fan." I give her my warmest, widest smile.

"Excellent." She seems to relax a little. Her glance skitters to my notebook. "I don't mean to intrude, but I'm curious. Are you new to town? Just visiting?"

Very curious, indeed. "Not new-new," I say, deliberately cryptic. "I grew up here, but that was a long time ago."

The chef narrows her eyes, as though she's searching her memory and might find an image of me buried deep down somewhere.

"Some of my staff have money on whether you're a restaurant critic, what with all the note-taking between dishes."

Ah. The chef can also be quite direct—that's more my language.

"God no. Your food is beyond critique." I tap a fingertip against my notebook. "I'm just working on something that has me totally transfixed. I'm sorry if that comes across as rude. This pencil is like a natural extension of my hand."

"Not at all." The chef flashes me a genuine smile now. "You just had us a little worried."

"Absolutely nothing to worry about." I mirror her smile. "I'll be back next Friday simply because I can't get enough of your food, Miss…"

"It's Cass and thank you. I'll put your name down then. For seven next Friday?"

"That would be wonderful. The sea bass tonight was out of this world." Now that I've profusely complimented her food, Cass seems to have grown a few inches. Her blond bob peeks out from under her hat and her blue eyes have something commanding but also intriguingly vulnerable about them.

"Thank you again. I'm so glad you enjoyed it." Cass shifts her weight around, as though she's unsure of what to do or say next. "You should really eat that soufflé before it sinks."

"Right." For a minute there, I completely forgot about my dessert.

"I'll let you get to it. Enjoy and see you soon." The smile she shoots me next reaches all the way to her eyes, lending her face a softness that throws me a little. I watch her head back into the open kitchen, but then intently focus on the dish in front of me instead of trying to figure out whether there was a vibe between us. Pity that sort of thing can't be calculated with a mathematical equation—I'd be all over that if it could.

The soufflé is light as a cloud and just the right amount of tart with a mere hint of sweetness, just the way I like it. At the bottom, there's a surprising crunch of dried cherries and I'm delighted yet again. Each bite is a dangerous indulgence, reminding me how easily pleasure can become a habit.

No wonder I keep coming back here. Did they really think I was a restaurant critic? Is that the energy I exude? I chuckle at how ludicrous that is. Then I glance into the kitchen. Cass is gesturing to a colleague, showing them something or explaining some culinary detail, but I'm too far away to hear.

Though my connections in town have dwindled, the few remaining can expect a thorough questioning about Chef Cass from Savor. I heave a small sigh.

No, no, no, Estelle, I admonish myself. Don't go there. Don't do it. Save yourself the trouble. But for someone who's fucked up every single relationship she's ever had, I'm desperately romantic and part of me has never given up hope—the rebellious, stubborn part of me simply can't.

At almost fifty, I should have learned my lesson—and I have. Besides, there's nothing wrong with admiring a chef's cuisine, another woman's superlative creativity. It's got nothing to do with romance. Silly me.

Because I don't feel like going back to my dad's empty house, I focus on my notebook again. I've long stopped caring how this makes me look. If anything, it provides a kind of shield. I always seem busy and hard at work. The pencil scratches against the paper with a familiar rhythm, like a metronome keeping time with my thoughts.

My dad left this particular problem for me on his deathbed and it feels as though I can't leave town before I've solved it. My father was the smartest man I'd ever met —and I've met some men in my day who were utterly convinced they were the cleverest specimen mathematics had ever seen—and his problems have always been the hardest to solve.

I'm not sure yet whether I'm happy that his challenge is keeping me here. I'm not that keen to go home. There's literally nothing waiting for me there. My house in Berkeley is just as empty as my dad's house here. And at least being here doesn't remind me of how spectacularly I failed at a job my father, once again, made look easy.

I sink into the problem, forgetting the world around me —forgetting I'm in one of the best restaurants this area has ever seen—and for another delicious half hour, it's just me and math. Exactly how I like it.

CHAPTER 3
CASS

"Earth to Cass. Earth to Cass." Suzy glares at me over the rim of her wine glass.

"I'm sorry, Suze." I drag my gaze away from the beach. I could have sworn I saw the woman with the notebook—Estelle Raymond, I know from our reservation system—trudging along the beach, but upon further inspection, it's not her.

"It's okay, Cass," Hunter chimes in. "Suzy's talking about the menopause again. I vote we change the subject."

Suzy rolls her eyes, and I'm with her. If Hunter can't handle his female friends discussing menopause—this thing that seems to dominate our lives whether we like it or not—he can find somewhere else to be.

"Talking about menopause is my job," Suzy is unperturbed by Hunter. "I'm a menopause consultant."

"You just said it." Hunter isn't one to give up easily either. These two keep me fully entertained on my days off. We've grown a lot closer since I became single again three years ago. "It's your job. We're not paying you. We're just friends hanging out." Hunter dramatically puffs out some air—it's more a gesture I would associate with his husband, Bobby. "Even Devon's started complaining about it. Honestly, I think it's contagious." He shakes his head. "And Sadie with her later-in-life surf club. If low estrogen is the criteria to be accepted, I, too, should qualify."

"No way, babe," Suzy says matter-of-factly. "I don't need to run your labs to know your estrogen is through the roof." She chuckles heartily. "Now, either you let me talk to Cass about this without snark or you respectfully fuck off." She punctuates her words by stabbing a finger in Hunter's direction, nearly knocking over the bowl of nuts between us.

Hunter gasps as he brings a hand to his mouth. "Are you sending me away simply because I'm a man? How dare you?"

"Not because you're a man. Because you're being obnoxious and ignorant about something that's important to us."

"Damn, girl. That's how I talk to Finn when I tell him off. You just made me feel this small and we both know I'm—"

Suzy cuts him off simply by holding up her hand. God, I love these two. They've been my lifeline since Sarah left. Hunter with his wit and Suzy with her invaluable advice on this phase we're both going through. A few years ago, she pivoted from a career as life coach to menopause consultant and she sure has her work cut out for her.

"Fine," Hunter finally surrenders. "I shall take this opportunity to learn from my wise sisters, what with Finn's baby mama and her lovely wife swiftly heading in this direction as well."

Suzy turns to me and holds my gaze. "I'd like to

suggest Savor as the venue for my menopause support group."

"You want to use my restaurant?" It doesn't strike me as the right venue for a gathering like that.

Suzy nods. "Yes, because it's swanky and cozy and beats any meeting room in Clearwater Bay. I don't want us to hide away in some dank basement to talk about our issues."

She might have a point.

"With your relaxed opening hours, I figured we could work something out."

"Yeah, I'll think—" My attention is hijacked by a group of five ladies with surfboards tucked under their arms strolling onto the beach. One of them has the most audacious mane of curls floating behind her as she walks. It's unmistakably the Friday-woman-with-the-notebook from the restaurant.

"Ah, there's my little sister." Suzy waves at the group on the beach.

"Sadie Ireland's dried-up pussy surf club, you mean," Hunter adds.

"What's with you today?" Suzy's eyes shoot daggers at Hunter. "I know the menopause is not your favorite subject, but you're being a lot more bitchy than usual."

Their voices fade as my attention drifts to the women on the beach. Estelle cuts a striking figure in her wetsuit. She moves with the grace of someone who hasn't yet realized they're being watched, that brief window of unselfconscious beauty before the world intrudes.

I shake off the thought as I'm reminded what my own body looks like. I only walk on the beach fully clothed these days. It's also one of the reasons I would never join Sadie's surf club.

Certainly not everyone in that little group on the beach has the same gorgeous physique as Estelle—although Sadie, obviously, does. All the Irelands, Suzy included, have been genetically blessed with a body that can withstand anything, most of all age. You should see Jack, their father.

"You could join, you know," Suzy says. "You're the perfect candidate."

"So could you." I suddenly sound extremely flippant. I tear my gaze away from the group and Friday Woman to send Suzy an apologetic smirk. In a family of surf-mad people, she's always been the odd one out.

She doesn't dignify what I just said with a response, and rightly so.

"Is that Estelle Raymond?" she says, instead. She squints into the setting sun. She shakes her head, looking unsure of who she has just seen.

"It is," I confirm. "She's been to the restaurant three times in the past three weeks."

"God, I haven't seen her in decades," Suzy says. "Her father died a few months ago. She must have come back."

"You know her?"

Suzy nods. "Used to, at least. We went to school together. She's my age."

We've been planning Suzy's big Five-Oh for months. Goodness, Friday Woman is close to fifty? She looks at least ten years younger. But that means she must also be going through what we've been discussing to Hunter's growing annoyance—menopause. Maybe she's keen to join other clubs as well as Sadie's later-in-life surf club. Maybe she'd like to join Sadie's sister's menopause support group. But what do I even care?

I focus my gaze back on Suzy although, admittedly, it's

kind of hard to drag it away from the beach—and from Estelle. The other ladies don't seem to draw my eye that much. It's just that, once it was confirmed that Estelle Raymond wasn't a weirdly often-returning restaurant critic, it became really hard to ignore how utterly gorgeous she is. Because she is. Those dark, lush curls, that sharp jawline, that intense gaze… and those lips.

What the hell? I haven't felt this pull toward another woman—this raw, physical attraction—in years. As the estrogen levels in my bloodstream started their harrowing ups-and-downs, my libido has been near non-existent. Dead, really. Gone. Not that I care, not anymore. Although, and I don't blame her for this for one single second, it's one of two big reasons Sarah left me. At least it was just one out of two.

"Let's do it," I say, as I try to regroup. "Let's have the support group meeting at Savor."

"I suppose I'm banned." Hunter grins at us. "Bottoms up, ladies. Next round's on me."

"I think he and Bobby are going through something," Suzy whispers as soon as Hunter has disappeared inside The Bay. "We need to give him some time and grace."

"Hunter doesn't bother me," I say. "Hot flashes do."

"Have you had more?"

"Several times a day now," I admit.

"Oh, Cass. Why won't you see Doctor Gupta?"

"You know why." It's much easier to look at the beach and let my gaze wander to Estelle than to talk about this. Besides, Suzy and I have had this conversation a million times. I can't believe she still expects it to have a different outcome than all the times before.

"You're too stubborn for your own good," Suzy says. "Why can't you trust me on this?"

I have to be careful when I talk about mothers with Suzy. Despite a lifetime of therapy—she has even become a counselor herself—her mother leaving when Suzy was a young girl is something she'll never fully get over. I respect that, but some things need to be said.

"I took care of my mom until her final breath. And I promised her."

I can tell Suzy wants to say something, possibly an iteration of all the things she has said to me before, but she bites her lip and swallows her reply. But I'm not as stubborn as Suzy thinks I am. Every time I have a hot flash, especially when it happens in the middle of service, I want to talk to Doctor Gupta and beg her to prescribe me hormone therapy. But then the flash recedes and I invariably think of my mother and what she was convinced of when she died—the cause of her breast cancer she was so certain of, even though, in the end, it was more an obsession than anything else.

Hunter comes out with the drinks.

"Ooh." He puts the wine glasses down. "Did I just walk into a menopausal spat?"

Suzy mock-slaps him around the ears while she shoots him a tension-diffusing grin.

As I take a sip of wine, I look at the small group of women huddled around Sadie. She's taking them into the water. My gaze is, again, captured by Estelle as she tiptoes along the water's edge. Her curls dance in the wind like they have a mind of their own.

If she grew up here with the likes of the Ireland family, she might not be a later-in-life surfer, but have some tricks up that tight wetsuit's sleeve. Now I can't look away if I wanted to. I have to see for myself.

CHAPTER 4
ESTELLE

What in the holy fuck am I doing here? I'd been climbing the walls in Dad's house, drowning in memories and dead-end calculations, when I remembered the flyer from The Bay: *Later-in-life surf lessons, for women only. Forty-five and older.*

The flyer didn't mention Sadie Ireland would be the instructor, but here we are. What an unexpected perk.

My wetsuit clings too tightly to all the wrong places, like a second skin that knows all my secrets.

Sadie Ireland speaks, and just like that, she has everyone's full attention. That smile, that voice, the way she moves—some people really do make it look easy. I've always known of the Irelands—they're Clearwater Bay's surfing royalty—but seeing Sadie now, I'm reminded that the universe doesn't distribute charm and athleticism equally. Some people just get more than their fair share.

I adjust the zipper at my back, wincing as it pinches. A bead of sweat trickles between my shoulder blades despite the crisp evening air, and I watch the other women stretching and chatting as if this is the most natural thing in the world.

My surfboard lies beside me, its once-pristine surface now scuffed and dulled with age. Like owner, like board.

I've surfed before, in my teens. Dad thought it would loosen me up, make me think about something other than mathematics. I hated it at first—the loss of control, the unpredictability—but then I found my footing, or more accurately, my balance on a wave. For one brief, perfect moment, the world tilted in a way that made sense. But that was a lifetime ago. Now I'm just old and rusty.

"Time to paddle out!" Sadie's call breaks through my brooding.

The others cheer like we're about to conquer the world. I force myself into the water, gritting my teeth as the cold shocks my ankles, climbs to my knees, races up my thighs. I try to remember this is supposed to be fun.

"You all right there?" Sadie's voice floats toward me, light and warm—like it used to on TV.

"I'm fine," I say, though my tone betrays the lie.

She paddles ahead, leaving me to wrestle with my board and my thoughts. The water's colder than I remember, heavier somehow, as if it too knows how long I've been away. Each stroke feels clumsy, my body refusing to remember what it learned.

But then I catch a glimpse of the horizon—that endless stretch of blue that hasn't changed since I left—and something inside me stirs. Because I'm from here, the ocean has always had a way of putting things into perspective, of making everything else seem smaller. For a moment, I forget about the wetsuit, the board, and the reason why I'm back in town.

The moment shatters when the wave hits.

It's small but perfectly timed, and before I can react,

I'm underwater. It's not dramatic enough to make me lose my board, but when I surface, sputtering water, my dignity is nowhere to be found.

I expect laughter, maybe a snide remark, but instead there's a cheer. Linda, the retired school principal, claps her hands in encouragement.

"You've got this," she yells.

I have to believe she's right, otherwise I might as well leave. So, I climb back onto the board, dripping and humiliated but also a little bit lighter. It's strange. I'm no longer any good at this, but the failure doesn't sting the way I thought it would. Maybe that's what happens when you've already failed at much bigger things.

Sadie flashes me a grin as I paddle past her. "Take your time. The ocean's not going anywhere."

Her words settle over me as I try to follow her advice and take my time. As though this isn't just a desperate attempt to escape Dad's empty house. As though there's something here worth coming back to. Maybe there is.

I shake off the thought and focus on paddling, letting myself sink into the rhythm. For now, it's enough to just move, for my body to do something other than sitting at a desk.

The next wave rises beneath me with deceptive gentleness. I paddle harder this time, Sadie's words echoing in my head—the ocean isn't going anywhere, and neither am I.

"Looking good!" Linda shouts, her enthusiasm contagious. "You've got the paddle down. Now you just need to trust your legs."

My legs. Right. Trust them. As if they haven't betrayed me in countless physical endeavors over the years, as if I haven't spent the last two decades letting them get soft behind a desk.

Sadie's voice carries from farther ahead, calm and steady. "Watch the crest, ladies. Feel the energy of the wave underneath you. When it starts to rise, that's your moment. Don't think, just go."

Don't think. As if that's an option. My brain's already running the numbers—curve of the wave, speed of the water, angle of approach. There must be a formula for this. But out here, in the thick of it, all that theory dissolves. The wave isn't interested in logic. It's already coming—fast, wild, and impossible to pin down.

I miss my timing and wobble on the board, arms flailing in a desperate bid against gravity. It doesn't work and I go under again.

Another dunk, another round of cheers. This time, I let myself laugh. There's something liberating about being this bad at something, about failing in front of strangers who seem determined to celebrate every disaster. Linda paddles closer, flashing a thumbs-up.

"Your wipeouts are getting more graceful," she says with a wink.

"Oh good," I reply, pushing wet curls from my face. "Maybe by the end of the lesson, I'll master the art of falling."

Their laughter carries over the waves, making me feel like I belong.

Sadie glides back toward me, balanced on her board with the kind of effortless grace that makes me both envious and oddly hopeful.

"You're clearly overthinking it," she says. "Surfing is about feeling. You have to let the wave guide you."

I nod, though her words feel like an impossible request.

Like trying to forget how to count. We paddle out together, and this time I try to focus on the rhythm instead of the variables. The water laps against my arms in a steady cadence as the horizon stretches endlessly before us.

Sadie signals for us to turn and wait for the next set. As I bob on the surface, my gaze drifts to shore. The lights from The Bay beach bar twinkle invitingly, casting a warm glow over the deck.

And then I see her.

Cass sits perched at one of the tables, her chef's hat nowhere in sight. Even at this distance, there's no mistaking that blond bob. She's with two others and I can't help but wonder whether I might know them.

"Estelle," Sadie's voice snaps me back. A wave is rising behind me. "Paddle!"

I throw myself into the motion, digging my arms into the water with every ounce of strength I have left. The wave catches me, and for a split second, I feel it—the lift, the rush, the undeniable pull of something bigger than myself.

I don't stand. Not quite yet. But I ride the wave on my knees, grinning like a fool as I glide toward the shore. It's clumsy and far from perfect, but it's progress. As the wave fades beneath me, I glance toward the bar again. Cass is still there, and she's looking in my direction. For a moment, I wonder if she saw me catch the wave, if she noticed my ungainly triumph.

By the time Sadie calls the lesson over, I feel every single one of my forty-nine years—and then some. My arms ache with a bone-deep fatigue, my legs have turned to jelly, and there's sand in places I don't want to think about. But I also feel different. As if the saltwater has rinsed away more than just the sweat of exertion.

We trudge toward the row of weathered changing cabins at the edge of the beach. Sadie still looks camera-ready, her wetsuit unzipped in that perfect I-didn't-even-try way. The rest of us resemble a pack of bedraggled seals hauling our boards up the sand.

"Anyone else feel like their body might mutiny tomorrow morning?" Linda groans, tossing her towel onto the bench inside a cabin.

"All part of the fun," Sadie calls back with a grin that makes it almost believable.

The cabins are small but functional, with hooks for wetsuits and just enough space to maneuver. I peel off my wetsuit carefully, grimacing as the tight neoprene clings stubbornly to my damp skin.

By the time I emerge in a loose pair of linen pants and a T-shirt that's seen better days, most of the group has already gathered by the picnic tables near the cabins. The air smells of sunscreen and sea spray, carried in on the breeze that rolls off the water.

Sadie slings her board into the rack and wipes her hands on her towel. "All right, ladies," she says. "Who's up for post-surf drinks at The Bay?"

Everyone easily agrees, so I do too, ignoring the flutter of anticipation in my stomach.

We walk up the path from the beach, the group's chatter light and buoyant, a shared sense of accomplishment buzzing among us. The Bay glows ahead, a beacon for tired limbs and parched throats.

Sadie waves toward the deck. "Looks like my sister's already beat us to it."

"It still feels strange seeing The Bay without Sam running the show," Linda says, shaking her head.

"Sam traded bar life for babies and bedtime stories," Sadie replies, earning a ripple of laughter.

As we draw closer, I can see Cass more clearly, leaning back slightly in her chair, one hand curled around a glass of white wine. The evening light does something to her—makes it impossible to look away.

"Let's grab a seat," Sadie says as we step onto the deck. "And have ourselves a well-earned drink."

For some reason I'm not ready to examine, my heart hammers in my throat as I follow her.

CHAPTER 5
CASS

Suzy rises from her chair, beaming. "This couldn't be more perfect." She welcomes Sadie and her surfers to the deck of The Bay with her trademark authority. "Cass and I were just discussing holding a support group for menopausal women at Savor and in walks my target group."

Suzy is the Ireland with the least qualms about anything.

"Hear, hear," one of the ladies says. "I'm in." She's standing next to Estelle, who is shuffling around awkwardly, as though, out of the water and surrounded by so many people, she doesn't quite know what to do with herself.

"No doubt there, Linda," Suzy says to the woman. She's probably one of her clients and if not, Suzy knows just about everyone in Clearwater Bay. She's our town's unofficial mayor.

"I'm going to leave you ladies to it." Hunter rises as well, freeing up the chair next to mine. "Let you discuss your hormones in peace."

He kisses me goodbye and offers his empty chair to Estelle.

Suddenly, Friday Woman is sitting next to me. She looks a little forlorn without her little notebook, as well as tired from that surfing lesson. From what I could see, she didn't have any surprising board tricks up her sleeve at all. I only saw her go under spectacularly a few times, always to loud cheers from her companions.

"Hi," Estelle says, tucking a wet strand of hair behind her ear. "You don't surf?"

"Hey." I shoot her a smile. "No. Dry land is decidedly more my thing."

"My treat, ladies," Sadie shouts over our brittle conversation. "Shall I just order a couple of bottles of white wine?"

There's lots of whooping and I glance around the rowdy group that has joined us as though it was always planned that they would once Sadie's lesson ended. I know the other four ladies from the restaurant—and Estelle as well now, I guess.

I just came here for drinks with my two best friends on my day off, but that's Clearwater Bay for you.

One of them, Julianne, a feisty woman in her sixties with short-cropped gray hair, also used to be my mother-in-law. Sitting here with her makes me realize, once more, why it makes sense that Sarah and I are no longer a couple —although it sure hurt like hell when she left.

The wine is served, glasses distributed, and a group conversation develops. Estelle doesn't interject much. She's more a quiet observer, although it's only logical she wouldn't have much to contribute since most of the topics relate directly to the town. Besides, when you're at a table with the likes of Suzy and Linda, not much is required from anyone else in terms of conversation.

I push my chair back a little and angle it to my side—to Estelle. She's wearing a tattered T-shirt and her hair is a wet mess, but she still easily rivals Sadie's TV-worthy good looks.

"How's that thing you were working on so relentlessly last Friday?" I ask.

"Oh, hm, yeah… not good." She rolls her eyes. "It's a math problem my father left for me just before he died, and I'm beginning to think he wanted to play one last prank on me by giving me an unsolvable problem that he knew I wouldn't be able to let go."

"I'm so sorry to hear about your father."

"Thanks, um, yeah, he passed a few months ago, but I'm only just now going through all his stuff." Her face doesn't betray deep sadness, but that doesn't mean anything. Perhaps Estelle is just very good at hiding her emotions. Especially when sitting with a group of strangers. "That's why I'm back in Clearwater Bay." She sips from her wine.

"Suzy reckons she knows you from school," I say.

Estelle squints in Suzy's direction. "Yeah. Goodness, that was so long ago. I never lived here again after college. My dad moved back after he retired, but that was only a few years ago, once his health didn't allow him to teach anymore. He would have just kept on going if his body hadn't stopped him." A touch of sadness does creep into her voice now.

"Where did he teach?" I ask, gazing into Estelle's light-brown eyes.

"Berkeley. Differential Equations." She shrugs. "Just like me. Well, used to."

"You were a professor at Berkeley?" I'm a little impressed, especially because numbers might as well be another language for me.

"I, um, resigned recently." Estelle is not forthcoming with more information. This is hardly the place for it.

"How long are you planning on staying in Clearwater Bay?"

"At least until I solve this fucking problem." When she smiles, her face opens up and her eyes catch the orange hues of the sunset—and she's even more shockingly beautiful.

For a split second, I consider asking her on a date, so we can have a proper conversation, but then I remember what Suzy and I were talking about earlier, and the reason why Sarah and I split up, and I think better of it—much, much better. Either way, Estelle Raymond is so incredibly out of my league, I wouldn't even dare to ask.

"So I might be here a while," Estelle says.

"Suzy's turning fifty in a few months," I say. "Even though you don't look it, you must not be too far off." An inconvenient blush heats up my cheeks. Damn it. But at least it's not a hot flash—yet.

"Oh, please." Estelle waves off my comment. She's not good at taking compliments then. "But yes. My birthday's only at the end of the year, though. In December."

"Are you at all interested in joining her support group?" I pry, my blush intensifying. Suzy's so right about how much we need this group if it's this hard to have a casual conversation about it, with another woman no less. My cheeks are burning up, for heaven's sake.

"Hm." Estelle makes a noise somewhere between a groan and a scoff. "Not sure that's for me, to be honest."

I almost ask whether she's a late bloomer but realize just in time that would be quite rude.

"You?" she asks, tilting her head, as though she's taking a good look at me for the first time and only now realizes that, give or take a few years, we must be the same age.

"The other night when you were at the restaurant," I admit, even though I have no clue why—must be brain fog, another fun symptom of the menopause—"I had to cool off outside during a massive hot flash."

"It didn't impact your food," Estelle says dryly.

I have to chuckle. "Good to know."

"Honestly, the inventiveness of your dishes floors me every time. How do you even think of putting certain flavors together? Things like that are just so completely beyond me. I don't have a creative bone in my body so I really respect that." Her smile lingers.

My pulse stutters, just once, before the heat rushes in like a slap. I've never had a hot flash triggered by a lovely compliment from an incredibly attractive lady before, quite possibly because I haven't been on the receiving end of those for a long time, but here we go. The blush on my cheeks spreads to my neck and, just like that, it feels like my entire body is on fire.

"Please excuse me," I mumble, jumping out of my chair as though I'm trying to escape an actual fire. How much more embarrassing can it get?

I duck around the building's corner, grateful for the ocean breeze against my burning skin. I try to breathe through it, but slowing down my breathing can only do so much.

Experience has taught me one thing: there's nothing to do but ride it out. The only small mercy of a hot flash is that it never takes long. It embarrasses the hell out of you. It makes you feel as though you've lost all control over your body. You feel sticky and sweaty and dirty. It's as though your insides are burning and trying to find a way out but your skin is already aflame as well.

But it doesn't last very long. Afterward, there's plenty of time and opportunity to face whomever you had to flee from.

At work, my staff know how to deal with it. It's just a thing that happens now. But it's different in a social situation like this. I certainly wasn't flirting with Estelle—I'm in no condition to be doing anything silly like that—but we were having a nice conversation.

"Hey, Cass. Are you okay?" It's my ex-mother-in-law, which is a blessing but also very much not.

"Hot flash," I manage to say, wanting to rip this too-thick pair of jeans off my sweaty legs.

"Do you want some ice? A wet towel?" Julianne has been where I am. I know because she told me all about it.

"It'll be over in a few minutes." I expel a few deep breaths and try to catch more of the chill in the air. But then another image of Estelle pops up in my head, of how her lips moved so sensuously while she said those wonderful things about my food, and another wave of heat crashes through me. I'm so overheated, I have to stop myself from sprinting into the ocean.

And then, as though it never even happened, as though it was all just a figment of my imagination, it's all over—except for my wrinkled blouse and the wet hair clinging to my forehead.

"Could you do me a favor, Julianne?" I manage a grin. "Could you get my purse from the deck? I can't go back there, and I just want to go home."

"Come on, Cass. You don't have to hide from us. Suzy was just talking about a support group for women going through this very thing."

"I know I don't have to hide, but... I don't have the energy to argue about this right now. Could you just do me this small favor, please?"

"Of course. I'll be right back."

Maybe it's silly and, according to Suzy, certainly giving in to internalized misogyny because of the patriarchy and whatnot, but I simply can't face Estelle after that.

"Hey." Oh, no. Damn you, Julianne. "Here's your bag," Estelle says. "Are you okay?"

"God, I'm sorry." I take my purse from her. "Thanks. You didn't have to, um, do that."

"I wanted to make sure you were all right." She pulls those damned luscious lips of hers into the smoothest grin. "Hot flash?"

"Yeah. Serves me right for talking about it so brazenly." What a stupid thing to say.

Estelle just shakes her head. "Can I walk you home? Make sure you don't have another on the way?"

This gorgeous woman wants to walk me home? *Me.* Really?

It doesn't mean anything, Cass, I tell myself. She's just trying to make some friends in the town she left behind all those years ago.

"That would be very nice of you," I hear myself say, because why the hell not?

CHAPTER 6
ESTELLE

Cass and I walk along the boardwalk to the house on the cliff where Savor is located. We fall into an easy rhythm, the ocean to our left, the sky blushing with the very last streaks of sunset.

"I hope this doesn't sound insensitive after what you've just been through, but I've yet to experience my first hot flash," I say.

Cass runs her fingers through her matted hair, swiping it away from her face.

"Lucky you."

"Yeah." If it sent her fleeing from the table, it must've been brutal.

"Somehow, it's still uncomfortable to talk about," Cass mutters. "Although, according to Suzy, we should all be talking about it all the time."

"Sounds like Suzy turned into a very wise woman." I glance at Cass's profile in the fading light. "Yet I prefer to talk about your cooking. Did I mention that sea bass was incredible?" I inject all the lightness in my tone that I have in me.

"Quite a few times, actually." Cass turns to me and smiles softly. "Now that you've seen me at my most embarrassing, can I ask you something?"

"Of course." I dig my hands a little deeper into my pockets.

"Why did you resign from your job?"

"I burned out," I admit. It's not that hard to do anymore. "Pretty spectacularly." When I found myself bawling over a grant application because I'd used the wrong font, I knew something was seriously wrong.

"I'm so sorry." Cass's voice is warm with compassion.

"I loved the research and the teaching, but the endless admin and committees, not so much." I sneak a quick glance at the side of her head, but Cass just listens intently. "It doesn't help that I'm a perfectionist. I just—I spent my entire life chasing that world only to realize, at the cusp of fifty, it's not what I want. My father dying somehow made that crystal clear." If someone hadn't made my dad retire, he'd have taught until his final breath. "Through some twisted subconscious logic, I believed I had to be exactly like him, follow the same path. I looked up to him so much."

Our footfalls slow on the boardwalk, as though what we're talking about requires a gentler pace.

"I'm so sorry you lost him."

"He was very ill toward the end and people don't live forever." I give a quick shake of the head. "Sorry, that sounded a little harsh, as though I'm glad he's dead, which I'm not, but he'd stopped being the genius I so admired a while ago. Then, mercifully, it all went pretty quickly, and he didn't have too long to suffer the indignity of no longer being able to use his once-brilliant brain. It was really hard for him."

"I'm still sorry." Cass bumps into me ever so lightly.

"Thank you."

"Thank you for walking me home. No more signs of hot flashes, thank goodness." Her restaurant comes into view, looming in the distance.

"My pleasure." I chuckle. "I figured it couldn't hurt to be friendly to the best chef in the town and its surroundings."

"I didn't open Savor until I was forty-five. It took me too long to follow my dream, what I really wanted, as well."

"What stopped you?"

"Life. Excuses. Fear, probably." She shrugs. "I worked in other chefs' kitchens for years, convincing myself it was good enough." She pauses. "It took my mother dying to finally push me into doing it. She left me just enough money to make it happen."

"I'm so sorry," I say, the only appropriate response to the revelation of a parent dying.

"She died way too young. Breast cancer." Sadness seeps from Cass's voice. "And she never got to see the restaurant she gave me."

I stop myself from wrapping an arm around her. We don't know each other well enough for that.

"Take it from someone who often gets mistaken for a restaurant critic," I say, "your mother would be so proud."

Cass chuckles and the sound is soothing, like the push and pull of the waves alongside us.

"Are you joking or do you really get mistaken for a critic a lot?" Cass asks.

"I often go to restaurants with my notebook as only companion, but, no actually, I haven't been mistaken for a critic before. That was just you."

"You mainly had my staff worried, but I guess I went along with it." We've almost reached Cass's house and our pace has slowed to a crawl.

"If the surfing doesn't work out, you can always try for a career as a food critic. Or both." Cass comes to a halt.

I cackle as I stop next to her. "Yeah right."

Her gaze finds mine. "Would you like to come in for a drink?"

I wasn't expecting that. I look a mess and I'm exhausted from that surfing lesson, from putting my body through motions it's not used to. I also don't want to give her the wrong idea.

So, of course, I can't say yes. Not tonight. Maybe not ever. I've made that mistake too many times before—letting someone in, thinking that maybe this time will be different, maybe this time they'll understand that intimacy isn't always physical, that love can be both tender and fierce without lust.

"I should go home, take a shower." I point at my hair that's a mess. "Sadie took it out of me."

"Sure. No problem." The warmth in her smile doesn't fade because of my rejection. "Thanks again for your kindness."

"My pleasure. I will see you on Friday."

"Good night." Cass gives a small nod and walks up the steps to Savor. I watch her until she disappears inside the building.

On the way to my dad's house, I replay our short walk and the surprisingly deep things we talked about. Ten minutes, and suddenly we're not strangers anymore. Or maybe Cass is just easy to talk to. One of those people who's so easy to be around, that they're made for the hospitality business. I glance backward, at her restaurant, happy for her. That it's hers. And that I get to go back on Friday under slightly different circumstances.

I also consider what might have happened if I'd said yes to a drink. Probably nothing, except rehydrating my body. But still. You'd think my heart was strong from all that breaking, but it's still too soft for my own good. For me to say yes to a drink with a kind and special chef I'm getting to know.

CHAPTER 7
CASS

In that hazy time between sleeping and waking, I see Estelle, graceful on her board, not tipping into the water but staying upright, negotiating one of the ocean's more challenging waves like she has done nothing else all her life. Because this is a dream, her long curls are not wet but bouncy and, somehow, naughty, and she's not wearing a wetsuit but a skimpy bikini.

A precise pounce on my full middle-aged lady bladder shatters my dream. My cat, August, barely eight pounds of ginger fluff, somehow manages to land with the impact of a bowling ball.

He settles into his morning ritual: first the rumbling purr against my ear, then the deliberate sweep of his fluffy tail across my face, like a feather duster with attitude. This has been my wake-up call every single morning since Sarah left.

"Gussie, for crying out loud," I whisper. "I was dreaming of a hot lady. Why can't you respect that?" I surrender to August's demands and rise, padding to the kitchen where his food bowl awaits. But maybe I should be happy my fluffy ginger woke me up. Who knows where that dream might have ended?

Clearly, though, that walk home moved something in me. And I feel something, perhaps even attraction—although, truth be told, that would be rather baffling.

Either way, Estelle refused to come in for a nightcap. The question was out of my mouth before I could think it through. She could have so many good reasons for refusing my offer. She's been through a lot lately, that much is clear.

I feed August and cast my gaze over the ocean. My apartment is above the restaurant and has a breathtaking view from the cliffs. I brew myself a cup of coffee and count the hours until Estelle will come to Savor. Damn it. What the hell is going on with me? Or should I just, innocently, enjoy this sensation of sudden attraction? There haven't even been any hints that she's gay, although it's as though I can sense it. Somehow, it's like I know that she is.

I sip my coffee, my gaze drifting over the ocean's gray expanse. The waves are wild this morning. They look untamable, yet I'm sure if I walk down the boardwalk, I'll see a couple of Irelands trying to.

As often happens during my morning coffee moment with the Pacific, inspiration strikes. An idea for a new dish pops into my head. Something I could present to Estelle on Friday to impress her in the language I speak best.

August finishes his breakfast with fastidious precision, then leaps to the windowsill in one fluid motion, settling beside me to survey his territory. As I scratch behind his ears, I say, as though he can understand me and is very valuable in my brainstorm process, "What do you think, Gussie? Shall we come up with something spectacular for Friday Woman?"

In response, August leans his soft head into my hand and I take it as a yes.

It doesn't take me long to make my way down to the restaurant, put on my chef's whites, and start experimenting.

After years of working in kitchens under shouty head chefs who squeezed their staff dry until they quit, I wanted to do things differently in my own restaurant. Staff retention is how I measure myself as a boss and apart from a pastry chef who moved to San Francisco and a sous chef who wanted a career change, my employees have all been with me since the very beginning of Savor. Because we are only open four days a week, from Tuesday to Friday, my staff get plenty of time off and they have weekends to themselves.

Today is Tuesday, three days before Estelle's next reservation, and we're only open for dinner, giving me plenty of time for experimentation.

I start with clams. They're fresh, briny, and taste of the ocean. The best dishes don't come from overthinking—they come from instinct, from curiosity, from standing in an empty kitchen and letting the ingredients tell you where they want to go. And perhaps, if I'm being honest, sometimes also from wanting to impress someone. Estelle is on my mind, but I'm putting the thought of her to the best use I know: inspiration.

I set a pot on the stove and let butter melt, the sizzle filling the space. Garlic follows, then shallots, softening into something fragrant. I pour in a splash of white wine and watch it hiss against the heat before it settles into a simmer. The clams go in next, their shells clinking against the pot. I clap the lid on and step back, inhaling deeply.

It smells divine already. The clams are starting to open, revealing their tender center. Remembering a divine bouillabaisse I once had in a small Greek taverna years ago, I reach for the Metaxa. I drizzle in just enough for warmth, depth, and for something unexpected.

The scent of the Metaxa, mingling with the briny sweetness of the clams, fills the kitchen. It's a fragrance that speaks of places I've been and memories I've held onto, infusing the dish with a little of my own story. Cooking is a way to connect without words. A way to say, "I hope you feel welcome here."

I add a touch of cream to the pot, just enough to mellow the sharper notes and bring a silky texture to the broth. I toss in a handful of fresh parsley for brightness and a dash of saffron for a hint of the exotic. The golden threads bleed their color into the sauce, like sunlight pouring into a room.

I taste the broth with a spoon, closing my eyes as the flavors unfold on my tongue. It's close, but not quite there. It needs something else—something to pull it all together.

I get a lemon from the fridge and slice it in half. A few generous squeezes, and the dish is transformed. The acidity lifts the flavors, sharpens them, gives them clarity.

As the clams fully open, I plate them in a shallow bowl, ladling the aromatic broth around them. With a few slices of crusty bread on the side for soaking up the sauce, the dish will be complete. It's simple but thoughtful. Elegant but comforting.

The plate looks like a celebration of the ocean itself—a tribute to the Pacific that stretches beyond Savor's walls.

Estelle walked me home out of kindness, and this dish

is how I walk her back. How I let her know that there's something in me that wants to connect.

I make a note to run this new dish as a special on Friday, not just for Estelle but for anyone willing to taste a little piece of my heart. The thought makes me smile, even as a small voice in the back of my head warns me to be careful. At least my kitchen is a safe place to take risks. If only matters of the heart were as simple as a recipe.

A knock at the back door startles me. I'm not expecting any deliveries and my staff won't be in for another hour, unless someone has decided to show up early. Wiping my hands on my apron, I swing the door open.

It's Sarah. She looks good. The way people do when they've truly moved on and built something new and beautiful. When she was here with Rose last Friday, she was beaming as well.

"I saw the light was on," she says, shifting slightly, as if debating whether coming here was such a good idea after all.

"How are you?" For her to drop by like this is definitely out of the ordinary.

"I wanted you to hear it from me." A humungous smile—the kind that looks unstoppable—takes over her face. "Last Friday, when we were here." A pause. "Rose and I were celebrating that, um, I'm pregnant."

"Congratulations." Of course, I'm happy for her. It's what she wanted. It's also the other reason we broke up.

A short silence falls. It's full of everything we were and everything we couldn't be. But her news doesn't hurt me. Not in the way I once thought it might.

Sarah lets out a nervous laugh that catches in her throat. She puts a hand on her belly and doesn't say anything else. She doesn't have to.

Despite the love we had, and all the ways we tried, we couldn't make it work. We both knew it had to end. And now, here she is, stepping into the life she always wanted. And here I am, finally at peace with not being the one to give it to her.

She studies me for a second longer, then bridges the distance between us, tentative but somehow sure. "Can I—?"

I don't let her finish. I pull her into a hug.

She melts into it, and for a moment, we're just two people who once knew each other in a way no one else did. There's no bitterness—just the understanding that we mattered to each other once, and maybe, in some way, always will.

When we pull apart, Sarah smiles. "I'm glad you're doing okay."

"I am," I say, which is true enough.

"I should go, leave you to whatever smells so delicious in here."

"Thanks for stopping by and telling me in person. I appreciate it."

Sarah squeezes my hand briefly before turning away. "Take care, Cass."

"You too."

Once she's out the door, I let out a deep breath. Although I'm happy for her, I will need a little time to process this news.

Meanwhile, I go back to my dish. I taste it again and adjust the seasoning a little. Because that's the thing about cooking—it's never truly finished. There's always room for a little more depth, a little more balance. And maybe, if I get it just right, someone will take one bite and understand exactly what I'm trying to say.

CHAPTER 8
ESTELLE

It's different when I arrive at Savor this week. I'm still at my table for one by the window, and the maitre d' is the same as last time, but I can't help but look out for Cass in the open kitchen. I've been thinking about her more than I've wanted to. Despite myself. Despite how I am and what life has taught me. And then I had to decide what to wear.

I'm not someone who puts much thought into their outfit. If it's blazer weather—which, in NorCal, it is more often than not thanks to the wind off the Pacific—it's jeans and a blouse, usually white or baby-blue, topped with a blazer. It's a look I perfected in academia and never felt the need to evolve beyond.

I should make a return trip to Berkeley to pick up some more of my clothes, but, up until today, I haven't felt the need to wear one of my swankier blouses. I have a green silk one that would have worked well tonight—although for what purpose exactly, I'm not even sure—but here I am. Dressed in a crisp white blouse and a beige check blazer, as if it even matters.

I study the menu, always a fun exercise because it changes every week. The special with clams and a broth made with Metaxa sounds intriguing, mostly because I have no idea what Metaxa is.

When I glance over to the kitchen, I smile inadvertently. I tell myself it's because I'm well on my way to making a friend in town, and I could do with a friend in Clearwater Bay. The other day, after surfing, I didn't even recognize Suzy Ireland, that's how long I've been away. She's someone I could get back in touch with, although I have no intention of joining her support group—yet.

I don't see Cass in the kitchen. I've yet to catch my first glimpse of her tonight. My stomach flutters in anticipation. Sometimes I think that what I lack in physical desire, my brain tries to compensate for by developing instant, ill-advised crushes. It's ridiculous. But there's something about Cass. Although I've barely spoken to her. I've tasted her food. But I'm not that foolish to become infatuated with a chef simply because of their tasty dishes.

When the server comes over, he says, "The chef has asked if she can serve a surprise menu tonight. Just for you."

"Really?" How delightful. There's that flutter in my stomach again.

When I glance at the kitchen now, I see Cass very clearly. She stands there in her whites beaming. She gives me a small nod. How bossy—and utterly charming.

"Of course. Please thank her from me. I can't wait." I order a glass of champagne because why the hell not? I only wish Cass was sitting opposite me so that we could enjoy this together. But she's got work to do. So do I, but tonight, I don't feel so inclined to work on my dad's problem. I've pretty much resigned myself to the fact that it's unsolvable, and I just want to take in every moment of being here.

I want to watch the other diners and study their faces when they taste their first bite of Cass's food. I want to revel in the view of this ocean that stretches as far as the eye can see. And I want to catch glimpses of Cass as she works, as she's in her element, as she does what she was born to do.

The two amuse-bouches are to die for, and then out walks Cass herself, straight toward me, carrying a plate as if it's the most normal thing in the world for the head chef to be serving a customer. She did do it last time as well with that divine dessert, but I haven't seen her give that special treatment to any other customer.

She's so deliciously tall and confident. She looks in control and not at all like the flustered woman I walked home after a hot flash earlier this week.

"Good evening." She sets the plate in front of me. "How's everything so far?"

"To fucking die for," I say, feeling suddenly brazen.

"Exactly what I was going for." She wants to say something more, I can tell, but it's as though her lips are unavailable for speaking because she can't stop smiling. Then she composes herself.

She gestures toward the plate. "For your starter, I wanted to keep things light but full of flavor. Local Dungeness crab with a touch of citrus and a little heat."

The dish is beautifully plated—delicate shreds of crab nestled atop something smooth and pale, tiny flecks of red scattered across like an artist's final brushstrokes.

"I assume the red is the heat?"

Cass smirks. "A little Aleppo pepper, just enough to wake up your palate."

I pick up my fork, hyperaware that she's still standing there, watching me. The moment stretches, charged with something I can't quite name, until she clears her throat and steps back.

"I'll let you enjoy your dish in peace." Her voice is decidedly lower than before—and I have no idea what's really going on here. As she turns, I catch myself watching the way she moves, the way her chef's coat fits just right over her broad shoulders.

Then I take my first bite. The flavors hit instantly—sweet crab, bright citrus, the silkiness of the emulsion underneath. Then the heat lingers at the very end, not overpowering but persistent, teasing my tongue just enough to make me want another bite.

I put my fork down for a moment. It's unfair, really, how good she is at this. At making food that doesn't just taste amazing but makes me feel something.

I glance over at the kitchen again. Cass is at her station, focused, moving with the ease of someone who is exactly where she belongs.

I take another bite, savoring it. I don't know what's happening here. But I know I don't want it to stop.

When the server clears my starter, I sit back, letting the hum of the restaurant wash over me. More tables have filled, voices blending into a pleasant murmur, glasses clinking in celebration. I sip my champagne slowly, aware of the way my body feels—loose and relaxed.

When I look toward the kitchen again—I can't keep my eyes off it tonight—Cass is nowhere in sight. I tell myself I'm not waiting for her—that I'm not expecting every course to be served by the head chef. That I'm just here to enjoy a good meal, like I have every Friday since coming back to Clearwater Bay. But when she heads toward me again, carrying a deep bowl, I know that's a lie.

She moves differently this time. Like she's bringing me something really important. She puts the dish down carefully in front of me.

"Your next course," she says. "Clams in a Metaxa broth, with saffron and citrus."

Steam curls upward, carrying the scent of the ocean and of something rich and complex beneath it.

Cass lingers for a second, her gaze flicking over my face. "I felt inspired this week," she says, almost as if she's trying to tell me something else entirely.

I dip my spoon into the broth, then bring it to my lips. It's exquisite. Layers of warmth and depth, the briny sweetness of the clams balancing against the heat of the Metaxa, the brightness of citrus cutting through like sunlight.

"This..." I shake my head, searching for words. "This is something special."

Cass beams me a smile. "I'm glad you think so."

And then she's gone, back to the kitchen, back to her world.

I taste another spoonful of broth, letting the flavors expand, trying not to think too much about how all of this is making me feel.

The rest of the meal passes in a slow, luxurious blur. Course after course arrives, each dish some sort of revelation, each paired with a different wine. Cass has more than delighted me with her surprise menu for one.

The dining room thins out as the evening stretches on, tables emptying one by one. The soft clatter of cutlery and murmur of conversation fade, replaced by the sounds of the kitchen winding down. My wine glass is nearly empty, the candle on my table burning low.

I could leave. I probably should. But something keeps me here, nursing my last few sips of wine slowly, watching the movement in the open kitchen as the staff wraps up for the night. I tell myself I'm just savoring the experience. That's what this restaurant is called, after all.

But when Cass finally emerges, wiping her hands on a towel, her chef's coat unbuttoned at the collar, I know that's not the whole truth.

"Still here?" she asks as she approaches.

"I didn't want to rush a perfect meal." I lift my glass slightly. "And I absolutely wanted to thank the chef in person."

She leans a hip against the table. "Will you have a drink with me now?"

"It's a yes from me tonight." My head is light and my body warm from the wine.

Cass nods toward the bar. "Come on, then. Let me pour you something special."

Although my legs feel unsteady, I follow her without hesitation.

CHAPTER 9
CASS

"Neat or on the rocks?" I lift the bottle of Metaxa, the same brandy that inspired tonight's seafood special. Estelle's eyes have grown soft around the edges, her smile even more generous than before. I should be pouring her water instead of Greek brandy.

"Chef's choice," she says. Her words are still crisp and clear, though her movements have slowed. "All your choices tonight have been excellent so I'd be foolish to start making my own now."

I drop ice cubes into both glasses, letting them crack before pouring. The ritual gives me a moment to steady myself before sliding onto the barstool next to Estelle.

"Thank you for a wonderful evening." Estelle holds up her glass, then winces when she gets a whiff of the Metaxa's strong aroma.

"Thank you for being such a loyal Friday evening customer."

"Put my name down for next week, please." She peers over the rim of her glass, her gaze both intense and mischievous.

"Sure, but… hm…" *Come on, Cass. There's no better time for this question.* "Wouldn't you rather have dinner *with* me instead of just having me cook for you?"

"What do you mean? You have to work on Friday night, don't you?" Maybe her brain functions are more impaired than she lets on—although she still looks good enough to eat in that pristine white blouse that stands out against her skin so gorgeously, just enough of its buttons undone to give you an idea of what's underneath but not nearly enough to stop you from guessing.

"How about tomorrow?" I ask.

"Savor's not open on Saturdays. I read all about your slow restaurant philosophy on the website." She finally takes a sip and it's as though the shock of the alcohol, paradoxically, allows her to see what I'm getting at. "Do you mean a private dinner? Just for me?" Her lips curve into the most divine smile.

"That's exactly what I mean."

"Hm." Her smile abruptly disappears as she swallows slowly. "I've had too much to drink so I will say yes for now, but I reserve the right to change my mind tomorrow when I'm sober."

Ouch. But I don't give up that easily. "Have you had enough of my food already?"

"Of course not, but, um… I'm not—" She glances at me, but only for a split second. "Is this… a thing? A date, I mean?" Estelle seems to have lost most of her cool.

I refrain from saying something cheesy like it can be whatever she wants it to be. Instead, emboldened by how much she enjoyed my special menu tonight, I take the direct route. "I'm single, into women, and I like you, so…"

"Oh." Estelle peers into the amber liquid.

Damn. I read it all wrong. I let her beauty distract me

into a state of near oblivion, into someone who misinterprets signals. I'm so out of practice, it's like I no longer know how this works. Add to that the confusing physical attraction I feel toward her and it's almost logical I've made this mistake. My poor brain is in complete disarray.

"I'm sorry. Can we rewind about five minutes?" I ask. "Can we please do that?"

"We can try."

Estelle's probably not even queer—I could have sworn, though. But my gaydar is very rusty as well.

"Obviously, I would love to have dinner with you," Estelle says, her voice almost a whisper.

"But?" I ask.

"But… I don't want you to get the wrong idea. I'm not —I shouldn't be dating. It's really not on my to-do list. Also, it's not you. It's definitely me. I—" She shakes her head. "I'm sorry."

"Dinner as friends, then?" I say, aiming for casual and missing by a mile. "I'm not exactly prime dating material either."

"That's really not what I meant," Estelle says.

"Yeah." I take a sip of my drink, letting its burn calm me down. "Although you did witness my hot flash the other day."

Estelle doesn't even chuckle at my lame joke. "Is that why you don't consider yourself datable?"

"I'd be lying if I said that had nothing to do with it, but it's a bit more complicated than that." I swirl the ice cubes in my glass. "My ex, Sarah, stopped by a few days ago to tell me she's pregnant. Our relationship ended a few years ago because she wanted kids and I didn't." I pause. "She's a lot younger than me, and then I hit menopause and, well, things took a turn for the worse rather quickly."

Estelle doesn't say anything right away, but her eyes soften with understanding. "I'm so sorry."

"It's okay. I'm happy for Sarah. She and her new wife, Rose, were in here last Friday, celebrating, although I didn't know about the pregnancy yet."

She's quiet for a beat before asking, "Was it difficult when she told you?"

"No, not anymore. But our break-up was very painful because it made me feel so utterly inadequate. Even though, in my heart, I knew that I had to let her go. I tried to hold on for too long."

I take another sip of my drink, the warmth of the Metaxa spreading through me, paving the way for this conversation that I didn't expect to have tonight.

Estelle just waits, letting me decide whether to continue.

I clear my throat. "It's hard to explain without sounding like a dreadful cliché, especially to someone who hasn't been through it. But menopause… it changed everything for me. My body, my energy, my… drive. Well, my sex drive most of all."

Estelle's fingers trace the rim of her glass. "That must be hard."

"That's one way to put it." And also a great way to extract the good vibe from any conversation.

I consider changing the subject and asking her about what she meant earlier, about why dating isn't on her to-do list. But I don't. Not yet.

I roll the glass between my palms. "I gained a lot of weight, too," I add, surprising myself even more. This is not something I tend to talk about.

Estelle catches my gaze, but she doesn't say anything.

"It shouldn't matter, right? But it does. I used to feel

strong and assured in my body. Now, some days, I barely recognize myself." I force a smile. "Not exactly a selling point in the dating world."

Estelle studies me with the same careful attention she's given each dish I've served her. "I think you look great."

Her words sound true enough—but I know better. At least I think that I do. Still, I shift in my seat, suddenly warm in a way that has nothing to do with the Metaxa. "That's very kind of you to say."

"It's not just kindness, Cass. It's an observation." She takes another sip. "I saw you walk through the restaurant earlier and you carry yourself so..." She pauses, her smile suddenly shy. "I might have had too much to drink to actually put it into words, but I enjoyed watching you walk toward me like that."

I don't know what to say to that. I can only hope my body won't respond with another hot flash, like the last time she paid me a compliment—as though my poor body has no clue how to behave around her.

Also, for the first time in a long time, I wonder what it would feel like to actually believe her. Her kind words spur me on to continue. I clear my throat.

"Sarah and I..." It kind of feels as though the support group for menopausal women is already having its first gathering at Savor, with Estelle and I as the only participants. "We stopped having sex. I stopped wanting it."

Estelle doesn't react right away.

"She tried to be patient," I continue. "I did too. But something in me just changed, and I couldn't seem to get it back. It wasn't just that I didn't want it—I didn't miss it. And when someone you love is waiting for you to... come back to them in that way, it starts to feel like you're failing them. Like you're failing yourself."

I chance a glance at Estelle. There's no judgment on her face, just consideration.

"That must have been difficult," she says finally.

I nod. "It was. For both of us. But, in the end, I couldn't give her what she needed."

Estelle's eyes meet mine. "And what do *you* need, Cass?"

I part my lips, but nothing comes out. The truth is that I don't know.

Estelle doesn't push. She watches me, her expression patient in a way that does something to my stomach. I could deflect, turn the conversation back to her, ask why she doesn't date. But I still don't. I sit with the question, let it linger like the last sip of Metaxa, slow and warm as it slips down my throat.

"I need to feel like myself again," I say finally. My voice is quieter than I mean for it to be. "Or at least figure out who this new version of me is and try to accept her."

Estelle nods, as if she understands. Maybe she does—somehow. Her empty glass scrapes softly against the bar as she pushes it aside.

"I hope that you will." She finds my gaze. "Figure it out." There's something different about her expression. A hint of sadness, perhaps? "I hate to leave on this note, but…" She points at her empty glass. "That one really tipped me over the edge of tipsiness and whatever comes next."

"Let me get you some water." I hurry behind the bar.

"It's fine, Cass. You've done too much for me tonight already." She slips off her seat. "I should go."

"Are you okay to walk home? I can call you a taxi."

Estelle shakes her head. "It's not far and I need the fresh air." She sucks her bottom lip between her teeth for a split second, then says, "But it's going to be another yes from me."

"Dinner tomorrow?" Something twists inside me.

Estelle nods slowly.

"A dinner between friends it is, then." How can it be anything else after what I've just told her? I suppose that's the best two undatable women—for whatever reason—can hope for.

CHAPTER 10
ESTELLE

On my way home, I wish Cass hadn't said that about her no longer wanting sex. It made me change my mind about dinner too easily. But a woman who doesn't want sex happens to be exactly what I'm looking for. I know it's not the same—not in the least—but still, maybe it's enough. Because, for all the years I've tried to convince myself that romantic love is not for me, that someone like me should find other means of fulfillment in life, deep down, I've always believed, with an intensity that has only increased with age, that, I too, deserve love. Even though all I have to show for all the times I've tried is a heart chock-full of scars.

Maybe that's why I've been drawn to Cass. Because I sense something different about her. Because her gaze doesn't devour me in an overtly sexual way. Because we have some sort of unspoken connection.

The Metaxa burns warmly in my stomach, a bit like how Cass makes me feel. Maybe it's because of her age that I sense a possibility. It would be foolish to pursue a woman at the height of her sexuality. Been there, done that, failed every single time.

I slow my steps as I reach the boardwalk, the ocean stretching dark and endless beside me. The night air is cool against my skin, the lingering warmth of the Metaxa curling through my veins. I press my hands deeper into my pockets, anchoring myself against the undertow of my thoughts.

The idea of love has always been easier in theory than in practice. In theory, I believe in soulmates. In deep, long-lasting connection. In the certainty of knowing someone sees you—really sees you—and chooses you anyway. But in practice, love has been a series of inevitable disappointments. Women who thought they could change me. Women who convinced themselves they could live without what I couldn't give them. Women who loved me right up until the moment they realized I wasn't enough.

Maybe things can be different with Cass. But I shouldn't get ahead of myself. Either way, I have another scrumptious dinner to look forward to tomorrow.

The waves are small and not too wild this morning—perfect for a beginner—but I'm still convinced I'll make a fool of myself. My body feels sluggish, heavy with last night's booze and thoughts I haven't been able to shake off. The things Cass told me and the things I didn't say.

My stomach tightens at the memory, and not just from the hangover. She laid herself bare, and what did I do? I sat there like a statue, my words trapped behind years of carefully constructed walls.

I paddle out, determined to focus, but my mind keeps replaying the way she looked at me, and what she said.

I settle onto my board, legs dangling in the cool water as I draw in a deep breath. The salt air stings my lungs, sharp but insufficient to slice through the fog in my head.

"You're overthinking it," a voice calls from nearby.

I glance over to see Sadie Ireland paddling toward me, a knowing grin on her face.

"You don't know what I'm thinking," I counter.

Sadie flows onto her board in one fluid motion, water streaming from her shoulders. "Fair enough, but I still know you're overthinking it. I can tell."

Before I can protest, another surfer glides up beside her. Her wife, Devon. I know her from the tabloid pictures from a few years ago of Sadie Ireland kissing another woman on this very beach.

Sadie nods toward her.

"Dev, this is Estelle. She took my surfing class this week."

Devon studies me. "How's it going?"

"I try," I say on a sigh.

Devon smirks. "That's your first mistake."

Sadie laughs. "She's right. You don't try, you just do. The ocean doesn't care how hard you're thinking about it."

Easy for them to say. They make it look effortless, all muscle and grace, their movements second nature in a way mine will never be. I adjust my position on the board, trying not to look as unsure as I feel.

Devon watches me for a second, then gestures to the waves rolling in behind us. "Next one's yours."

I shake my head. "I don't know—"

"Exactly." She paddles a little closer, balancing on her

board like it's an extension of herself. "When you feel the wave catch you, just pop up. Don't hesitate."

"And if you wipeout," Sadie adds. "No big deal. Just get back on the board and go again."

Their confidence in me is baffling. But maybe I just need to borrow a little of it. I take a deep breath, reposition myself, and start paddling as the next wave rises behind me.

"Now!" Devon shouts.

I push up too slowly, too hesitantly, and the wave surges past, leaving me wobbling awkwardly before I topple into the water.

When I surface, Sadie is grinning. "Not bad."

Devon chuckles. "Not good, either."

I huff out a laugh, brushing wet hair from my face. "Again?"

Sadie winks. "That's the spirit."

By the time I catch a wave—really catch it, even if only for a few exhilarating seconds—my arms are burning, my legs unsteady, and my lungs full of the salt-bright air. But I do it. I stand. Wobbly, barely in control, but upright. And for that fleeting moment that the ocean carries me, nothing else matters.

Not too bad for a sedentary mathematician.

Sadie whoops as I splash back into the water. "There she is!"

Devon grins. "Told you. Less thinking, more doing."

I float on my back for a second, staring up at the wide, cloudless sky, letting the water cradle me. Maybe there's something to what they keep hammering on—less thinking, more doing. Less doubting, more trusting.

I paddle back toward them, shaking the water from my hair.

"We'll make a surfer out of you yet," Devon says.

"I wouldn't hold your breath."

Sadie smirks. "We're surfers, which automatically makes us more patient than most."

I ride one more wave—not well, but better—and then wade back to shore, my body tired but my mind a little lighter.

As I squeeze the water from my hair, the salt drying on my skin and the ocean still tugging at my feet, I tell myself that maybe it's time to stop letting doubt dictate my every move, to stop analyzing every possibility before I've even let something begin, to stop believing that hesitation will protect me when all it's ever done is keep me standing still.

I stare at my reflection in the mirror. Dinner with Cass shouldn't feel this momentous. It's just a friendly meal, after all—we clearly established that. Yet it feels like something more because of what she confided in me.

I grab my lotion and smooth it over my arms, the scent grounding me as I try to ignore the nerves buzzing beneath my skin. It's just dinner. Yet I'm standing here like I have something to prove, like I need to present myself in a certain way.

As I button up my blouse, my fingers hesitate at the last one, hovering over my collarbone.

Less thinking, more doing.

I let the top button stay undone. Maybe it's okay to be seen—if just a tiny bit.

CHAPTER 11
CASS

I run a hand through my hair, trying to make it look casual enough for a non-date. Because this isn't a date. Even so, I still changed my outfit twice.

I glance at the clock. Estelle will be here any minute. I reach for the bottle of wine and pour myself a small glass to steady my nerves. Then the bell rings and I buzz her up.

As expected, Estelle looks gorgeous. Her curls frame her face in a way that makes my breath catch for a moment. I invite her in, trying very hard not to be too impressed by her easy beauty. She looks nothing like the woman who left the restaurant last night. She's stone-cold sober, for starters. And I haven't wooed her with my food yet.

She hands me a bottle of wine and a gift-wrapped package. "For you." She grins.

I put the wine to the side and focus on the package. She brought me a gift. How thoughtful.

I tear the paper carefully, revealing a wooden frame, the glass slightly worn but intact. Inside is a black-and-white image—an old postcard, by the look of it—of the very building we're standing in now. The restaurant. My home. But decades ago, when it was something else entirely.

Surprised, I glance up at her. "Where did you find this?"

"My father's house," she says. "He had a whole collection of Clearwater Bay memorabilia. I thought you might like it."

I meet her gaze. "I love it."

"Good," she says. "I wasn't certain whether you'd find it sentimental or just clutter."

I glance at the photo again, at the old bones of this place, the way it stood against the cliff's edge even then, battered by wind and salt and time. "It's not clutter," I say. "It's history."

She smiles, and I invite her to sit. I catch myself staring, at the way her blouse shifts against her frame, the way she moves with the kind of grace that makes me too aware of my own body, of its heft and hesitations.

August comes over to inspect the stranger in his home.

"I hope you don't mind cats."

"Not when they're cute like this." Her approach toward Gussie is equally thoughtful. She lets him sniff her hand first, before petting him. Gus responds by jumping onto the couch next to her.

"Estelle, meet August. Gussie, Estelle." I almost say, 'our new friend', but it would sound too silly.

"It smells incredible in here." Estelle leans back, one hand scratching behind August's ear. I know it's ridiculous to be jealous of a cat, and yet.

I put the frame she gave me on the sideboard, prominently on display, and ask what she would like to drink.

"I was thinking just water after last night, but I'll have whatever you're having."

"I have a local sauvignon blanc open. How about a small glass of that alongside a large glass of sparkling water?"

"Sounds perfect." She smiles up at me. "Is there anything I can do to help?"

"Of course not. You're my guest."

"It hardly seems fair. Just because you're this amazing chef, you shouldn't have to do everything." She looks as comfortable and relaxed in the couch as August does.

"It's what I do." I nod at my cat. "Besides, you have your work cut out for you."

I head into the kitchen to fetch the drinks. Estelle might have been tipsy last night, but I wasn't. Yet I told her all these things about myself. It feels a bit unnerving.

"I went surfing this morning," Estelle says, a stupid grin appearing on her face. "That actually makes it sound as though I can surf, which I can't. Anyway, I wanted to clear my head, get rid of my hangover, and Sadie and Devon were in the ocean as well. When I signed up for surf club, I honestly had no idea Sadie Ireland would be teaching. I dare to guess that, once word spreads, there will be more than five middle-aged ladies taking her class."

I shrug. "Sadie's been back in Clearwater Bay for years. Most people are used to her now, but I understand it can be a lot to process for a newcomer."

"Do you know them well?"

"Her sister, Suzy, is one of my best friends and her twin brother, Sam, is married to my ex's best friend, so..." I nod. "We run in the same circles."

"It must be nice to be so embedded in the town."

"It's lovely here. Do you enjoy being back?"

"I guess so. Even though I haven't spent any significant time here in so long, there's something about coming back to the place where you grew up. I feel like I don't know anyone here anymore, though."

"We're a friendly enough bunch."

"Hence… why I'm here at yours now."

"Hey, um, I wanted to say… sorry if I pushed you last night. That wasn't my intention."

"I'm here, so…"

"Yeah." Looking at her, sitting in my couch—August about to roll over and show her his belly—I can't help but feel like, physically, we're such a mismatch. I don't even know where I found the audacity to ask her out last night. I must have been a bit high on myself and a great night of service and her kind words about my food. She's not dressed up, yet she looks like she's ready to enter the poshest room. Like she would turn every single head.

After we exchange some small talk—mostly me filling her in about the goings-on in Clearwater Bay—I invite her to the table.

I head into the kitchen, happy to feel fully in my element for a few moments. This might be a dinner with a new friend, yet she still destabilizes me a little. I let muscle memory take over—my hands know what to do. After thousands of services, plating comes easy.

By the time we're halfway through the meal, conversation flows easily, the initial formality of the evening giving way to something looser.

Estelle asks about the restaurant, about how I ended up in Clearwater Bay—I'm not a native, like her—and I tell her about leaving San Francisco, about needing something slower, about how I wasn't sure this place would ever feel like home until, one day, it did.

She listens intently, resting her chin against her palm, her eyes steady on mine. "Do you ever regret leaving the city?"

"Not the move. But… I guess I sometimes miss who I was before."

Estelle considers this for a moment. "And who was that?"

"Someone who had a lot more fun," I say.

Her lips curve, just slightly. "You look like you have plenty of fun."

I let out a low chuckle. "The most I have to look forward to these days is a support group for menopausal women."

Estelle lifts her fork, spearing a bite of octopus. She doesn't respond to my quip with words. Instead, she takes a bite, closing her eyes briefly as she savors it.

I watch her expression shift. I hear the faint hum of appreciation she makes in the back of her throat. That sound every chef lives for. The involuntary *mmm* that means you've done something right, created something that bypasses thought and goes straight to pleasure.

She opens her eyes and says, "This is incredible. You must have had fun preparing this. I can taste the fun you had in making this."

It's a simple dish—grilled octopus, tender from hours of slow braising, finished on an open flame for just the right amount of char, served over a bed of lemony white-bean purée with a drizzle of olive oil.

"I did," I admit. I watch as she takes another bite, the candlelight flickering in her eyes, and wonder how I got here, having dinner with a woman who makes me feel as if maybe I could possibly learn how to have fun again—albeit just as friends.

"Last night," I say, trying to keep my tone light, "you said dating wasn't on your to-do list."

"Yeah."

"I don't want to pry," I say, despite my curiosity. "But I keep thinking about it. I keep wondering why."

Estelle breathes out softly, not quite a sigh, but close enough. "I've had my heart broken so many times…" She pauses.

I nod, waiting.

Her fingers tighten around her glass. "You were very open and honest with me last night, and I really appreciate that, but I'm not sure I'm ready to return that favor."

"Okay." I send her my softest smile. "Of course."

She leans back in her chair, a shadow crossing her face. She looks away, from the table and from me. Maybe my question wasn't as innocent as I thought it was.

"I will tell you, but…" Her scoff cuts through the air. "This is the kind of information that has sent many a woman running for the hills."

I raise my eyebrows. I don't know what to expect, but she's got my full attention.

"I—um…" She finds my gaze, suddenly defiant. "I'm almost fifty, and for decades now, I've worked on myself to no longer feel bad about this. And I don't, but it's still a hard thing to say because of the effect it has on other people."

"Go on," I gently encourage her.

"I'm asexual. Ace. As in, I don't have sex. I don't feel that desire."

Oh. Fuck. I'm utterly speechless. Although one of my

best friends—Suzy—is aromantic, I'm stumped for words. Because it's not the same. Not even close.

"I'm sorry, I feel like the most ignorant boomer on the planet," I manage to say after a few awkward seconds of silence. "I don't really know how to react to that."

"You could run for the hills." I can hear all the times her heart has been broken, right there in the crack of her voice.

"I'm on a cliff and it's just ocean behind me," I joke stupidly.

"I'm not ashamed of who I am, but, um, well, neither shame, nor pride, have much to do with how my relationships turn out."

"Yeah, I can imagine." It all makes sense now. That's why a gorgeous, brilliant woman—a professor, no less—like Estelle is single. I take a slow sip of wine because I need a second. A moment to process, to not say something clumsy or trite or, worst of all, something that makes her regret telling me.

There's a sudden tightness in her face, like she's waiting for impact. I hate that she expects it, that she's bracing for something.

"I honestly don't know what to say," I admit, keeping my voice low. "Which probably isn't the best thing to say, but…" I chuckle awkwardly. "I guess I'm afraid to say the wrong thing."

Her shoulders relax a fraction. "That's okay. I know it's a lot."

I look at her. "Still, I should say something." It's not because it's hard for me to understand, or because it's the first time I've met someone who's ace, that I can't try.

"I'm not running for the hills," I say. "This body isn't

very good at running anymore, anyway." I hold her gaze. "Besides, why would I? As your new best friend in town?"

CHAPTER 12
ESTELLE

I'm completely okay with who I am, yet I've never met someone who isn't thrown by my coming out. Especially because it's usually someone who's romantically interested in me, and nothing puts a damper on all things romance more than revealing you're ace. But I did inform Cass last night that dating isn't on my to-do list.

Though if I'm honest, part of me looked forward to tonight as if it were a date. A not entirely conscious part, because I do know better—I have all the scars on my foolish, hopeless heart to remind me when needed.

"My new best friend, eh?" I'm not blind. I've seen Cass check me out—especially tonight, before my confession.

"As long as you don't want to go jogging or surfing together," Cass jokes.

I laugh along because it's the easy thing to do under the circumstances—this is hardly the time for a body positivity pep talk.

"In that case, I really should reciprocate this dinner invitation, although my lack of cooking skills might put too big a strain on our budding friendship."

"We could just go for drinks at The Bay instead." Cass puts her cutlery down.

"Let me just enjoy this final piece of exquisiteness before we continue this conversation." I make a show of how tasty Cass's dish is—not a hard thing to do—then wave my hand over my empty plate. "You're a genius, by the way."

"Just a good cook," she says matter-of-factly.

"So." I reach for my wine glass. Now that I've told her about myself, I'd like to ask her a more inquisitive question. "You haven't been with anyone since you and your ex broke up?"

"No." Cass tops up our wine glasses.

"No dates? No nothing?"

"It took me a while to get over because we didn't break up out of lack of love. God, I loved her, but… There were so many obstacles and sometimes love isn't enough, you know?"

"Oh, I know." How I wish I didn't. How I wish I could still innocently—stupidly—believe that love is always enough.

"What would be the point of dating, anyway?" She shrugs. "And the Clearwater Bay dating pool for middle-aged lesbians is also fairly small."

"Hm, isn't later-in-life lesbianism a big thing these days?" I joke.

"Maybe in Berkeley. Among college types and whatnot."

"So you truly consider yourself undatable?" I prod a little.

"Look at me," is all she responds, as though that's an actual answer.

"I am looking at you and, well, you did ask me out last night."

"While you didn't exactly say no, you hardly said yes either."

"For good reason." I point a finger at myself. "If we're in a contest of who's the most undatable, I think I win hands-down."

"It's not a contest, but no fucking way." She rests her chin on an upturned palm. "I'm sure you've heard this a million times before and I hope it doesn't irk you, but you are rather, um, hot."

A chuckle rises from my throat. "It doesn't irk me when you say it." Although she has read that right, it has most certainly irritated me plenty of times before. "But being 'hot'"—I curl my fingers into air quotes—"doesn't make me good at dating. The opposite, actually."

"You said you had your heart broken too many times?" Cass's expression softens further.

"Ten times to be exact." I smile sheepishly. "I do like numbers, but ten times is too many. My heart…" I shake my head. "It's not because I don't have sex that I don't fall in love." Unfortunately. "But it's never enough. I'm never enough."

"I'm so sorry, Estelle."

"We all have our cross to bear." I laugh at myself. "Sorry, I didn't mean to sound so dramatic."

"It's just that, to me," Cass says, "love without sex doesn't sound like the complete impossibility you say it is."

"You just told me your ex was not okay with you no longer wanting sex." Cass has no idea.

"My ex was also twenty years younger than me. We

wanted different things—things that became crystal clear when I hit menopause."

"No kids for you?" As if her cat responds to the word 'kids', August turns up and jumps into Cass's lap. She pushes her chair back to give him space, then gently strokes his head.

"Can you imagine having a newborn when you're going through menopause? I also run a restaurant and I would have been near seventy when our kid went off to college." She shakes her head. "I loved Sarah but it just felt completely unreasonable." Gus rubs his chin against her fingers. "The thing is, when we met, Sarah didn't want kids. That all changed when her best friend had her first baby. She got a bad case of baby fever, and I can't hold her change of heart against her. I will never begrudge a woman for her biological desire to have a child, but I couldn't do that with her. Her new wife is much younger. It's all just so much more… suitable."

"What about you, though? Sarah has a new wife and a baby on the way. What do you have?"

"I have August." She looks at her cat with all the affection in the world. "I have Savor. I have my friends. It's a pretty good life."

"Yet you'd like a bit more fun?"

"I'd like for my body not to betray me so much. I'd like to be able to go out and not worry about hot flashes. I'd like to have a goddamn orga—" She cuts herself off. The clipped word hangs suspended in the air between us.

"You can say the word orgasm in my presence, you know." I inject lightness into my tone. "I'm not triggered by it."

"You've never…" Cass arches up her eyebrows. "Um—" Her cheeks flush. "You've never had an orgasm?"

"No."

"God. It's—"

"I know it sounds weird, but it's just how I'm wired. It's not something that I miss or crave."

"I can't climax anymore," Cass says. "My body seems entirely unwilling—or unable."

Oh, fuck. Don't go there, Estelle. This is a time to be sensitive, not to rise to a challenge. I try to ignore the tug in my chest—that old, dangerous thought. Because this is how it always begins. And it always ends the same.

"I'm sorry," I mumble.

"It's fine." As if he can't handle this conversation, August abruptly jumps off Cass's lap. "How about dessert?" Maybe Cass can't handle it anymore either.

"Um, okay." I accept Cass's swift gear change. In fact, I welcome it. And I have good reason to.

While Cass rummages in the kitchen, I take a moment to process our conversation—to absorb the effects of coming out. And to brainstorm ways to keep this as a potential friendship and not let it turn into something more. Because I am romantically attracted to Cass. I like her. Being around her is easy but also exciting. But I have my reckless little heart to consider.

She strides out of the kitchen with two plates in her hands. I can't help but smile when I see her walk toward me. She is by no means a light-footed, dainty woman—and it only makes me like her even more. Also, deliciously paradoxically, she's not above complaining about her body and its middle-aged weight gain, while serving a generous portion of dessert not long after. She puts another gorgeous plate down in front of me.

It's beautiful in an understated way—dark and glossy, with a delicate dusting of powdered sugar on top. A single, thin curl of chocolate rests at an angle.

I hover my fork over the pristine surface of the dessert. "What masterpiece am I about to devour next?"

"A dark chocolate cake." Cass settles back into her chair. "A little bitter, a little sweet. Kind of like…" She tilts her head as if assessing me.

I narrow my eyes. "Don't say me."

She grins. "I was going to say life, but sure, if the shoe fits…"

If anyone is like this cake, it's Cass—and it's probably the main reason why I'm here tonight.

I take a bite and it's exactly as she described. Dark and rich, with just enough sweetness to soften the edges.

"Oh my god." My mouth full of yummy goodness, I shake my head. I try to savor my bite, but I end up swallowing it greedily because it's just too damn good. "You're not the first chef I've dated," I blurt out. "I think food might be my sex."

I didn't mean to be so flippant, but I think something in that chocolate has intoxicated me.

"Hold on a minute." Cass does an impressive job of not losing her cool—it must be all those years working in high pressure environments. "First of all, when did this become a date?"

"It's not." I shake my head. "I'm sorry. That came out wrong. I meant friend-date."

"Are you still friends with the chef you used to date?" She's looking at me with a very self-satisfied grin on her lips and I can't tell whether it's because of this divine dessert she served me or for another reason—or both.

"Heavens no." The chef left me with Scar Number 8. "I sure hope we never fall out, because your food is too good to live without." I glance at the delicious cake on my plate.

A short silence falls, the only noise the clattering of our forks against porcelain. It's the kind of awkward silence I'm desperate to fill, but I've blurted out enough inanities these past couple of minutes. Instead, I patiently wait for Cass to say something.

"Because food is your sex?" It sounds utterly ridiculous after that silence.

"Obviously…" Maybe I can still save this, come out of this looking better than I deserve. "I can't compare the two. I've heard people talk of foodgasms and such, but, well, for obvious reasons, I wouldn't know whether that term is correct."

"Oh, it is. I've seen it happen plenty of times." Cass surprises me. She's throwing me a conversational lifeline.

"Only *seen* it happen?"

She chuckles low in her throat. "In my extremely expert opinion, you can't compare the two." She pushes a strand of hair away from her forehead. Are those beads of sweat pearling on her brow? "I mean, I guess it depends. But sex is…" She pauses, then moves her hand about as though what she was about to say next needs to be waved off.

"It's okay. You don't have to hold back on my account." She's looking decidedly flustered now, which—again—delights me too much.

"Oh, no. That's not what I was doing. You're the one who started talking about this, but… my thought ran out of steam." She scoffs gently. "Kind of like my own sex life, really." She pulls her lips into a smile that completely contradicts what she just said.

I have to laugh because, so far, tonight has been nothing short of joyful—and I truly do believe that Cass might become my new best friend in this town.

CHAPTER 13
CASS

Because I have no idea what's happening here—is a gorgeous asexual woman actually flirting with me? And what does that even mean?—I gather the dessert plates and take them into the kitchen.

She's asexual and I've admitted to not having any sex drive left, still, this evening doesn't feel like some sort of Victorian, overly chaste dinner date between two possible friends. In fact, it feels like the exact opposite.

I rinse the plates and leave them in the sink. The irony is also that, when I'm with Estelle, my libido doesn't feel so dead anymore. There are flickers of life. Because, yes, she's hot—as I clumsily let her know—but even more so because she's a mystery.

On the surface, she's a Berkeley math professor with burnout, but then she comes into my house and reveals she's asexual, only to then—and I might suffer from brain fog, but I'm not too far gone to discern this—rather brazenly flirt with me. That really is too much for my poor menopausal brain to handle.

"Can I help?" Silent like a cat—August has a way of

sneaking up on me like this—she has approached the kitchen.

Look at her. She's like an apparition in my doorway. As though some divinity has sent her from the heavens of hotness for the sole purpose of letting me know that physical attraction is still an option for me. That there are women out there whose hotness supersedes the havoc my hormones have wreaked in my body.

"Are you okay?" Her question cuts through my impertinent thoughts. "You have a funny look on your face."

Or maybe this is yet another glorious symptom of menopause. A new one that affects the brain and makes the most out-there illusions seem perfectly plausible. Nothing surprises me anymore when it comes to this.

"Just, huh, a lesser moment," I mumble.

"I'm sorry if I made you uncomfortable. I was feeling a little uncomfortable myself, to be honest." She puts a hand on her chest. "All my own doing, just to be clear. And, erm, I guess I was acting out, you know, like nearly fifty-year-old women tend to do." Her smile is so crookedly perfect, it dislodges something in me.

I'm beginning to think that Estelle is some sort of test. Because she's so stunning and lovely and enigmatic, but she's also asexual. Then again, she has contradicted herself before. She says she's undatable, yet here we are, on what definitely feels like a date. Because, as far as I can tell, that really was a slip of the tongue. She can declare this a non-date all she wants, but I still know what a date feels like. And I most certainly know the difference between flirting and having a purely platonic chat with a friend.

"I guess I'm a little confused." I lean against the counter.

"Yeah, me too." She heads farther into the kitchen—closer to me. "Very confused, actually."

"About what... specifically?" My voice has become all thick and husky.

"You. Me." She takes another step closer but leaves a respectable distance between us. "Whatever's going on here." Another smile. "Mainly me, though."

"Truth be told, you are quite confusing." I swallow slowly.

"I know." She tilts her head. "And I know how infuriating that can be." She bites her bottom lip.

From that point on, all I can see are her lips. My entire focus is pulled toward her mouth and all I can think of is how much I want to kiss her. But I can't kiss Estelle. Does she even kiss?

I'm stuck—nailed to the goddamn floor.

And she's right. There is something infuriating about her. What is she even doing in my kitchen? Clearly, she's not helping.

"Cass. I—" She gazes into my eyes. "Can I come closer? Is that okay?"

I can only nod.

She steps right into whatever's left of my personal space. She's so near, I can smell her perfume—I can feel the heat of her body radiating onto mine. And, oh my, is she hot.

She fixes her gaze on me, and the moment hangs suspended between us, like a drop of water before it falls.

Then, she leans in and kisses me.

It's soft and tentative at first, as if she's testing the feel of it—like she might not remember how it is to kiss. I breathe into it, my eyes fluttering shut, letting myself be fully in it—because I'm not going to pull back now. Hell no. I enjoy the delicious pressure of her lips against mine like I'm a woman in the prime of her life instead of in the dry depths of menopause.

Then, her hand finds my waist, her fingers light but certain against the fabric of my blouse, and I'm about to lose my mind. What the hell is happening? I escaped to my kitchen for some much-needed refuge from the escalating tension in the living room, and now she's kissing me, in my kitchen.

And it's the kind of kiss that steals nothing, but gives everything. A kiss that goes on and on and effortlessly fills the space where my earlier questions lingered. Because when someone kisses you like this, at least for the time the kiss lasts, there's no room left for questioning.

When she finally pulls back, she doesn't leave a lot of space between us. Her breath is still warm against my skin, her forehead resting against mine.

"I don't know what this is," she murmurs.

"Me neither." It's pretty clear Estelle does kiss and—judging by how excellent she is at it—that she's had plenty of practice. "I certainly didn't expect you'd kiss me," I whisper. Turns out there's plenty of room left for confusion.

"I didn't come here to kiss you," she whispers back, and her voice is so soft and low, her lips so close to mine, it almost feels like another kiss. "But—"

"But?" My forehead still rests against hers, making it impossible to get a good look at her face. That's as far as it goes? I want to ask, but I'm not sure if I should. I'm not sure of anything anymore, except that I would like to kiss her again. Her hand rests on my hip and, for the first time in my life, I'm unsure whether I can touch her like that.

Whether I can put a hand on the hip of the woman who's kissing me.

In response, Estelle just gently shakes her head, and mine along with it.

Then, I say the most lesbian thing possible. "Should we talk about this?"

"That's probably a good idea." But Estelle doesn't pull away. Instead, her forehead slides down my cheek as she tilts her head, and kisses me again.

Her tongue is like the smoothest velvet and her lips so pillowy, so moreish, that I wish kissing equaled talking and we could just do this for the rest of the night. That it would magically explain what is going on here. What she's thinking. What she's after. What she's willing to give and where the line is.

A kiss can be magical—this one's pretty bewitching—but it can no longer quiet the thoughts that swirl in my brain. My body might be oddly keen to continue, to just kiss and kiss her, but my brain simply can't allow it.

I pull back now, deliberately putting some distance between us by moving away from the counter.

I spent many long nights lying awake next to my beautiful partner, wondering why I could no longer bear for her to touch me, and it messed with my head to no end. Although not the same, this situation is even more puzzling. Perhaps because this isn't so much about me.

"Goodness, Cass," Estelle says, her hip against the counter. "I understand if this is a little perplexing."

"No, I mean, yes… we agreed this wasn't a date, but then you flirted and… I don't even do this anymore." What a thing to say.

"I like you so much," Estelle says. "I'm interested in

you for, um, so many reasons. Some of them…" She shakes her head. "Not… that acceptable."

It's like every time Estelle tries to explain something to me, a brand-new mystery is created.

"Come on." I march back into the living room—I need to get out of the kitchen. I nod for her to follow me. I quickly refill our wine glasses and sit in an armchair that only has room for one. "Let's talk," I say.

CHAPTER 14
ESTELLE

I can't tell Cass that something she said made her—in my own way—irresistible to me. Although, come to think of it, it would be wholly dishonest not to divulge it. I didn't come here to trick, nor kiss her—let alone seduce her.

"There are so many things about you that appeal to me," I say honestly. "I don't mean your cooking, although that's magnificent. That goes without saying at this point." I might have hammered on it a bit too much in order to hide some other emotions. "I like that you're straightforward. I like that you know what you want. I like that you're very honest about the stage of your life you're in. I like your sense of humor and your kindness. Your respect for me and what I told you."

"Jesus." Cass fans her face with her fingers. "Way to make a middle-aged lady blush." She's no longer in a mood to mess about, though, that much is crystal clear. "All of that sounds very acceptable. Like music to my ears, actually."

I shake my head. "I'm sorry. I can't tell you. Not tonight." She might very well run for the hills if I do.

"I can't make heads nor tails of you." Nothing Cass says ever sounds unkind. Her words are always tinged with a softness that is addictive. "Can you tell me what *you* want?"

"Maybe we can go on a proper date? One that we call by its right name from the start." I put all my warmth in the smile I send her. "If you want."

"We certainly would have a lot to talk about."

I take it that means she has a lot of questions for me. It's not a yes, however.

"So, you want to go on a date," Cass repeats what I just said. "Even though you've said several times that dating isn't on your to-do list and you're undatable."

It's confrontational to hear my own contradictions repeated back to me. Cass is right. I did say those things. And then I kissed her.

"I do." I take a sip of wine and wish it was something stronger, like that brandy from yesterday.

"To what end?" she asks.

I'm not the only one in this room who's been hurt. I bet Cass's heart has plenty of scars as well.

"I would like to get to know you better."

She huffs out some air. "I don't know if you're being coy or just honest. It's driving me up the wall."

"I'm not being coy. I'm being as honest as I can be." I take a beat, then swallow what I'm about to say next.

"I want to, Estelle… Of course, I do."

"But?"

"You confuse the hell out of me. I don't know what to think. You're one big mixed signal. A very pretty one, at that." She shakes her head. "I know it's not sex you're after. And why would you, with the likes of me?"

How I wish Cass wouldn't refer to her body as though it's become some useless burden she has to carry around. But I get it.

"I'm sorry for being confusing. You might not think so after tonight, but I actually prefer things to be obvious and clear cut. Yet, confusion and a certain level of chaos is what I end up projecting."

"To be blunt." Cass shifts in her chair. "After what you told me, I didn't think kissing would even be on the menu."

"It is."

"But… how does it make you feel?" She finds my gaze and is brave enough to hold it.

"I would love to explain all of this to you during a proper date." I'm desperately pushing for a yes because if she says no now, if she ushers me out of her house, I fear I might also be ushered out of her life.

"Of course I'll go on a date with you," Cass says. "I can't say no after that kiss, but… I'm worried it doesn't mean the same to you as it does to me."

"Don't worry about that. Please." It's easy enough to say, much harder to do. Eighty percent of my relationships might have been salvageable if there had been less worrying.

Cass smiles gently, then sags deeper into her chair. "I was enjoying my quiet life, dealing with my hot flashes, finding my groove as a single lady, and then you turn up with… all of this." She briefly arches up her eyebrows. "I should probably stay away from you, but I already can't resist you." She scoffs. "You probably have no idea how crazy that sounds to *me*." She puts a hand on her chest, just below her clavicle.

"Maybe when you put together two women who consider themselves undatable, you get the opposite."

"I'd like to see you calculate that in your little notebook."

I burst into a chuckle. It might not be as hard as the problem my dad set me. I'd make it work somehow.

"I can show you my calculations on our date. I'd like to take you out to thank you for tonight. And last night."

"Show me with food, that's more my language." Cass might be a little confused, but she's by no means put off—or intimidated.

"Deal. Although it's a pity I can't take you to the best restaurant in town."

"Burgers at The Bay are fine. Maybe you can show off your newfound surfing skills for me first."

"Oh, god." I giggle because we're now firmly past the hurdle our impromptu kiss has thrown up. "Only if you join me."

"Never," Cass says. "I prefer to watch."

On that note, August strolls into the living room and utters an exasperated meow, as though commenting on something very untoward that's happening.

"He's hungry," Cass says. "He's a very punctual cat." She pats her lap, but August refuses to jump in. "Very bossy as well."

"I'll let you feed your cat." I push myself out of the couch. I could stay here for a good while longer, but I might end up kissing Cass again—and I don't think I should. "I'll see you for burgers at The Bay on…" I crouch down to scratch August behind the ear. "My calendar's wide open."

"What day is your surfing lesson?" Cass rises. "I can meet you there."

I shake my head, unable to suppress a smile. "No. A proper date, we said. I'm not going to turn up in a wetsuit."

"Why not? From where I was sitting, it looked pretty good on you."

"So you were watching me?"

"I was curious about your skills. Suzy told me you grew up here and I know that for most people that means they have surfer blood."

"As soon as I learned to count, I turned into a math nerd." I push myself up, eliciting another offended meow from August. "If you have any math that needs doing, I'm your girl." This conversation is getting more irrational by the minute.

"I'll think about it." Cass nods at the frame I gave her—it seems like a lifetime ago that I arrived. "Thank you for that. I really appreciate it."

"Thank you for another amazing meal. It was special, like the person who made it."

"My pleasure." She walks toward me, her arm extended as though she wants to put her hand on my back, but she retracts it. "My oh-so confused pleasure, Estelle Raymond."

I reach for her hand and take it in mine.

"Shall we say Monday?" Cass squeezes my hand softly. "Seven o'clock?"

"I'll skip surf club. Happily." Our hands intertwined, Cass walks me to the door.

"We can do lunch instead on Tuesday," Cass offers.

"No, dinner on Monday evening sounds perfect." I turn toward her. "I had an impromptu private lesson with both Sadie Ireland and her wife this morning."

"Both Sadie and Devon?" Cass grins. "You must be a pro by now."

"Close enough." I slant toward Cass and kiss her softly on the cheek. "Good night. See you soon."

I slip out the door before I can create any more confusion.

CHAPTER 15
CASS

There it is again. I lean closer to the mirror, tilting my chin to the light, my fingers searching for the offending strand —a single hair sprouting defiantly from a spot it has no business being. I pluck it quickly, wincing more out of frustration than pain. It's not the first time I've found one there, but this morning, it feels like a personal attack. Because I can't help but wonder whether Estelle noticed it last night—when she kissed me.

Luckily, I have no time to reminisce further—I've done enough of that already during the night, my body blowing hot and cold like never before—because Suzy's coming over for lunch.

I wait for her in Savor's kitchen, laying out the ingredients I will need for this simple but most delicious dish.

Suzy doesn't knock. She just waltzes in, kisses me on the cheek, gives me a once-over, and says, "Hm."

"Good day to you too, Miss Ireland."

"There's no better vibe reader in this town than *moi*, and I'm getting vibes." She settles on a stool on the right side of the stove.

I pour her some coffee and slide it over to her.

She waits, patient as ever, sipping her coffee.

"Something happened last night," I admit readily. I run my fingers along my jaw, brushing the spot where that damn rogue hair was earlier. "I'll tell you all about it, but first: grilled cheese sandwiches."

"Oh my god. Yes and yes, please," Suzy groans. "I'm starving."

My ingredients are ready: crusty slices of sourdough; extra-sharp, aged cheddar; a bit of Gruyère for depth; and butter, because a perfect grilled cheese lives and dies by how well you butter the bread.

The pan clicks softly against the burner as it heats. I cut a slab of butter and press it into the bread, feeling the resistance before it softens into something pliant.

I'm glad for the time it buys me because while I'm dying to tell my best friend about that kiss, it's not just *that* I will be telling her about. I have to give her the whole story—and Suzy happens to be the perfect conversation partner for that.

The butter sizzles as I lay the bread down in the pan. The scent warms the air. I sprinkle a touch of flaky salt over the slices, then layer the cheese, allowing the heat to work its magic.

With my back half turned to her, my voice barely audible over the sizzle, I say, "Estelle kissed me last night."

"Say what now?"

I turn around and look into her flabbergasted face.

"Context please," Suzy says.

"Hold on." I flip the sandwiches, watching as the bread turns perfectly golden, the cheese melting into something lush and inviting. I take a few breaths, then plate the sandwiches, slicing them diagonally so the cheese oozes at the edges. I give one to Suzy.

She picks up the plate, inspecting the sandwich with the reverence it deserves. "You're such a queen in the kitchen." Suzy takes a bite, closes her eyes for a second, then sighs. "Okay, I'm ready. Tell me everything."

I lean against the counter, cradling my own sandwich in my hands. "It's not so much the kiss that has thrown me," I say. "The kiss was amazing."

"I sense a but." Suzy glances at me.

"It's hard to get a handle on what it means, because…"

Suzy studies me in silence, then takes another bite.

"Before we kissed, she told me that, um, she's asexual." This might not be for me to say, but Estelle didn't tell me it was a secret.

Suzy stops mid-chew, eyes widening slightly. "She is?"

I nod.

Her gaze sharpens. She swallows, then asks, "And she kissed you?" Suzy seems to chew that over as much as her grilled cheese sandwich.

"Yeah."

Finally, she puts her sandwich down and wipes her fingers on a napkin. "Tell me everything you're thinking."

"I don't know what to think. I'm so confused. The whole evening was so incredibly confusing."

"Well, then, let's figure it out." Suzy sends me a knowing smile. "She's asexual. And she kissed you. Perhaps you're assuming that's a contradiction."

I rub my temples. "Logically, I kind of know it's not. Or it doesn't have to be. But…" I struggle to articulate the rest. "It's not just the kiss. It's a lot of the things she said."

"Like?"

"Like that she doesn't date. That she's had her heart

broken too many times. That she's never enough for the women she's with. All of that, but then she started flirting with me, ending with a kiss I really did not see coming."

"Okay." Suzy picks up her sandwich again, tapping a finger against the crust. "As you well know, attraction and intimacy don't have to fit into the neat little boxes we were raised to believe in."

"You sound like an after-school special."

"That's what it takes sometimes." She grins.

I shake my head, yet I can't help but grin back. Even though I know all this—I don't live in a bubble of ignorance—it's good to be reminded sometimes.

Suzy continues, "Asexuality is a spectrum. Just like everything else. Some aces never want sex. Some do, under the right conditions. Some want romance, some don't. It's not a one-size-fits-all thing."

I run my thumb over what's left of the golden crust of my sandwich. "I get that. But I don't know where Estelle falls on that spectrum. Or what she wants from me."

Suzy examines my face. "What do you want from her?"

I blink at her. "I don't know. I don't think I want anything from her." That might not be entirely true. I sure wouldn't mind another one of those kisses—but not before I know where they will end up.

She lifts an eyebrow, seeing right through me, no doubt. "Are you sure?"

I press my lips together and shrug.

"You're probably overcomplicating things. Estelle kissed you because she wanted to. Not because she's secretly trying to trick herself into something she doesn't want. Not because she's confused about her identity." She pauses. "Although I get why this is messing with your head."

I glance at her. "You do?"

"After Sarah, you're not really open to anything romantic."

"That's right and you know why." It's really convenient to have a menopause consultant as a best friend.

"I do, but maybe there's an opportunity here."

"An opportunity?"

"Do I need to spell it out?" Her tone's sharper than usual, but her smile softens it. "Low libido meets asexuality…" She tilts her head. "Maybe this is a match made in heaven."

It sounds a bit like what Estelle said last night. "It's that simple?"

"Probably not, because this is life and humans are incredibly complex, but you never know." Suzy leans over and puts a warm hand on my arm. "Why don't you just see what happens instead of obsessing over what it means?"

"I might just do that because we have a 'proper' date tomorrow."

"Wonderful." Suzy all but applauds me. "Word of advice: don't tell Hunter. He'll go nuts." She retracts her hand.

I shake my head, ignoring her comment. There's something else I have to tell her.

"The other day, Sarah stopped by."

"Really?"

I wipe at a stubborn spot on the counter. "She's pregnant."

"Fuck." Suzy tilts her head. "And how do you feel about *that*?"

"I'm happy for her. I really am. She wanted kids. And Rose is… well, she's a good match for her." Most certainly a better match than I ever was. "She'll be a great mom."

"And yet, it has thrown you."

"A little bit…" It's only normal that the news of my ex being pregnant would unsettle me. "It's not really about Sarah. I guess it made me realize how much I've convinced myself that certain things just aren't in the cards for me anymore."

Suzy doesn't jump in right away, which is one of the things I love about her. She lets me sit with my own words for as long as I need. She once told me that it took endless hours of life coach training for her to be able to do this.

Finally, after we've been silent for a while, she does speak. "Could it be that Sarah's pregnancy is reminding you of the version of yourself who wanted to make things work with her? Even when you knew, deep down, that you couldn't."

"Oh, I don't know." I sort of meant what I said to Estelle last night about enjoying my quiet, non-tumultuous life.

"And now, you've met someone who, on paper, might be very compatible, and it's throwing you for a loop."

I let out a sharp breath. "It's not just that. It's *me*." I tap a hand against my chest. "I don't even know if I'm capable of being with someone anymore."

"Of course, you are."

I shake my head. "After Sarah, I shut that part of myself off. I had to." No sex. No relationships. Easy-peasy.

"I know." Her voice is warm and gentle. "And for a long time, that made sense. But what if this is different?" Once Suzy gets going, it's hard to stop her. "Why don't you just see what happens?" She pats my arm, her touch very different than before.

"Burgers at The Bay tomorrow," I say. "We'll see."

"I'll try not to meet up with Hunter for drinks there at the same time." She shoots me a crooked smile.

"You'd better not."

"You'd better call me with news as soon as you can."

"As I said, we'll see." I clear our plates.

"As long as you keep making me grilled cheese sandwiches like this, you can do whatever you want." Suzy blows me a kiss and then smiles at me the way only a best friend who knows you through-and-through can.

CHAPTER 16
ESTELLE

I'm only pretending to brood on the problem in my notebook. I'm about an hour early for my date with Cass, but I couldn't stay at my dad's house one minute longer.

"Penny for your thoughts." A vaguely familiar voice pulls me from my reverie on the deck of The Bay.

I look into Devon's friendly face, the early evening sun catching the fine salt spray in her hair.

"Are you working?" She rests her hands on the chair opposite me. "I don't want to disturb you."

"No. You're not disturbing me at all." I quickly close my notebook and send her a smile. I could do with some small talk, some light conversation to ease my nerves—because I am nervous. What if Cass changed her mind after all my confusing antics? "Join me?"

"I'd love to." Devon sends me a sly grin. "I need to keep an eye on the women my wife is teaching how to surf, especially hot newcomers."

A loud chuckle escapes me. "First of all, I'm not exactly new to town, and well, hot is debatable, so I'll stay out of that."

If anything, Devon is smoking hot, what with her sun-kissed skin and high cheekbones. I don't care much for tattoos, but that sleeve on her arm is a true eye-catcher. No wonder Sadie Ireland married her. They're the sort of couple that makes you believe in love again, even when you're trying your hardest not to.

"Are you taking Sadie's lesson later?"

"No, um, not this week." I clear my throat. "I'll be back next week for sure."

"Good." Devon nods while she pushes a ginger strand of hair away from her face. "I think every middle-aged woman should learn how to surf, not only for the physical health benefits, but even more so for the mental ones." When she flashes me a bright wide smile, faint laughter lines are visible around the corners of her mouth. "Although my sister-in-law wholeheartedly disagrees with me on that and she calls me completely biased when it comes to all things surfing."

"The learning curve is quite steep," I say.

"Anything really worth learning should have a degree of difficulty. If you could just grab a board, take to the water, and glide on a wave, where would be the satisfaction in that?"

"Oh my god, that would be so fucking satisfying," I blurt out.

"You say that now, but it's not really true." Devon's very matter-of-fact about this.

A server stops by to bring us some water.

"Any particular reason you're not surfing tonight? The weather's great for it and the waves are perfect."

"Um, yeah." An inadvertent smile tugs at my lips. "I have a date. Here. Later."

Devon grins at me. "That's an excellent reason to skip

surfing with my wife." She flashes me a grin. "Anyone I know?"

"Cass."

"Cass from Savor?"

I nod, butterflies doing something untoward in my stomach.

"Right." It's hard to read Devon's face. "Cass, huh?" Her head seems stuck between a shake and a nod. "Okay." She takes a sip of water. "How did that come about, if I may be so curious?"

News of our date will be all over town in no time, I imagine. Not an issue for me, but I can't be sure how Cass feels about that, what with her actually living here.

"I, um, got a little too addicted to her food and kept showing up at Savor. We got talking and…" I open my hands as if I've just given Devon a precise lowdown despite leaving out about ninety percent of the details. "Here we are."

"I know Cass well," Devon says. "Her best friend, Suzy, isn't just my sister-in-law, we also work together."

"Oh, what do you do?"

"I'm a life coach. Suzy focuses more on menopause consulting now, which doesn't make her less of a life coach. On the contrary, I would say."

"A life coach, huh?" My life could do with some coaching right about now. "So you have all the wisdom?"

Devon shakes her head. "No, but I've worked on myself a lot, I've helped a ton of clients, and I've studied my ass off, so… I do know a thing or two." She leans forward. "Mostly, it's about listening, though. Most women just need to be heard." She leans back in silence, as though she's ready to hear whatever I have to say. A gull lands on the railing beside us, head cocked as if it too is waiting for what I say next.

Maybe she has a sixth sense as a life coach, maybe her experience listening to so many women has helped her recognize a woman struggling with something.

I consider Devon's words. I don't doubt that most women need to be heard, but talking doesn't always come easy to me. I try regardless.

"I came back to Clearwater Bay because I burned out," I say, sort of surprising myself. "My dad died a few months ago and I tried to go back to work afterward, but it was suddenly all too much and I couldn't care about work as much as I did before. As when he was still alive."

"That's a hell of a one-two punch," Devon says.

"Yeah." I glance past her, watching a group of young surfers wander along the boardwalk, carefree and relaxed. "I thought coming here might help me reset, but I'm definitely not there yet."

"These things take time," Devon says. "It's probably good that you came back."

I wrap my hands around my water glass. "I'm doing all the right things according to the internet. Taking time off, learning a new skill like surfing, getting plenty of fresh air." I force a smirk.

"Going on a date." Devon grins at me.

"Mom. Mom!" A kid runs up to our table. "Mom, come on, you promised." He hovers over Devon, dripping water onto her.

"Estelle, meet my son, Finn. Finn, Estelle."

"Hi." The boy looks me straight in the eye. "Nice to meet you, Estelle," he says. Finn's adorable and obviously raised to be polite.

"And you, Finn."

"He wanted to join Sadie's lesson. He figured he could teach the ladies a thing or two," Devon says. "It's my job to keep him away." Devon gets up. "We're doing a sunset surf."

"I'll get your board," Finn says and runs off.

"He's such a little surfer dude," Devon's voice is soaked with motherly love. She sends me a smile. "Hey, um, if you want to talk more, I'm an excellent listener. You know where to find me." She raises her hand. "Have a great date. Cass is lovely."

"Thanks," I mumble as she walks off with the confident gait of a woman who's about to do what she loves most in the world.

I'm engrossed in watching Sadie and her surfers take to the water when Cass arrives, a fashionable ten minutes after seven.

"No regrets about not being able to join them, I hope," she says. She most certainly looks good enough to kiss again. Her eyes are bluer in this light and her hair is delightfully windswept from the walk over.

I rise so I can kiss her on the cheek. She smells like freshly picked flowers.

"None." I glance at her. "You?"

"No, but on second thought, The Bay might not be the best place for our first *proper* date."

"Do you want to go somewhere else?" I ask, but she's already sitting down.

"It's okay. For now." She points at my notebook. "Did you manage to make the numbers work?"

I chuckle low in my throat. Cass's company simultaneously relaxes and excites me. It's a strange feeling. "Always."

The server comes by and we order a bottle of white wine. "That good sauvignon, please," Cass adds.

"I was early and got talking to Devon, actually." I nod at the water. "She's out there surfing with her son."

"Finn's a good kid. At least when they get the surfing bug, they can't get up to any other mischief." Her face softens. "His dad, Hunter, is my other bestie. He was here last week before I, um, had my little incident."

I remember a guy offering me the chair next to Cass, which, come to think of it, might be the reason we're sitting here again tonight. Maybe if I hadn't sat next to her after surf club, we wouldn't have got to talking and I wouldn't have worried about her hot flash. I probably wouldn't have walked her home. I would most definitely have gone back to Savor, though.

"How are the incidents?"

"I had one just before I came here so fingers crossed that's it for tonight."

The bottle of wine is brought to the table. Cass pours us each a glass.

"To our first proper date." She lifts her glass.

"I was a little worried you might not show," I admit.

"I didn't hesitate for even a split second." She leans over the table. "Although, um, I talked to Suzy about last Saturday. About our dinner and that... kiss." She leans in even closer. "I told her that you're ace. I hope that wasn't out of line, but Suzy, she's aromantic. She gets it. If it's supposed to be a secret, it's definitely safe with her."

"It's okay. It's not a secret. It's just who I am."

"Phew." Cass leans back. "I was worried about it. Admittedly, I—um—yeah..."

She's adorable when flustered like that. "You don't know how to deal with it. It's okay."

"I don't want to rush things or speak out of turn or anything like that, but you're going to have to give me pointers, because… I don't know the protocol."

"The protocol…" I have to chuckle at the word. "For me, and this is very personal, but for me, no touching below the waist." I've said this so many times, it comes out easy and natural enough. The reactions to it haven't always been the same, however. "Anything else goes."

"Okay." Cass takes a sip of wine. "Thank you for telling me that. That, um, clears things up considerably."

"I didn't mean to be so coy about that. That really wasn't my intention. In hindsight, I was more coy than honest with you."

"You were flirting." Cass smiles. "Brutal honesty doesn't always work when engaged in the subtle art of flirting. I accept that."

"I was flirting, wasn't I?"

Cass nods. "Hence my confusion. I've never had a beautiful woman tell me she's asexual and then kiss me like that before, so…"

It's funny how we can so openly talk about everything that was so difficult to address only a few days ago.

"It's just that," Cass continues, "in my experience, a kiss often leads to… more." She locks her gaze on mine. "But that will never be the case with you?" Her tone rises at the end of the sentence, telling me it's another question she needs answered.

"Not necessarily," I say, no doubt adding to her confusion.

"I know it's a spectrum." She's curious but unafraid—another thing to like about her. "I guess what I'm asking, if this is something I can ask you, is where are you on this spectrum?"

"And we haven't even ordered our burgers yet," I joke. But I'm the one who kissed her and, for that, I do owe her an explanation.

I take a sip of wine, staring into the pale liquid. Then I meet her soft blue gaze.

"I do have sex, but I only give. I never receive."

This stuns Cass into silence. I give her the time she needs to process.

"But the other day you said you didn't have sex."

I nod. "It was the easier thing to say at the time. This is more third date information."

"You're the numbers person…" She pauses. "I've told you about me. About what I'm going through. You're managing my expectations and I think I should do the same with you. Sex for me… it's not a given. Not necessarily because I don't want to, but my body…"

"It's okay." I open my hand to her. "It's absolutely not required. It's an option, within my boundaries, but it's not something I ever expect. It can be off the table or on the table. That's totally up to you. I will always respect your choice."

She peers at my hand. "I'm very much in an off the table stage." She traces a fingertip over my palm. "Although, to be completely honest…" With her other hand, she points at her forehead. "I think my brain is trying to trick me into things my body can no longer live up to."

"What does that mean?" Cass can be coy, too.

"It means that I find you insanely attractive. As in off-the-charts, out-of-my-league, kiss-me-again-now hot."

I trap her wandering finger in my palm. "You're totally

in my league, Cass, and I would very much like to kiss you again."

"Not here, though." A blush creeps up her cheeks.

"We could give the surfer ladies something to talk about." I keep hold of her hand in mine. It feels good there.

"Let's keep the kissing for later," Cass says. "How about those much-talked-about burgers now?"

CHAPTER 17
CASS

My mind blows as hot and cold as my body does these days. It's unmistakable that I feel something, that the old engine has some steam left in it, especially since Estelle told me that 'she only gives, never receives'. But I'm hardly going to jump into bed with her to find out what that means exactly. It's not that hard to imagine.

We order our meal, drink more wine, even dazedly stare into each other's eyes once in a while like lovestruck teenagers.

"Can I ask you a personal question?" Estelle breaks the easy silence.

"It's only fair."

"It's not about fairness. You've told me plenty about yourself." Estelle's voice is soft—velvety, like her lips. And her eyes. God, those eyes. The lightest of brown with a hint of green—an infuriatingly complex color that I can't stop studying. "I was just wondering, as you suffer so much from hot flashes and the other delights of menopause, whether you've considered hormone therapy?"

"Of course." It's hard for me not to get defensive about this subject—because it touches on such a sore point. "My best friend is a menopause consultant. She's on my case about it all the time."

"Okay." Estelle just tilts her head.

"My mother died of breast cancer ten years ago. She was only sixty-eight." There goes my voice. Ten years without her, and I still can't say it in a normal tone. "She took hormones and until the day she died, she was convinced that it was the cause of her cancer. That it killed her." I swallow hard. "Nothing I said could convince her otherwise and she made me promise... She made me look her in the eye and promise her that I would never take hormones so I wouldn't have to suffer the same fate she did."

"Oh my god, Cass. I'm so sorry." Estelle extends her hand toward me again.

"I gave her my word." I gladly put my hand in Estelle's. "And I'm keeping it." I hold up my other hand. "Spare me the lectures, please. I've heard them all a million times before."

"I wasn't going to lecture you." Estelle gives my hand a gentle squeeze. "My lecturing days might very well be behind me."

Mercifully, our food arrives. The Bay does damn good burgers—and that's high praise coming from me.

Estelle doesn't waste any time. She digs in with so much gusto, it catches me off guard. It's almost as though she's making love to the burger instead of just eating it, the way she groans and suddenly loses all decorum.

"I love the burgers here," she says, after she's had a couple of greedy bites.

"I can tell." I purse my lips into a mock-pout. "One might get jealous."

"One really mustn't." She puts her burger down. "They don't compare. This burger is delicious in its own way, while your food is on another level altogether compared to most fine-dining restaurants I've been to."

"Maybe I should make you a burger."

"Maybe you should." She licks some juices off her finger and the old engine is surely revving now. "I'm there for it. Any time you like."

"It's on," I barely manage to say. I tuck into my own burger—or hide behind it, more like.

"I'll hold you to that." Estelle starts munching on her burger again and, this time, I simply enjoy the view. It's pure joy to watch her eat, how she delights in it and—obviously—doesn't care how it makes her look, even though we're on a date.

Our conversation stops while we eat and I catch myself feeling a certain sense of pride—of look-at-me-now—at sitting outside The Bay with her. Estelle can say she's not out of my league all she wants, but that's not how I see things. If she hadn't already kissed me, I'd have to pinch myself because I'm sitting opposite this gorgeous woman.

Earlier, when I suffered through another hot flash, it made me feel as if I was the most unkissable person in the world. And it's not just that—because there's still the unruly mass that is my body. Despite my attraction—because, honestly, it's impossible not to be attracted to her—I'm glad sex is off the table. I wouldn't dream of letting Estelle see me naked. I couldn't bear it. So maybe Suzy was right. Maybe we are a match made in heaven, because I sure do like her.

After we've finished the burgers, wiping our greasy

hands on our napkins, I pick up on something she said earlier.

"Your lecturing days are really behind you?"

"I could give you one of my lectures if you want. I'm pretty good at it." She flashes a sly smile made all the more seductive because of the pillowy quality of her lips.

"Please, don't teach me math. I hope that's not what a third date's for."

"What's it for, then?"

"Getting to know each other better. Asking about future plans, for example."

"Fair enough." Estelle nods. "I'm lucky, actually. My dad left me enough money that I no longer have to work if I don't want to. And I really don't want to right now."

"Really?"

"I may be smart and have a flair for mathematics, but my father was one of a kind brilliant. His skills were in high demand by a number of companies and organizations and they paid him handsomely for his work."

"I'm sorry I never got to meet him." For the life of me, I can't remember retired math professor Mr. Raymond walking the streets of Clearwater Bay. "I don't think I've ever seen him in town."

"You wouldn't have." Estelle's voice sounds a bit more gravelly. "He didn't go out anymore. He didn't have the confidence. He had the beginnings of dementia and—" She pauses to swallow something out of her throat. "For a man with a brain like that, it's worse than losing your pride." She shakes her head. "In the end, it was a mercy for him that he died relatively quickly, because it was agony—for him, and for me to see him like that." Her beautiful brown eyes fill with moisture. "He was such a great father. I loved him to absolute pieces." A tear slides down her cheek, but Estelle doesn't try to catch or hide it. "Some people are just natural born parents. My mother wasn't, but my dad really made up for that. He taught me everything. No matter how busy he was, he always had time for me." She tilts her head backward briefly. "I miss him so much, but the year or so before he died, he wasn't the father I'd always known. As though he wasn't a full person anymore because of his illness. It was awful, but he had a good life and he gave me an amazing life." She reaches for the dirty napkin and dabs it at her tears.

I swiftly dig a pack of paper tissues out of my purse and offer her one. "Here."

She takes it. "I'm pretty sure third dates aren't for crying either, but there you go." Her radiant smile has dimmed into a forced grin.

"They can be for whatever we want them to be." I give her my warmest smile. "I know how hard it is to lose a parent. Someone you love with all your heart."

"Yeah. Sadly, they just can't live forever." She discreetly blows her nose. "My dad was eighty-three and I guess you could say at the end he was ready to go. It's not the same as your mom."

"No." My turn to swallow a lump out of my throat. "My mother…" Even though she passed ten years ago, at times, it still hits me as if she only died the previous week. "She was a go-go-go kind of woman. She couldn't sit still for five minutes. She always had plans and such an incredible zest for life." If only I could talk to her, just ask her one last question, just have five more minutes. "To see her die from cancer." I huff out some air. "I should be able to talk about this by now, but sometimes I can't." I inhale deeply. "I vote we steer the conversation away from dead parents."

"To life." Estelle picks up her wine glass, but it's empty.

"More?" I take another breath, and it's easy enough to shake off my grief when sitting opposite her.

"Why not? I don't have to work tomorrow." She leans back in her chair.

"I do, but I don't have to get up early." And most of the time my work doesn't feel like a job, I think, but don't say out loud because of Estelle's burnout. That's probably the last thing she wants to hear—although she did just say she doesn't have to work if she doesn't want to, which is not the worst position to be in.

I pour more wine and even though we touched on a melancholy subject, I don't feel sad, because I'm sitting with Estelle on the deck of The Bay and I can't think of any other place I'd rather be.

"Uh-oh." Estelle's gaze is pulled to the shoreline. "I think Sadie's lesson has finished. Things might not be so quiet here anymore once they've changed out of their wetsuits."

"Do you want to get out of here?" Was it only a week ago that I sat here with Estelle for the first time? It feels like so much has happened since. She's taking up so much space in my life already.

"That's a safe bet. They're a pretty rowdy bunch for middle-aged ladies." She makes quick work of her wine and pushes herself out of her chair. "Let me settle the bill. I'll be right back."

I have no choice. Automatically, my gaze follows her as she heads inside. Her ass looks mighty fine in those jeans and the way that blouse is tucked in so tightly easily convinces me that—unlike me—Estelle doesn't carry much excess fat on her body. While with anyone else, it would make me feel insecure enough to cut a lovely date short, with her, it doesn't—because I don't have to show myself to her and it takes off so much pressure. Maybe—and I won't know this until I work up the nerve to ask her—she sees people differently. Maybe physical attraction is not something that's in play for her when dating. It would certainly explain why she's on a date with me.

My lips pull into a smile when she walks toward me.

"Do you want to go elsewhere?" I ask.

"How about you walk me home this time?"

"I'd love to."

"Word of warning, my dad was a scotch collector." Estelle leans into me and slides her hand down my arm. Her fingers slip between mine and we walk hand in hand along the boardwalk. We wave at Sadie and her ladies, who must be having all sorts of thoughts, and there's that ripple of pride again running up my spine. If anything, Estelle's very good for my self-esteem.

"I do like a good scotch." I revel in the warm touch of her hand against mine. Maybe, when sex is off the table, all other touches are magically magnified, and simply walking hand in hand along the ocean can feel like an intimate kiss.

The waves roar beside us and we don't speak for a while, until we have to turn inland. Estelle's father's house is a few blocks from the beach.

"Apologies in advance for the mess and the dust." Estelle gently extricates her hand from mine so she can unlock the door. "I'm not much of a cleaner and my dad was basically a hoarder."

"You don't cook. You don't clean," I joke.

"I'm no trad wife." Estelle bats her long lashes for an instant, then opens the door and ushers me in.

She wasn't kidding about the mess, nor the dust. She stops in the hallway for a moment, as though the state of the house surprises her as well.

"We can also just go to yours." She shrugs. "I'm trying to see the place through your eyes and I now realize it's not, um, you know, as it should be, but I don't notice it anymore. It's like I've become blind to the shambles this place is in." She turns to me. "I wasn't really thinking about this when I invited you over."

"What were you thinking about?" As if I care about the state of Estelle's late father's house when I'm standing so close to her I can smell her perfume.

"Scotch, of course." Her grin is so mischievous, it's obvious she wanted to say something else entirely.

"Then by all means, take me to your scotch." I reach for her hand again, as though I already miss it, and I'm taken aback by what her touch in the privacy of this house does to me. It feels as though my clit has woken up from the longest hibernation and, hesitantly but unmistakably, says to me, "Hey, I still exist. I'm still a part of your body."

Thank goodness Estelle pulls me into the living room, stacks of paper everywhere, toward a bar worthy of a top-notch restaurant.

"Daddy Raymond liked a tipple," I say, admiring the dusty bottles crowding the shelves.

"Funnily enough, he was more a collector than a drinker. He added a lot of bottles while not many got thrown out." Estelle sighs. "It was a nightmare when he moved back here, but he wasn't one for downsizing, either."

"When did he move back to Clearwater Bay?" I have my eye on a bottle of Macallan.

"Three years ago, when he turned eighty and the dean finally convinced him to leave the university—not an easy thing to do." Estelle reaches for the bottle I was eyeing. "This one?" She nods approvingly. "Excellent choice."

While we head to the living area, Estelle grabs two glasses. "In hindsight, I think that's when his dementia started to become an issue. In Berkeley, he was still known for his sharp mind, but his body wasn't very able and willing anymore." She pours us each two fingers of scotch. "But he didn't want to stay in his house in Berkeley after he left the university. He didn't say it as such, but it hurt him too much to no longer be a professor. It truly was his pride and joy. Clearly, he'd made enough money to no longer have to teach, but it was everything to him." Estelle gazes into the amber liquid. "I think it might be one of the reasons I held on for so long at my own job at Berkeley. I didn't want to disappoint him by quitting. I would never have quit as long as he was alive. I'd rather have dragged myself through day after day, completely mentally exhausted, than having to tell my father that I no longer wanted to be a professor at his beloved Berkeley." She exhales deeply, then holds up her glass. "The day I got tenure might have been the best day of his life. You should have seen him." She shakes her head. "To Richard Raymond, a wonderfully complicated genius and the best father a girl could ever wish for."

I tap my glass against hers. "To Richard Raymond." While I take a sip, I make a mental note to google Estelle's genius of a father tomorrow—if I manage to think of anything else but her.

CHAPTER 18
ESTELLE

For the first fifteen minutes of sipping my dad's scotch with Cass, I'm a little embarrassed about the mess, but this isn't my house. Although technically it is, because Dad left it to me—along with a hefty sum I never saw coming. But being with Cass is relaxing. Combined with the scotch and our pleasant evening, the state of the house is the last thing on my mind.

Of course, her words from before are sticking in my mind: 'sex is off the table.' *Hallelujah.* But I shouldn't get ahead of myself—not with a woman I've only just met. After all, I once fell deeply in love with an amazing asexual woman, convinced I'd won the romantic relationship lottery, only to have her make a swift shift on the spectrum and start wanting to experiment with sex. It didn't work out. It never does. I take another sip.

"Is it fair to assume," Cass's buttery voice cuts through my thoughts, "that you might linger in town a while."

"Look around you." I point at my dad's stuff that couldn't be more prominently on display around us. "I still have some work to do."

"What are you going to do with all of this?"

"Go over every single sheet of paper." I nod sharply. "I have to. God knows what he was working on when he had good days. I owe it to him to find out."

"What about the problem he left you? Have you solved it yet?"

"No," I say on a sigh. "At this point, it's impossible to know whether I can't solve it because it's unsolvable or whether it's too difficult. The two options are equally possible."

"If you need help with any of this." Cass points at a stack of paper threatening to topple over. "I'm available."

"You have a restaurant to run." Looking into Cass's kind face gives me that cozy warm feeling again.

"Savor is always closed on the weekend, so I'm free Saturday *and* Sunday." Some women simply look even better with a glass of fine scotch in their hand—Cass is one of them.

"That's very kind of you, but I need to do the first stage on my own. I need to go through his work and only then can I start disposing of old furniture and clothes and whatnot."

"Just say the word and I'm here." Cass's eyes are so blue—and all tenderness and generosity.

"Thank you." I don't look away as I take another sip.

"Can I ask what happened to your mother?"

"She died a long time ago, when I was only sixteen."

Cass narrows her eyes, and it makes her look even more compassionate.

"A car accident," I say.

"I'm sorry. That must have been so hard, especially at that age."

"I had my dad. He was always the more attentive and

caring parent." I take a beat "Don't get me wrong, losing a parent is horrible, but all that time alone with my dad shaped me in so many ways." I trace the rim of my glass with my fingertip. "We became this peculiar team of two math nerds against the world. In the morning, he'd quiz me on theorems over breakfast. Every evening, we'd solve puzzles instead of watching TV."

Cass leans forward slightly. "He sounds remarkable."

"He was." The scotch burns pleasantly as I take another sip. "He created this bubble. Just us and numbers. He made life safe and predictable after that devastating loss." I'm surprised by my own candor. "Unfortunately, I soon found out that people aren't equations. They don't behave according to established rules."

"People are definitely not equations," Cass says softly. "Though sometimes I wish they were. It would make running a restaurant so much easier."

Her attempt at lightness makes me smile, so I happily play along. "Can you imagine? If server A moves at X velocity while carrying Y plates…"

"I'd have the most efficient restaurant in all of California," she says.

Our laughter mingles in the dusty air of my father's living room, and for a moment, despite where we are, and what we're talking about, it feels just right.

"After my mother died," I continue, picking up the conversation where we left it earlier, "my father became even more absorbed in mathematics. It was his refuge. Mine too, I guess." A thought occurs to me. "Maybe that's why I can't solve his final problem. Maybe I'm not supposed to. Maybe it's just his way of keeping me connected to him a little longer."

Cass's expression shifts subtly—a flash of recognition,

as though I've inadvertently given voice to something she, too, has experienced.

"Some connections last well beyond what seems possible," she says.

I study her face. She meets my gaze without flinching, and it knocks something loose inside me.

"I kept all my mother's cookbooks," Cass says. "They're on a shelf in the restaurant's kitchen, taking up precious space. They have little notes in her handwriting. She'd write 'too salty' or 'needs more thyme.'" Cass swirls the scotch in her glass. "I read them sometimes, not for the recipes, but for those notes. It's like hearing her voice again."

"That's exactly it," I whisper. "My dad's voice is in these papers. In the way he'd circle a variable twice when he was excited, or the little exclamation points next to a particularly elegant solution."

Something passes between us—a kind of understanding. A mutual recognition of loss and what it does to you.

We raise our glasses in a silent toast. My father would have approved—not because he was romantic, but because he believed in things aligning when they should. Cass and I, sitting here in the chaotic mess of his house, finding comfort in each other, would have pleased him.

"What about your father?" I ask, now that we're on the subject.

"My parents divorced when I was in culinary school. I somehow completely lost touch with my dad after that. We haven't spoken in a very long time." She shrugs. "As far as I know, he's never tried to contact me again," Cass says. "And I'm not exactly hiding. Savor has been written about in plenty of publications."

Her words hang in the air, part dismissal and part

question—one that doesn't demand an answer, yet might welcome one all the same.

"Do you ever wonder?" I ask.

"If he reads about me? If he feels a stab of recognition when he sees my name?" Cass's mouth curls into something too complicated to be called a smile. "Less often now. Time has a way of doing that."

Outside, the wind picks up, rattling the old windows. Inside, we exist in the kind of bubble my dad used to create for me—for us—in this house.

"When I was younger," Cass continues, "I used to rehearse what I'd say if I ever ran into him. I had this whole speech prepared—eloquent and cutting, the perfect blend of indifference and insight." She laughs softly. "Now I think I'd just ask how he's been. Isn't that disappointing?"

"Not disappointing," I say. "Just human."

She meets my eyes. There's something new in her gaze—like she's seeing more than before. "For a mathematician, you're quite good at human emotions."

"A lifetime of observing from the sidelines has its advantages." I let a wry smile play across my lips.

Our glasses are empty. The bottle stands between us, like a question about what happens next. I reach for it, but Cass leans in and lays her hand on my wrist.

"I really should go," she says. "I have to work tomorrow."

"Of course." Her hand slips away.

We rise and stand close together for a moment, neither of us quite ready to call it a night.

"Thank you for tonight," Cass says, her voice lower than before. "For those truly spectacular burgers at The Bay and the utter privilege of watching you devour one."

I chuckle. "I worked hard on those burgers, as you well know."

"Like a devoted trad wife should." Her smile transforms her face again. She looks at me as though she sees right through the front I've spent years perfecting—as though she sees the parts of me I usually keep hidden.

Unhurried, we walk to the door. At the threshold, Cass turns to face me. The light hits her face just right, catching that irresistible curve of her mouth. I've only known this woman for a week, yet standing here feels like the pinnacle of a much longer journey.

The air between us shifts, again. Time slows. I can see every detail of her face in perfect clarity—the lone, tiny freckle left of her nose, a tiny scar near her temple, how her pupils dilate slightly in the light.

I step forward, trying not to presume. My heart hammers against my ribs, a counterpoint to the absolute stillness of the moment. Her breath catches almost imperceptibly, but I see it.

I slowly raise my hand, giving her every opportunity to step back, to reconsider. When my fingers finally make contact with her cheek, the touch is featherlight. Her skin is warm and inviting.

She doesn't pull away—I wasn't really expecting her to, but I've learned the hard way that you just never know. She leans into my touch. My thumb traces the curve of her cheekbone. Cass exhales softly.

Inch by inch, the space between us shrinks. I can smell the scotch on her breath. Our foreheads touch first. Her hand finds my waist.

When our lips finally meet, it's with the inevitability of waves reaching shore. The kiss is slow but certain. Her mouth is warm, and she's all there.

It's a kiss that says more than we're willing to admit out loud. When we finally part, breathless and slightly dazed, I keep my hand where it is, unwilling to break contact completely.

"I'll see you soon," she whispers.

"Yes," I say. "You will." Only then do I let her leave.

CHAPTER 19
CASS

The morning after my sublime date with Estelle, I wake before Gussie can pounce on me. Instantly, my mind drifts to that goodbye kiss. It really was something else. I play it over and over in my mind.

Estelle's lips already have an addictive quality—and I've only kissed her twice. But it's not only the yearning to kiss her again—and to see her again as quickly as possible—that I feel. I vividly remember my clit roaring back to life when my tongue slipped into her mouth. She's so damn sexy. And I can't believe I told her that, for me, sex being off the table is preferable. But she hadn't kissed me again when I said that. My clit was still as dead as a doornail when I exclaimed those words with utter conviction.

I'm not so sure now, just as I'm not sure about my body's reaction. It might just be a hormone fluctuation that spiked because of Estelle's glorious kiss. Maybe there's only one way to find out whether my attraction is genuinely physical—whether my body can keep up with meeting such a spectacular woman.

I run my hand over my belly and, instantly, I'm put off

by its bulky curve. There's too much of me—*okay, stop it.* If ever there was a more unsexy thought than 'I'm too fat to masturbate', I've yet to encounter it. But I haven't done this in so long. Not only because of lack of desire but also because the last few times I did try—on Suzy's recommendation—it simply didn't work. My body totally refused to cooperate.

Once, I did manage a sufficient degree of excitement to get into it but the orgasm, if you could even call it that, was a total dud—like a reluctant wave retreating back into the ocean instead of crashing to shore. But mostly, I just couldn't get there. As though my body was trying to tell me that the good times were well and truly over. And I didn't even care. It didn't bother me because I was single and unattractive—especially to myself—and, frankly, I had far better things to do with my time.

But that was before Estelle, and before last night when I definitely experienced a few upticks in lust. Perhaps I owe it to myself to try—Suzy would be so proud of me. It's not hard to imagine Estelle in bed with me—a place she might never find herself—because she's all I see as soon as I close my eyes. That intense, commanding gaze. Her lips slightly parted. How warm and close she was when she leaned in. But also the connection we shared, the things we talked about, the ways in which we seem to click so effortlessly.

I circle my nipple and it instantly becomes hard at the thought of Estelle's lips wrapping around it. Those divine lips that left such an impression, I can still feel them.

I've learned to take my time with myself, to not expect miracles from my fifty-three-year-old body. My fingers don't go near my clit until my brain is completely suffused with all things Estelle Raymond.

I only give. I don't receive. Those words seem to be etched in my brain just as much as the exquisite slope of her cheekbones and the curve of her jawline. What would she have to give exactly? How would she give it? None of that might be rocket science, but it has an extra tinge of mystery because of all the other things she has confided in me. And she sure had a way of licking sauce off her fingers. Oh, fuck. Her fingers. They might not be entirely off-limits, after all.

Okay. I'm ready. I let my fingers drift lower, circling gently. But it's as though I'm out of practice and I don't really know how to touch myself any longer. I take a breath and start again because this is hardly rocket science either. Of course, I haven't forgotten how to do this—a body isn't a manual you can misplace. I suck my finger into my mouth, much like Estelle did with hers last night, and my clit reacts instantly, as though it, too, wants a whole lot more of her.

When I bring my hand back between my legs, it's as though my body might actually still be capable of this. For a few moments, I forget where I am and what I'm doing while I relive our kiss again, its maddeningly slow approach followed by that sensual joining of our lips. I amp up the speed of my finger but it has the opposite effect, as though the desire I obviously have for Estelle won't translate to my body. As though that arrow of lust that runs up my spine when I think of her has no path to my clit, like some critical connection has been severed.

Frustrated, I give up. Perhaps too easily, but I don't care enough and I need the full strength of my hands for cooking later.

As if he knows what I've been up to and was patiently

waiting by the door—*as if*—August rushes in and hops onto the bed with a dramatic meow.

"I know exactly how you feel, little fella," I say.

I wisely decide not to linger in bed, to focus on last night rather than on this morning. Despite my failed attempt at reviving my aging body, there's a new lightness in my step as I go to feed my cat.

"Once again, only one word for you, Mama Cass," Bobby says. "D.I.V.I.N.E!"

I cooked with extra flair tonight, or maybe everything just tasted better because I have a crush on Estelle and infatuation is more delicious than the best-made jus.

"Thank you, darling." It's the end of service and I pull up a chair to Bobby and Hunter's table.

"No hot flashes in the kitchen tonight, I take it." Hunter grins at me. "That broth was so good, I considered proposing to it."

"What's going on here?" Bobby waves his hand at my body. "Is your menopause over? There's something distinctly different about you, Cassie."

I give a one-shouldered shrug that's meant to be mysterious.

"What is it?" Hunter studies my face.

A grin tugs at my lips. "Nothing," I say, despite that grin, because it's so much fun toying with them.

"Okay. I guess we're off then." Hunter pretends to rise, then falls back into his chair. Two can play that game.

"Believe it or not, but I've met someone," I say.

"You're right," Hunter says. "That is hard to believe. Was it at Suzy's support group?"

"Babe, this is serious," Bobby admonishes his husband. "If Cass has met someone who makes her look as though she won the lottery of life, we have to leave the snark aside." He looks me right in the eye. "Who is it and where did you meet? Do we know her?" He brings his hand to his mouth. "Presuming it is a she."

I chuckle because they crack me up, but also because of the sheer elation of telling my friends about Estelle. Beautiful, brilliant Estelle, who kissed me until I saw the stars on the backs of my eyelids last night.

"I met *her* here, at the restaurant." I can hear how my voice goes up in pitch, as though it has a mind of its own when talking about Estelle. "Her name's Estelle. She's back in town after her father died."

"Black, big hair, drop dead gorgeous?" Bobby asks.

"Yes," I confirm.

"I've seen her around." He shrugs. "I tend to notice beautiful women who are not from around here," he says matter-of-factly, but then swiftly takes it up a notch. "How did you swing that?"

"Bobby." Hunter punches his husband in the upper arm.

"Apologies if that came out wrong," Bobby corrects himself. "What I mean is that you are our good friend, Cass. We are aware of your, um, woman issues. You've also told us several times that you're not looking and, basically, not interested in anything romantic right now."

"I wasn't looking, but she was just… there." I point at the table by the window Estelle's been dining at for the past three weeks. "And no offense taken, Bobby. I know what you mean. She's way too hot for me, but… I don't know, maybe we're at a stage in our lives where that matters less."

"Oh, Cassie." Bobby reaches for my hands. "That's really not what I meant. Please know that."

"Oh, it's fine." I pull my hands from his and wave off his comment.

"So you met her at Savor and then what happened?" Hunter asks.

"She joined Sadie's surf club. We all had a drink together last Monday after you left." Hunter clearly doesn't remember offering Estelle his chair.

"Damn it. I missed her?"

"You couldn't handle the amount of estrogen, remember?" I arch up my eyebrows.

"That sounds like him," Bobby says.

"I had a hot flash. She was very kind and walked me home. When she came to dinner again next, she stayed for a drink, and I invited her to a private dinner upstairs. Things have kind of spiraled from there."

"Tell me exactly what you mean by 'private dinner' and 'spiraled.'" Bobby looks at me as though I'm a news anchor delivering the most important news of his life.

I'm still wearing my chef's hat and it's suddenly too hot. I pull it off and say, "We might have kissed." I sink my teeth into my bottom lip, as though wanting to catch whatever taste may—impossibly— still linger. "And then, last night…"

Bobby gasps as if I'm about to announce that we're getting engaged.

"We went on a date and ended up at her father's house, where more kissing ensued."

"Just kissing?" Hunter asks because he's utterly predictable.

"Yes, just kissing." Whereas I could tell Suzy about Estelle being ace with no qualms, that's not a conversation

I should have with these two. "And talking, of course. We get along so well. She's very smart. Apparently, her dad was some sort of mathematical genius." This doesn't impress my friends half as much as it did me. But they didn't sit opposite Estelle sipping fine scotch while looking into her dreamy eyes. "She's kind and funny and, well, extremely fucking hot."

"Plot twist, girl," Hunter says. "I did not see that one coming." He flashes me a boyish grin and drums his fingertips on the tabletop. "When can your gay besties meet her?"

"It's a bit early for friends' introductions," I murmur. I don't want to jinx whatever fragile thing we have between us by inviting Estelle to meet my boisterous friends.

"You just want to keep her for yourself a while longer," Bobby says. "I get it."

"How about brunch at ours next weekend?" Hunter doesn't take no for an answer.

"We'll see, babe. We'll see," I say.

"But when I see her in town, I am allowed to introduce myself as your friend?" Bobby asks, as if we're in high school instead of midlife.

"You can do whatever you want," I say.

"Is she staying a while or just passing through?" Hunter asks.

"Possibly staying a while. Her father has a lot of stuff that needs going through."

"How thrilling." Bobby smiles warmly. "I'm so happy for you, Cass."

"It's unexpected, but… yeah, it's wonderful." And also very early days.

"Either way, you and I are having drinks next Monday at The Bay while Sadie teaches the middle-aged ladies of

Clearwater Bay how to surf," Hunter says. "Aren't you thinking of joining now?"

"I will if you do," I tease.

Hunter is very fit for a man in his mid-forties, but he didn't grow up near the ocean and, to his son's disappointment—and despite several attempts—he's never taken to surfing.

"It's ladies only," Hunter says, as if that's the only thing stopping him.

"I'm sure Sadie would make an exception for her wife's baby daddy," I say.

"Let's share a bottle of chardonnay instead." Hunter winks at me.

"Make it sauvignon and I'm there."

CHAPTER 20
ESTELLE

When I walk along the beach, my gaze keeps being pulled to the building on the edge of the cliff. To Savor. It's Thursday afternoon and Cass and I have texted back and forth a bit, mostly to confirm my standing booking on Friday evening, but I can tell from the brevity and timing of her texts that she's busy, which makes perfect sense for someone running a restaurant. I've only tasted the output of her efforts, but Cass must put in a lot of energy, time, and skill to produce dishes like that.

Still, as though it's the only place they want to go, my feet carry me toward Savor. I want to see Cass. In private as opposed to walking into a full restaurant tomorrow, with her hidden away in the kitchen.

I text her as I approach, asking if she has a minute.

A minute for what? ;-)

She texts back, instantaneously this time. Maybe despite being busy, she has missed me, too.

I send back:

Step outside to find out

I wait for her on the deck of the restaurant, my gaze trained on the door. When it opens and Cass emerges, wiping her hands on her apron, my treacherous, hopeful heart skips a beat. Cass always walks with purpose and when that purpose is me, it makes me feel extra special.

"What's the emergency?" She keeps a respectable distance, as though not wanting to encroach on my personal space.

"This." I open my arms to her.

A smile breaks on her face. She's stunning when she smiles like that and my silly little heart hammers a little harder in my chest. Cass walks straight into my embrace and I wrap my arms around her. Her body is warm and she smells of something I can't decipher—probably a new dish she's working on with an ingredient I've never heard of. Her arms curve around my waist and I nuzzle my nose against the soft skin of her neck.

"I know you're busy," I whisper. "But I couldn't wait until tomorrow evening."

"I'm glad you came," she whispers back. "You're always welcome here."

I pull back from our embrace so I can look into her dreamy eyes. "I didn't just come for a hug," I say.

"What else are you here for?" She sinks her teeth into her bottom lip. "I'm sure Gus would be delighted to see you again. He told me your cheek rubs are out of this world."

I chuckle as I touch the place where her jaw curves into her neck—that little hollow that feels like it was made for this exact kind of tenderness.

Cass is taller than me, which means I have to reach up

when we're this close. It does something to me—arches my neck and leaves me exposed in a way that feels a bit like surrender.

She seems more than eager to meet me halfway. The space between us tightens, heavy with the kind of tension that only exists right before a kiss.

I kiss her, and instead of racing, my heart slows—like it knows something I haven't caught up to yet. I kiss her and my crush on her deepens. Her tongue is soft and her lips warm as they meet mine again and again. Each time our lips touch, it's a little different—more pressure, a shift in angle, something small that makes it better than the last. She pulls me even closer and moans into my mouth again.

Being with Cass makes me feel like everything will be all right. And isn't that one of the best feelings there is? Maybe safety is the most underrated kind of intimacy.

My hand moves to the small of her back. I smile against her mouth, as if to say how unexpected this is. How, every now and then, the universe manages to get something right.

An adventurous seagull careens right by our heads, pulling us from our divine kiss.

"Now I'm extra glad you came." Cass says. "I'm sorry I don't have a lot of time on weekdays, but I promise I'll be all yours this weekend."

"Don't apologize for that." I tug at her apron. "I love that you're a chef." Maybe I shouldn't have said something silly like 'food is my sex', but I can't unsay it, and it no longer matters because I'm standing here with Cass, the sky behind her as blue as her eyes, the ocean wild and beautiful next to us. "I can't wait for tomorrow."

"I can't wait to see you in my restaurant." She grins at me. "It looks different with you in it."

We giggle like lovestruck teenagers. That's kind of how I feel. Compared to when I arrived in Clearwater Bay a few weeks ago, exhausted and grieving and having no idea what to do with myself, being with Cass makes me feel like I'm on top of the world. Like I can do anything I damn well please. Brand-new energy flows through my muscles and there's a dizziness in my blood. I might as well admit it to myself. I'm already falling in love with her. Usually, I'd be more careful, but after what I've been through, the distraction is very welcome.

"I'll let you get back to work." I thread my fingers through hers, not quite ready to let her go back inside. "I wouldn't want to be the cause of a less-than-perfect carrot on someone's plate."

"That would be a disaster." Cass shuffles her feet, not ready to go yet either, it seems. "Hey, um, tomorrow, after your meal, will you stay a while? Have a post-service drink with me?"

"It would be my pleasure."

"Great." Her cheeks pink up. For a second, I fear for another hot flash, but perhaps it's just infatuation—like what I have burning inside of me. "I look forward to it."

The door of the restaurant flies open. "Boss," a young woman shouts. "We need your opinion."

"I'll be right there, Kelly."

"Sorry, Cass. I didn't know you had company. Take your time." The woman swiftly closes the door behind her.

"Go." Before I drop her hand, I plant a delicate kiss on the inside of her wrists. "Do your thing and I'll see you tomorrow."

"Deal." She pecks me ever so lightly on the cheek and heads back inside.

On my way home, I linger by The Bay, perhaps hoping to run into Devon again. I looked up her website and while life coaching wouldn't ordinarily be my thing, I really enjoyed our brief conversation earlier this week. But the waves are high and rough today and there's not a soul in the water. I'm contemplating an espresso when a buff Black man starts waving at me from the deck of The Bay.

"Estelle?" he calls, waving like we've known each other for years.

"Um, yes." I approach him. "That's me."

"I didn't mean to startle you." He flashes me a wide grin. "I'm Bobby, a good friend of Cass's." His grin grows even wider. "She told me about you a few days ago. I've been keen to run into you."

There's forward, and then there's Bobby. "Okay." But he's Cass's friend, so I'm naturally interested in him. "I was just contemplating a coffee."

"Then by all means, join me." He makes a show of pulling back a chair and making sure I'm comfortably seated.

We order double espressos—"Why have a single when you can have a double?" Bobby states matter-of-factly—and then I'm alone with this man who, instantly, makes me feel at ease while also making me miss my friends back home.

"So, you're the mysterious Estelle." Bobby doesn't have a hair left on his head but his eyebrows are very impressive when he waggles them like that. "My husband and I went to dinner at Savor on Tuesday and she told us all about you. Girl, I'm telling you, Mama Cass was glowing as if she'd just won a Michelin star." He bats his lashes now. I've only known him a few minutes but I'm already thoroughly entertained. And I'm beside myself with what he says about Cass.

I soon learn that Bobby is the kind of guy who only needs a small nod of the head from his so-called conversation partner to carry on a monologue. His personality seems almost too much for a town like Clearwater Bay.

"I'm sorry to hear about your father passing away." Apparently, he also has the gift to say the right thing in the appropriate tone of voice. By the time our espressos arrive, I'm already rather fond of him.

His eyes are warm and kind when he peers at me over the rim of his tiny cup.

"By the way." He puts his drink down. "Cass probably didn't tell you, but you're invited to brunch at ours next Sunday."

"Is that so?" I've barely spoken to Cass, but I doubt she would spring this on me last-minute.

"I get it if you two have better things to do on a Sunday morning, but even middle-aged ladies need to eat, right?"

I have to laugh, because calling someone a middle-aged lady ten minutes after meeting them is very bold, indeed.

"Not that you look a day over thirty-nine," he says. "Cass was right. You are extremely H.O.T." He actually fans his face with his fingers.

"Thank you." Bobby is hardly the first flamboyant, loud-mouthed gay man I've met in my life. Playing along can be rather fun. "This middle-aged lady takes that as a B.I.G. compliment."

"We love Cassie." His demeanor shifts into a more subtle range. "Ever since Sarah, she's been struggling." He—finally—pauses for a breath. "So, Estelle, tell me all about yourself." He all but drums his fingers on the table —maybe a double shot of caffeine wasn't the best idea for someone with his puppy dog energy.

I give him the broad strokes of the past few months, only touching on my burnout, and ending with that night at Savor when Cass believed I was a restaurant critic.

"Cass said you might stick around a while?"

"I don't know. Everything's kind of up in the air right now."

"Yeah, I get it." His turbocharged energy has tamped down considerably. "I do miss San Francisco sometimes, but this is a great town. Lots of lovely people. Lots of romantic beach walks. Both Sadie and Sam Ireland live here."

"Sam Ireland?"

"Sadie's hot twin brother." There go the eyebrows again. "Not that he would be of much interest to you."

"How long have you lived here?" I ask. Moving back to Clearwater Bay was never my intention, but I don't have much inclination to go back to Berkeley either—and I do own a house here, no matter how old and shabby it is.

"Almost six years." Bobby whistles through his teeth. "God." He shakes his head as though he can't quite believe it himself. "That's what happens when you fall in love with Sadie Ireland's wife's baby daddy."

"I'm sorry, could you repeat that, please?"

"Oh, it's complicated, all right." His face softens with all the love he has for the people he just mentioned. "My husband, Hunter, has a child with Devon, Sadie's wife." Glee lights up his eyes. "I know, it sounds like a really bad soap opera, but it's actually quite fun."

"I met Finn the other day. So he's your husband's son."

"My stepson." There's definitely more than a hint of

pride in his voice. "Lovely kid. He's ten now and absolutely hilarious. We're thick as thieves." He leans back in his chair and slings one leg over the other. "And when we've had enough of him for the day, we just tell him to go next door, where Devon and Sadie live." He grins. "Just kidding. Sort of."

"Sounds like you all get along."

"Yeah." He nods slowly. "Obviously it's not all sunshine and roses all the time, but we have a great community here."

"What do you do?"

"I make wooden furniture." He wiggles his fingers as though he's itching to sand down some wood right now. "I know I don't look it, but I'm very good with my hands."

"What do you mean, you don't look it?" I beam him my warmest smile.

"I'm as camp as they come, but I make a mean fucking chair, girl." He cocks his head. "If you come to brunch at our house, you can sit on one of them."

"I'll talk to Cass. I promise."

"Good. I look forward to it." He sits up straight. "I wish I could stay, but I was on my way to pick up Finn from his grandma's. I'm on stepdaddy duty." He rises. "But I sure hope to see you soon, Estelle."

I watch Bobby for a while as he walks off along the boardwalk and consider everything he said. Cass has some really nice friends in this town and if, somehow, I do decide to linger on, I wouldn't mind getting to know them all better.

But it's still very early days for all of that.

CHAPTER 21
CASS

Since Estelle last came to Savor, we've had two proper dates and one half-date. Now she's back at her table by the window, and my focus is all over the place. For the life of me, I can't keep my eyes off her. It's as if after kissing her again an extra layer of hotness has been added to her entire being. And the way she sits there, back straight, hair wild, tasting my food as if it's the most precious find on the planet, makes me nearly burn a scallop twice. First it was hot flashes during service, now it's this.

I manage to make it through service because I'm a chef and that's what we do. We muddle along while time speeds up and we never have enough hands to perform all the tasks that need doing. I may adhere to a slow restaurant philosophy but that doesn't mean things aren't hectic during a fully booked Friday evening.

Just like last Friday, we sit at the bar of the near-empty restaurant where I pour us an outrageously expensive glass of Napa Cabernet Sauvignon.

"Thanks for staying." I look into Estelle's brown gaze and everything is already so different than last week. I don't know her that well yet, not the details that make up the magnificent human that she is, but I do know some things. That she's a great kisser, for instance.

"There's nowhere else I'd rather be." When she smiles, I feel it everywhere. I've got it good. Suzy likes to say that menopause is like a second puberty—and that's very much how I feel when I'm with Estelle. "Although, apparently, we're invited to brunch at Bobby and Hunter's on Sunday."

"We don't have to go." Bobby called me this morning to tell me all about his impromptu-but-illuminating coffee with Estelle—knowing him, there probably wasn't that much impromptu about it. "I promised to help you out at your dad's house."

"I'd much rather go to brunch at a gay couple's than go through more of my father's incomprehensible papers."

"Really?"

"Of course. Bobby was lovely. A bit—" She pauses, possibly to search for the right word.

"Full-on? In your face? No-holds-barred?" I offer.

"Amongst other things." Estelle extends her leg and puts her foot on the footrest of my bar stool.

All I want to do is lean in and kiss her again, but that would be highly inappropriate with my staff finishing up in the kitchen.

"How about we take these glasses upstairs?" I ask. "It'll be more private."

"You're the boss." Estelle grins at me and I don't know what to do with myself. Ever since she stopped by yesterday with the sole purpose of kissing me, I've been wondering how dating her is different because of her being ace. It doesn't feel different. In my experience, kissing always leads to something else—to more. But I guess with her, even when I invite her upstairs and there's clearly an element of not being able to keep our hands off each other—her as well as me—the kissing has nowhere to go. Whereas I'm perfectly okay with that—I think—it's all a bit strange.

"Give me a minute." I head to the kitchen and as soon as she clocks me, Kelly catches my gaze.

"We've got it, boss. Go. Be with your lady. Enjoy. I'll lock up."

"Thanks, Kelly, you're the best."

"Don't do anything I wouldn't do," she jokingly shouts after me.

"Come on." We take the bottle and two wine glasses to the privacy of my apartment.

After Estelle and August have greeted each other like old friends, we end up sitting very close to each other in the couch.

It's hard not to burst into a silly grin every time I look into Estelle's face. Even the way she holds her wine glass, cupped in her hand, is sensual. It's also hard not to kiss her, which is the very reason I brought us here, but I'm confused by how fast this is moving—especially if kissing is the end station of what we will physically do together.

"Can I ask you another one of my ignorant questions?"

"Curiosity is the opposite of ignorance," she says, making me feel like a million bucks again. "It's perfectly normal to have questions."

"After you told me you were ace, I didn't think things would be so… physical between us. I didn't expect you to kiss me like that."

"Like how?" Estelle must have had a variation on this conversation a dozen times and she can probably read me like an open book.

"Like... foreplay."

"Would you rather we didn't kiss?"

As she asks the question, all I can do is stare at her lips with all my defenses down. "Heavens, no." I shake my head for emphasis.

"Do you want more?" There's not a hint of judgement in her tone.

"No, I mean... I don't know. Maybe." I huff out some air. "I'm sorry for being so un-suave about this." I have to search for my words again. "I guess I was wondering how you feel about sleepovers?" *Sleepovers?* As if we really are teenagers. My cheeks might as well be on fire that's how hot they're burning.

"Everything is debatable, except one thing," she says. "We can talk about anything you want, Cass. It's important that you ask me whatever you need to ask me. It's okay. I won't be embarrassed and you don't need to be embarrassed either, although I understand it can be a bit awkward."

"And that one thing would be that I can't touch you below the waist?" I ask.

Estelle nods. "In a sexual way."

"Okay." I take a sip of wine. "Has it always been this way for you?"

"Yes, although it took me a long time to figure out. Obviously, when I started developing feelings for other people, I experimented, just like everyone else." Her gaze is as soft as her voice. "I basically did everything with some girlfriends, but, um..." She pauses. "Well, let's say I could not believe my eyes when I saw how sex affected my partners. I literally couldn't fathom it, because I don't feel it. I never have and I never will—I know that now." Her shoulders sag a little. "I've been to so many doctors. Psychiatrists. Neurologists. Every kind of therapist you can think of. You name it, I've seen them." She looks away now. "Because I felt abnormal and I wanted answers. But sometimes there is no answer." She expels the smallest of sighs. "Except that I am partially asexual." She tips her head. "Which probably only raises more questions with you."

"Thank you for sharing." She's right, I have so many more questions.

"Not a problem. I'm happy to share. Honestly, the number one job of an asexual person is disentangling confusion." She chuckles. "It's what we spend the energy on we don't use for sex."

I'm so glad she just made a joke. It lightens the earnest vibe that has descended on my living room. A tension not caused by Estelle, but by my lack of knowledge. I happily chuckle along, ignoring the fact that her openness and the ease with which she talks about herself, quite ironically, only makes her more attractive to me.

"I'm perfectly happy not having sex, but I'm equally happy giving. I leave that entirely up to my partner."

"That kind of sounds like the dream of quite a few women."

"It may sound like it, but most women are givers. Because of how women are socialized, they have no idea how to just receive. Especially an orgasm."

"Really?" I've never considered this.

"Trust me."

"Is that why you have all those scars on your heart?"

Estelle nods. "Yes, among other things."

"Are you saying I should be careful what I wish for."

"I don't know, Cass." Something slowly shifts in the air. "What do you wish for?"

"What I *really* wish for—" I owe her this degree of honesty—at least in this we can give and receive equally. "Is for my body to be able to experience pleasure again."

Estelle nods as though she completely understands, whereas, if I've understood correctly, she's never had an orgasm in her life.

"If my face looks funny, it's because I'm biting my tongue," she says.

"What do you mean?" Her face is all broody gaze and lips I want to kiss for days. "Why?" Did I put my foot in it? It's highly likely in a conversation like this.

"I want to say something that I perhaps shouldn't."

"Please, don't let me stop you." My curiosity could not be more piqued.

"This is going to sound a bit out there, but I could… help you with your, um, pleasure." She briefly sucks her bottom lip between her teeth. "Ironically, I'm pretty good at that, because I don't focus on myself."

I need to keep my jaw from slacking. This is next-level flirting. This is wooing me into bed. Or am I reading this all wrong? Jesus. From the get-go, it's been like this.

"That does sound a bit out there." I have to push the words past the dryness in my throat because this isn't just confusing, it's also incredibly arousing.

"It's definitely something we could do together." She circles her fingertip along the rim of her wineglass. What happened to the woman who, minutes earlier, sitting in that same spot, exclaimed that she could take or leave sex?

"Estelle," I say on a sigh, "your signals are so mixed, I fear I might lose my mind."

"I know." She exhales. "But it's a weakness of mine to... want to awaken something inside a beautiful woman I have a crush on."

I take it the woman she's referring to is me. "But what do you get out of it? Does it give you pleasure? Do you experience any... sexual desire?"

"Pleasure, yes, but not the same kind of pleasure you would get from it. It's different for me. But I do get a kick out of making a woman come, although, for me, it's not sexual."

"Oh, boy."

"But as I said, it's not a must," she has the audacity to remind me.

"It's not?"

"Absolutely not."

"I'm attracted to and confused by you in equal measure," I say. "And I thought this was going to be simple. No sex. No complications."

"It can be."

"Not really. Not after what you've just said..."

"Because you're curious now?" Her lips tilt into a grin.

"Oh, yeah."

"That's okay. I'm not going anywhere."

"But... even though I'm curious, I'm not ready for..." I shake my head. "I can't, um, yet." I may be attracted to Estelle—and the brazen hope in her words—but I'm still a woman in the middle of menopause who gained twenty pounds in the past few years with a body that always seems to want to do the opposite of what I want it to.

"Do I look like I'm in any kind of rush?" She lets her head fall sideways onto her outstretched arm. "Let's take it slow."

"Maybe we can start with a simple sleepover," I say,

even though I'm not at all sure about sharing my bed with another human—August is more than enough.

"Sure." She smiles lazily at me. "How about tomorrow?"

"Okay." Despite everything, saying yes to Estelle is easy. She won't judge me—and I don't have to be naked.

CHAPTER 22
ESTELLE

I pack a small bag to stay over at Cass's. All day, I've been expecting a text from her saying she'd like to postpone or even cancel our sleepover date, but my phone's been blissfully quiet.

I'm a little nervous when I head over to hers because I opened myself up to her in a way I haven't done—haven't allowed myself to do—in a couple of years. Not since the last scar on my heart grew over a wound so deep, I feared it might never close.

But Cass has a calming effect on me and there's nothing more I like to do than spend time with her—and make her blush a little, if I'm being totally honest. And all of this because a former colleague at Berkeley made me promise to go to Savor as soon as I arrived in Clearwater Bay.

I didn't return to my hometown to meet someone—to develop a crush on Savor's irresistible chef—yet here we are. I lock up my dad's house, glad to have a night away from the dust and the heaviness of it, sling my bag over my shoulder and walk over to Cass's house for a sleepover followed by brunch at her friends' house tomorrow. If I keep this up, I might start feeling as though I belong here.

"Brunch tomorrow is on," Cass says instead of kissing me hello when I arrive. Her energy is all over the place. "Although invitations might have gotten out of hand."

It's as if she's walking away from me whenever I try to get close. Perhaps I did spook her last night—in hindsight, I did come on a little strong. I do that sometimes.

"And I'm making you the perfect burger tonight." She rushes into the kitchen as though the meat's already in the pan.

I follow her. "Hey." I try a smile. "What's going on?"

"What's going on?" she repeats. "I don't know where my head is. I barely slept last night. I had night sweats like you wouldn't believe. Don't worry, I changed the sheets. I —I…" She loses steam. "Can you tell me where my head is, please?"

"It's right here." I bridge the distance between us and gently place my palms on the sides of her face. "It's okay. Everything is fine, Cass."

"I'm all over the fucking place. Today of all days."

Slowly, I slip my hands downward until they rest on her shoulders.

"Sometimes, I think I should just take the fucking hormone pills and be done with all this mess."

"You don't have to suffer because you're a woman." I only realize how condescending that sounds after I've said it. I give her shoulders a soft squeeze. "How can I help?"

"I don't know. I'm sorry." Her eyes moisten.

"Oh, come here." I slide my hands downward a fraction. "Can I hug you? Is that okay?"

She just nods.

I curl my arms around her and, immediately, she puts her head on my shoulder and starts sobbing, as though she held it all in until I got here.

I hold her and let her cry until my shirt is dark with her tears.

"Oh, fucking fuck," she murmurs. "Jesus." She sighs deeply. "What a great way for our infamous sleepover to begin."

"I don't have to stay if you don't want me to. If you have any doubts."

"Me? What about you? You've witnessed one of my hot flashes, now a lovely mood swing, and you might wake up in a puddle of my sweat… That doesn't sound very enticing for you to stay."

"I have no doubts," I say. "I'd like to stay."

Another sigh, then she slowly pushes herself out of my embrace. "Can we start again, please?"

"Yes." I lower my hands until they find hers. "Hello. Good evening. I won't ask how you are."

"Hi." Her shoulders un-hunch. "I'm much better now that you're here, actually." She slants forward. "And I'd like to kiss you."

"That can be arranged." I fold my arms around her waist again and gently touch my lips to hers. Her face is still wet from crying and she looks a bit of a mess—she *is* a bit of a mess—and her vulnerability touches a nerve deep inside me.

"Are you really going to cook for me again?" I whisper when we break from our kiss.

"Maybe I just want to see you eat a burger again." She

has her sense of humor back. She swipes at her cheeks, then says, "As a way of sleepover foreplay." Oh, she definitely has her sense of humor back. She even throws in a wink.

I let out a loud laugh and it feels so good to stand in Cass's kitchen and just laugh with her, despite her little episode.

"How come you're forty-nine and not experiencing any symptoms of perimenopause?" she asks.

"Lucky, I guess." I've wondered about this and maybe I am just lucky or maybe my hormones behave differently—or maybe both.

"Let's avoid the M-word for the rest of the night, shall we?" Cass says.

"Sure." August presses himself against my shin. While I crouch down to pet him, I ask, "Who else is coming to brunch?"

"Suzy, Sadie and Devon. The usual suspects, really."

"Brunch with Sadie Ireland. Do you hear that, Gussie?"

"Meow," he says.

"I don't want to diss the burgers at The Bay," I say between greedy bites, "but yours is a million times better."

Cass just looks at me with a big smirk on her face.

"What?" I tease, because I know why she's looking at me like this. She told me in no uncertain terms.

"How can you eat so messily and still look so utterly gorgeous."

"It's my gift, I guess. You prepare the delicious food and I look good while eating it."

"What I love even more is how you have no qualms owning that you're beautiful."

I sense the possibility of a tricky conversation—again—but maybe this is a good time for it. Cass has alluded to her own issues with her body a few times now.

"Ah, beauty," I say, while licking a drop of sauce off my finger. "It's really all in the eye of the beholder."

"Maybe, but, um…" I give her the time she needs to articulate her thought. "Put us next to each other and ask a hundred random people who is the more attractive and ninety-nine of them will pick you."

I nearly drop my burger. Cass's body issues might actually be a bit too much for me to handle.

"You couldn't be more wrong." I put down my burger. "Do you truly believe that?"

"Yes, but you are exceptionally stunning."

"But, Cass, so are you." I want to offer my hand for support, but it's too dirty.

She scoffs. "Me? Nah, and please do me the courtesy of not trying to convince me otherwise. I have mirrors. I know what I look like."

"Are you having another mood swing?" I've been so busy devouring my delicious burger, I hadn't noticed she barely touched hers.

"I'm having a bad day full of insecurity." She shakes her head. "I'm sorry."

"Because I'm staying over?"

"Because I'm afraid that as soon as I take off one layer of clothing, you'll be out of here."

"Okay." I rise. "Let me just clean up, then come with me." I head into the kitchen and wash my hands. I will happily give up the remainder of my burger to make Cass feel better about herself. "Come." I reach out my hand to her. She takes it. I guide us to the nearest mirror. I stand next to her as we look into it together. "Let me tell you what I see." I hold on to her hand. "Look into those gorgeous blue eyes," I say. "I've done it a couple of times and the only outcome was that I couldn't stop kissing you." I bump my hip lightly against hers. A smile tugs at her lips, but is not ready to break through yet. "And those lips. Phew. Again, can't stop kissing them." I let go of her hand and bring mine to the side of her hip. "And guess what? Women have curves. We've always had them. Some more than others, but there's nothing wrong with curves. In fact, I like curves because they're soft and womanly and who doesn't like that?"

"You're very sweet." She leans into me a fraction. "But I can't help but wonder whether my physical appearance is even important to you." Her eyes find mine in the mirror. "I hope that's not insulting. It's not my intention, but… it's another one of those pesky questions running riot in my head."

"Oh, Cass." My body and I haven't always seen eye to eye, but even when I couldn't possibly understand it, I never hated it the way Cass seems to hate hers. I hold her gaze in the mirror. "I think you're beautiful. I love how tall you are. I love how you march around in your kitchen. I love your whole vibe and the confident way you carry yourself." Which seems to have totally slipped away for now, but she really is having a terrible day, that much is obvious.

"Thank you." Her voice is so soft, I can barely make it out. "I do know what I'm doing," she continues. "I'm pushing you away because I'm scared."

"Trust me, no one understands that better than me."

"You do?" We keep standing like that, our eyes glued to each other in the reflection of the mirror.

"Fuck yeah, Cass. I'm aware that I'm 'conventionally attractive', whatever that even means. I know what people see when they look at me—a tall Black woman with good cheekbones and great hair. But the number of times I've been told I'm beautiful will never make up for all the times I've failed at relationships. For all the times I've had my heart broken for not being enough. In the end, it doesn't mean anything, because it has never gotten me what I really wanted." I lean my head against her shoulder, relishing in how strong it feels.

"Which is?" Cass curves her arm around my waist.

"Pretty much the same as everyone else." I lean into her embrace. "A loving, respectful, long-term relationship with someone who accepts me for who I am." I can't hold her gaze. "Maybe it's too much to ask of someone else. After all, it took me a few decades to fully understand and accept myself. To ask that of another person might simply be… too much."

"No, please, don't lose your faith in love. There's so much about you to adore." Her grasp on my waist tightens. "Do you want me to list all the things I like about you or are we getting too cheesy too quickly?" Her body shakes against mine as she laughs. "Fuck, Estelle. You're so kind and patient and understanding."

"Not to mention very good at eating burgers." I turn in her embrace and look Cass in the eye again.

"And I just committed the worst sin a chef can commit. I let your food go cold." She slants her head. "Let me make you another burger."

"Why don't you kiss me instead?" I say, hoping that Cass will let me stay. I'd like the comfort of sleeping in her arms tonight—sometimes it feels like an emotional luxury I can no longer afford.

She closes the distance between us and kisses me deeply.

CHAPTER 23
CASS

How come Estelle is still here? I can only conclude that she must really like me. Despite all my antics, and the dreadful day I've had in anticipation of this date, it's exhilarating. There's still a lot of time to screw things up, as there always is, but there's also so much promise.

We end up on the couch, just like last night, so close our knees are touching.

She's telling a story about a co-worker at Berkeley who had an affair with her teaching assistant and I'm listening, although not as attentively as I could. Instead, I'm taking in the exquisiteness of her gestures and how her lips curve when she speaks and the way her voice sometimes dips into a deliciously low register, smooth and warm, like something you want to wrap yourself in. As she speaks, I fall for her more by the second.

How can I not fall for her? By her own admission, she's far from perfect. I know so well perfection is an invention of capitalism in order to make us buy more stuff we don't need—also Suzy's words—but when I look at Estelle like this all I see is perfection. And even though I'm scared, I want her to stay. Whatever ledge I was on regarding that, she talked me off it with her sweet words and boundless patience.

"Please, stay," I reply, wholly inadequately, when she has finished.

"That story was not meant to turn you on," she jokes—it must be a joke, but that's the other thing about Estelle. She's clearly good-natured and able to see through my dramatic behavior, but she's also full of surprises, and I don't know yet whether they'll end up being good or bad. She says one thing, then contradicts herself with her actions, at least from my perspective. She's the opposite of boring. She keeps me on my toes *and* lets me fall apart. Just like anyone else, she's many things, and I can't wait to unearth all her secret layers.

"You turn me on," I say, because her directness has rubbed off on me. And it's true, because a big part of my anxiety is caused by this new desire bubbling up inside me—a desire caused solely by Estelle Raymond.

No wonder I've been so confused, agitated and on edge. I truly don't know where my head is at. Just as I have no clue how my body will react to her presence in my bed. I can try to predict things all I want, but it's a waste of energy. The only way to find out is to have her stay the night. The worst that can happen is me suffering a brutal night sweat, like the one I had last night. It had been a while since my sheets were drenched like that.

"I'd love to stay." She puts a hand on my knee. "You set the pace. You're in charge, okay?"

"Sure." In response, I turn fully toward her and kiss her. At first, I'm worried about the kind of message it may send—that I might not respect her boundaries—but then I let my worries go and I fully enjoy the sensation of her lips on mine, of her tongue in my mouth, the pressure of her hands on the back of my neck and, admittedly, the wild pulse in my clit.

Estelle leans against the doorframe, watching me as I brush my teeth. I'm still clothed but she's only wearing boy shorts and a tank top and I can't stop sneaking glances in the mirror. I do hear Suzy's voice in my ear when I admire Estelle's perfect physique and compare it to my imperfect one: "It's the patriarchy, Cass, to reduce women to how they look." But it's hard to be righteous when the view is so breathtaking.

Then the moment has come. I can't slip under the covers in my jeans. I wouldn't want to either. I want to feel as much of Estelle's skin against mine as she will let me—because this is also an exercise in exploring boundaries.

"Do you want me to look away or do you want me to help?" This is not Estelle's flirty tone of voice. It's all warmth and understanding—and how she got me this far.

"Help," I say, surprising myself. It might be the arousal speaking, which is swiftly winning all the battles in my head right now—another old-but-new sensation.

"It would be my pleasure." She takes a step toward me and, slowly, undoes the top button of my blouse. Then another. And another.

Instead of worrying about the gradual exposure of my skin, for the first time since she has told me, I get a flicker of understanding of what it might be like to want to touch her and not be able to. Because how she undresses me is electrifying and, for a moment, all I want to do is press my lips to that delicious patch of skin next to the strap of her tank top. Or the soft swell of her biceps. Or, by god, the outline of her nipple pushing against the fabric. She might have explicitly told me that touching her above the waist is okay, but I'm too trepidatious for that. The moment is too delicate. Our connection too recent.

She has reached the bottom button and pulls open my blouse. I ignore the curve of my belly. It's not that hard under the circumstances, with my blood raging in my veins as though I'm at least twenty years younger.

What does she feel? Will I ever know and, if I do, will I be able to comprehend it? I should, because I know perfectly well what it feels like for your body not to respond to a sensual touch. To an intimate approach by a loved one. But I can't possibly imagine it in this moment because Estelle has just flipped open the button of my jeans and is now lowering the zipper and who the fuck is this woman and what is she doing to me?

Least of all, I recognize myself. I may accuse Estelle of saying one thing and doing the opposite, but I'm no better. I'm not usually this fickle—if anything, according to my ex, I was much too stubborn when it came to this. When it came to enjoying intimacy with this changing body I just couldn't get used to.

So what am I doing here? My jeans decidedly on their way down and, oh fuck, what will she do once they're off? I soon find out, because Estelle is very adept at undressing a woman and before I know it both my jeans and blouse are draped over the back of a chair and I stand before her in just my underwear.

"Do you want me to take off your bra?" she asks.

I don't think—I can no longer think. I just nod.

She looks me in the eye as she brings her hands behind my back and unclasps it. Ever so slowly, she guides the straps off my shoulders. As opposed to my jeans earlier, this takes forever. Inch by inch, she bares my breasts, and all I can think of is how improbably hard my nipples are. And, also, how much I want her.

None of this is plausible. My level of arousal is beyond anything I've experienced in the past five years, since the sudden death of my libido with no resuscitation possible. When my body started acting so erratically, I grew more and more disgusted by it. Then the extra pounds came. Then, nothing. Until Estelle Raymond came to town—and told me she was asexual.

"You're so beautiful, Cass," she whispers, and the most absurd thing of all is that I believe her. I don't question her words for a single second. Because there's no room in my brain for doubts. My mind is suffused with lust, and my clit thumps wildly against the fabric of my panties. I honestly didn't know it could still do that.

She slides my bra along my arms and throws it over her shoulder, as though she can't keep her eyes off me for even a short moment.

"Can I touch you?" Her voice is so soft and low and smooth, it feels like a caress.

Again, I just nod.

She cups my breasts in her hands so delicately, as though they are the most precious objects on Earth. So much for just spooning tonight. Featherlight, her thumbs skate along my nipples and I lose a little more of my breath—and of who I've been the past couple of years.

"I want you," I say, because I'm supposed to be setting the pace. *Yeah right*. But oh, do I want her.

As though she's been waiting for me to say those very words, her grip on my breasts intensifies. Just as my clit has roared back to life, my breasts are suddenly hyperresponsive to her touch. It certainly didn't feel like this when I tried touching myself the other day. All I felt then was inadequacy and indifference—a pretty lethal combination when trying to coax your body toward orgasm.

Her solemn expression as she gazes at my chest changes into something mischievous. She doesn't say anything, just leans closer and I expect another heavenly kiss, but her head dips lower and she wraps her lips around my nipple. The warmth of her mouth nearly floors me. An arrow of lust shoots through me, from the depths of my core straight to my clit.

Her tongue skates along my nipple and it's as though all the lust I've been unable to feel catches up with me in the space of a few moments. I don't even care if this results in a climax because this sensation already feels like a huge win. For once, instead of letting me down, my body is giving me pleasure. Or maybe I'm allowing it to. Or maybe the hormones in my blood have gone haywire because of this woman with her mouth on my nipple.

Estelle lets go of my nipple and looks me in the eye. "Come." She's the one who leads me toward my own bed. Somehow, it feels right. Everything about her feels exactly right. Although, to be honest, I would very much like to peel that tank top off her. I'd love to see her breasts, wrap my own lips around her nipples. But I don't because we need to have another conversation about that first.

We lie on the bed and she glues her body to my side. Her fingertip circles my improbably hard nipple.

"Is there anything I should know? Anything you want to tell me?" she asks.

I can't think of anything, except... "Please, don't be offended if I don't come. It's most certainly not you. It's me." I may be excited beyond any point I've reached in years, but my inability to climax might not be impacted by that. I have no idea. All of this is a surprise to me.

"Sure," she says, in a way that doesn't sound like acceptance at all. "Do you have lube?"

It's a logical question but I have to think really hard with a brain that's not capable of that right now. Does lube have an expiration date?

"I don't know. Maybe in the drawer on your side of the bed," I manage to say.

"It's okay." Estelle's finger still circles my nipple. "Let's not worry about that." Her voice is just as enticing as her fingertip. Like she has a special register for sex. Jesus, this woman.

She moves in and kisses me on the lips this time. I bring my hands to the back of her head and pull her closer. Automatically, my hands glide down, but I stop them when they dip too low. It's really not that hard to let all of this be about me, especially considering the effect Estelle has on me.

Her fingers dance over my skin, slow and sometimes fast. Her lips are on mine, then back on my nipples, then roaming across my neck, my shoulders, my belly. All the while, my clit rages like a wild bird suddenly trapped in a cage—like it can't believe what is happening here and wants to make damn sure I'm aware. But it's impossible not to be aware of my clit. All the energy in my body seems to have gathered there. Every time Estelle's fingers skim along my skin, my clit beats harder. Every time her lips find mine, her breath hot and full of promise against my mouth, my clit thumps with impossible vigor.

It's as though my bed has become a time machine taking me back to a time when I enjoyed sex with every fiber of my being. When it was an intrinsic part of my life, as vital as food and water. When sex was joyful and carefree and not the emotional minefield it became that last year with Sarah. When I could no longer give her what she wanted no matter how hard I tried—because I stopped wanting it for myself.

Estelle's lips find my ear. "I'm going to lick your pussy," she croons into my ear, and it's no longer a question. It's a fact—a delicious, breathtaking fact.

My mouth goes dry, and, for a split second, I fear for a hot flash, but this time around, my body is on fire for very different and much better reasons.

She kisses me again and the thought of her soft tongue on my clit is almost too much to bear—like more than I deserve. But I shake it off easily, perhaps because of the things she said to me, or simply because of how she is, or because of this moment which is special and unique and unexpected in the best possible way. There is no questioning sensual energy like this. Its only purpose is to be enjoyed.

She hooks her fingers into the waistband of my panties and tugs—slowly but purposefully—until I'm bare beneath her gaze. I spread my legs for her—another action I haven't performed for anyone in long years. The intimacy of it is both intimidating and thrilling. To show yourself like that to someone new, at my age, is not a given, yet she has made it so. She must be a magician—or some sort of sapphic sorceress.

She trails her lips along the inside of my thighs, taking her time, showering me with soft, hot kisses. The closer she gets to my throbbing mess of a clit, the more my breath stalls in my throat. The sweet agony of anticipation translates into goose bumps all over my skin and a red-hot sensation in my flesh.

My hands are in her hair, which tickles my belly in the most delicious manner. It makes me feel as though she's everywhere, although she's very much focused on the money spot right now. Her breath is hot against my clit. Her fingers roam across my nether lips, tickling, stroking, driving me ever more insane.

Then, at last, her tongue swipes along my clit. Not teasingly like I had expected, but fierce and full of intention. *Oh, fuck.* I'm such a goner—not for an orgasm, although its chances are increasing tenfold by the millisecond—but for her. For Estelle Raymond. If I wasn't already, I'm falling head-over-heels in love with her right here, right now, in my bed.

Her tongue is deft and hot and everything I need. I feel her everywhere. Against my clit but also, perhaps ridiculously, in my heart. None of this should be possible. Still, it's happening. Oh yes, it's definitely happening. It's as though she can read my body without me having to say or do anything. Like she picks up on every micro-movement of my hips, on every ragged inflection of my moans, on how my fingers cling to her scalp.

She *is* a sapphic sorceress with a magic wand for a tongue. It's the only explanation I have for the euphoric sensation rolling through my flesh. For the wave of lust that pulls me under—like one of those waves that is a giant wall of water I sometimes see from my kitchen window. There's no escape. And the sudden inevitability of it takes my breath away. Is this even me in this bed, with this gorgeous woman's head between my legs? If it is, how did I possibly swing this? How are my limbs suddenly going slack with the certainty of orgasm? How are the hormones in my blood making this happen? Which cocktail is riding through my veins because of Estelle—truly, simply, only because of her?

I thrash my head from side to side because I can't believe this, yet I feel it all the way down to my toes. I howl noisily and unabashedly, a sound I've never before uttered. Estelle's tongue works its magic on me as if it's nothing. As if I come like this every day of the week. And the pure joy that spreads through my flesh forces tears to stream from my eyes. The orgasm is long and strong and takes every last ounce of energy I have left in my middle-aged muscles.

I'm still half-paralyzed when Estelle's face appears before me, her chin glistening, her smirk more sweet than self-satisfied, although there's definitely also a hint of that.

"No need for me to be offended, then," she says, while gently swiping at the tears on my cheek.

"Fuck," is truly all I can say. I want to cry, but I already am. I want to ask how, but I already know. It's her.

She glues her body to mine again and puts her head on my shoulder, an arm curved warmly along my chest.

"Let me know when you can speak again," she says, a smile in her voice. "No rush. You set the pace."

CHAPTER 24
ESTELLE

Cass breathes heavily beneath me, her chest rising and falling. I'm so happy that she got what she wanted—that her body could experience this pleasure and, also, that I was the one who was able to give it to her.

Not to brag, but I've witnessed so many climaxes in my life, I no longer wonder what they feel like. I've long accepted that this kind of pleasure is not for me, but I get my own kind of pleasure from giving. And this was one hell of a present. Cass still hasn't regained the power of speech.

I'm bracing for what comes next, once she's recovered enough to ask the question I always, invariably, get after the first time with someone new. Human beings are so utterly predictable.

"Jesus effing Christ," Cass whispers after a few more minutes have passed, her voice brittle, as though she strained it with that wildcat scream earlier—August might think there's an intruder in his territory.

I push myself away from her shoulder, where some

wetness from her tears has pooled, moistening my own cheeks, to look at her.

"I don't know what to say." A wide smile spreads on Cass's lips.

"You don't have to say anything." Something flutters in my stomach. Cass has come a long way from that meltdown in her kitchen when I arrived, to this.

"We will have to test whether this is a one-off occurrence or repeatable." She giggles. "For science."

"I happen to be a mathematician who is very interested in science."

Cass shakes her head. "I don't know how to thank you."

"This was *my* thank-you for all the amazing food you've prepared for me."

"In that case, let's skip brunch tomorrow and I'll make you the best grilled cheese you've ever had."

My turn to chuckle. "It's definitely not a quid pro quo."

"My body will probably take some time to recover from this. I might not be able to move tomorrow from all the trembling my muscles did." Something solemn passes over her face. "All jokes aside," she says, "I am grateful because… I forgot what it felt like to be completely transported like that. I—" Her voice falters. "I don't want to make too much out of it, although it is a big deal to me." She pauses. "I have no idea how this happened. What went on in my body or my brain or both to make this possible. It's all quite unfathomable and the only differentiating factor is you."

"Differentiating factor?" I repeat. "You sound like a mathematician."

"You must be rubbing off on me already." She doesn't look as though she's joking. "You're so incredibly kind,

Estelle. It's like your kindness has just completely... melted me or something. I don't know how to adequately put the feeling into words."

I have to swallow something out of my throat now. "You were very brave, showing yourself to me like that."

"You made it easy. You make everything easy." Cass gazes up at me with sparkling eyes, still moist from crying earlier, and all my own defenses melt into a useless puddle as well. "I'm so going to fall in love with you. You'd better watch out."

"Watch out for what?" That tingle in my stomach grows a little bolder.

"Oh, I don't know. I just—" She blinks a few times, as though warding off more tears. "I was so not expecting someone like you in my life."

"Ditto."

"And, um..." She runs a fingertip over my arm. "Now we just... stop? Go to sleep? There's nothing, um, you need?"

There we go. The inevitable question. But it's only logical. I've yet to meet a woman who doesn't want to reciprocate. It's not in the female DNA to just receive.

"I already got everything I need." I want to kiss her again, which is usually an acceptable response to this question, but Cass isn't done talking.

"If we, um, were to do this again..."

"Which we've already established we should because of science."

"We do kind of owe it to middle-aged ladies, a notoriously under-researched bracket of the population, to investigate this further."

"That goes without saying."

"You said no touching below the waist." Cass goes

directly to the point—and I'm glad for it. "What about above the waist? That tank top looks mightily good on you, but…"

"You want to see what's underneath?"

She nods in response.

"You can touch my breasts. It's okay."

"But it doesn't turn you on?" she asks.

"It doesn't," I confirm. "But if it turns you on, that works for me. Although that's where I draw the line."

"Okay." She smiles softly. "Got it. I think."

"I know this is new for you and a little complicated, but we'll get used to it."

"It's not that complicated," Cass says and I don't contradict her, even though I know from experience it's not true. It always gets complicated at some point.

I just smile down at her and enjoy this special moment between us. She just said she's falling in love with me. This charismatic, passionate woman who makes the best burger I've ever tasted. And now I've seen her—really seen her—not just her naked body, but Cass Little in complete surrender mode. Not something I'll get enough of easily, although I might have to, because I will never be able to reciprocate that particular flavor of vulnerability.

"Big spoon or little spoon?" I ask.

"You'd think, with this body, I'd be the outer spoon—"

I bring a finger to her lips to silence her. "Now that we're in bed together, I will no longer accept you talking about your body in a deprecating way."

"Hm," Cass says. "Is that a glimpse of the bossy professor I just caught?" She arches up her blond eyebrows. "I just meant that I'm taller than you."

I'll never know whether that's actually true, but I

choose to accept it as the truth because the moment calls for it. "You want to be little spoon?"

"It's in the name, isn't it?"

I chuckle. "Sure. It'll be an honor to be your big spoon."

"I have a lot of experience with kitchen utensils." Cass can barely stop herself from bursting out laughing. "Let's see how you stack up." She shoots me a quick wink and turns on her side, her back to me.

I wrap an arm around her and sidle up to her. I hold her close and let out a contented sigh. I've slept without a woman in my arms for far too long.

When I open my eyes, I look straight into a furry ginger face. "Meow," August says.

"Sorry, I tried to keep him away from you," Cass whispers. "He doesn't know what to do with himself."

"Morning to you too, August." I rub his chin and he leans into my hand.

"He might be falling in love with you too." Under the covers, Cass's hands find mine.

A warm sensation spreads in my chest. August is adorable, but he's also in the way. I want to look at Cass. I curl my fingers tightly around her hand. With my other hand, I try to maneuver August to my other side in order to get a better view of his owner. Gracefully, he jumps over me and I can finally look into Cass's gorgeous face.

"How does your body feel? Not too sore, I hope?" An inadvertent smile breaks on my face—not a habitual occurrence this early in the day.

"My body mistakenly believes it's twenty-five years old again." Cass smiles back.

"How do *you* feel?" I ask, shuffling closer. "Did you get some sleep?"

"I did, until those pesky butterflies in my stomach started on their night shift."

"But no night sweats?" I put a hand on her belly as though my touch can silence those butterflies—as though, even if I had that power, I would even want to.

"You would have noticed if I'd had a night sweat, I assure you." She pushes herself into my touch. "How did you sleep?"

"Surprisingly well."

Cass bring a hand to my cheek. "Last night was... *amazing* sounds inadequate."

"I'm glad." I'm aware that also sounds a touch inadequate.

"So much for that take-it-slow, platonic sleepover." She giggles like the twenty-five-year-old her body believes she is. "I still have no idea what happened to me last night, what came over me..."

She did tell me that I was the only differentiating factor in the equation.

"The only explanation I can come up with is that I caught some feelings."

"Caught some feelings?" A grin spreads on my lips. "Sounds serious. Do you need a doctor to help you with that?"

"Even when you make silly jokes, you sound sexy." She briefly catches her lip between her teeth. "You're so incredibly sexy. Is it okay for me to say that?"

"Of course."

"Do you know what my very first thought was when I

woke up?" Cass looks so utterly delightful in the morning light, her blue eyes twinkling and her smile bright with mischief.

"No idea."

"Where can I find lube on a Sunday in Clearwater Bay?" She removes her hand from my cheek and covers her eyes with it, as though she just said something shameful.

"You're purely thinking in the interest of science. That can only be applauded." I peel her hand away from her face. "And to answer your question, aren't we going to brunch at a gay couple's house? They probably buy lube by the liter."

"I'm not asking Bobby and Hunter for lube." That smile now seems a permanent fixture on her face.

"Don't worry. I'll take care of it."

"No, no, no." Cass rolls on top of me. "Do not give them that satisfaction. We will never hear the end of it from Bobby. Promise me you won't ask my gay friends for lube."

"Fine, I'll ask Sadie Ireland instead."

We laugh together, our bodies convulsing in unison. The joint glee turns into kissing and before I know it, Cass's lips are trailing down my neck. Abruptly, she stops and slides off me.

"Sorry. I got carried away."

"It's okay. Really." I reach for her. "It's fine. You can't physically hurt me. I just don't… feel it the same way that you do."

"When I kiss your neck, it doesn't arouse you?" There's the first hint of disappointment—one of the most difficult emotions to conceal in your tone of voice.

"No." I don't follow up with a 'but' or sugarcoat it. The

truth has been too harsh in the past, but it doesn't make it any less true.

Cass nods. As though she senses that she needs something to do with her hands, August shows up next to her. She scratches him softly behind the ear.

"I'm just a little scared to..." Cass's voice is small and tight. "Get carried away. To cross your boundaries in the heat of the moment. That would make me feel terrible."

"It's going to happen because you're human, but it's okay. I have a voice. I'll let you know."

"And it will be less awkward than this?"

"Yes," I say, although I can only hope. "A new situation always takes some getting used to, but it will be fine. And I won't let you cross my boundaries. You can trust me on that."

"Okay." She slants her head. "What's your take on showering together? I don't want to brag, but the view from my bathroom window is pretty spectacular."

While I'm not a hundred percent comfortable with getting completely naked—a prerequisite for a shower—with someone else, this morning with Cass, I can easily see it as just another way to show her what my limits are—because the sooner she knows, the better.

CHAPTER 25
CASS

Every single one of my friends fawns over Estelle as though she is the greatest temporary inhabitant Clearwater Bay has ever seen. I totally get it. Every nice thing they say to her—or to me about her—couldn't be more true.

"She's gorgeous," Bobby says.

"She's incredibly smart," Suzy says, after only fifteen minutes of conversation with Estelle, but you can't argue with Suzy's intuition for things like cleverness in people.

"Very promising on a surfboard," Devon exclaims, staying the most levelheaded as usual.

"I can't believe it," Hunter says as he drags me into the kitchen. "What's the catch here, Cass? Because as far as I can see, that woman that my gay husband may very well want to leave me for, is fucking perfect." He's being very Bobby about this. "There has to be something and I want to know what."

"There's nothing," I say, although, obviously, nobody's perfect. Neither is Estelle but after the orgasm she drew from my body last night, she might as well be the queen of

Clearwater Bay. "I'm so smitten. I didn't see it coming. Not even a little bit."

"I can tell. You've barely touched my muffins," Hunter says matter-of-factly. "Very unlike you."

Suzy joins us in the kitchen. I'd love to talk to her in private, tell her what happened last night—how my body reacted in such an improbable way to Estelle—but I'll have to wait until Hunter leaves.

"If you won't tell me," Hunter says, "I'll find out for myself." He pecks me quickly on the cheek. "I'm really happy for you, Cassie."

"What does he want to find out?" Suzy asks.

Before I reply, I drag her into the empty living room, farther away from the backyard where everyone has gathered around the feast Hunter and Bobby have prepared to welcome Estelle.

"He's convinced she can't be as perfect as she looks," I whisper.

"That's a little cynical." Suzy rubs her chin. "And Hunter is usually the least cynical of the two." She tilts her head. "He might be subconsciously worried she'll end up hurting you."

"Suze," I interrupt her assessment of Hunter. "I had *the* most mind-blowing orgasm last night."

Eyebrows bunched together, she stares at me. "You did?"

"Seriously, my body's still in recovery, although it's also in a state of complete euphoria. It's like she… unlocked me or something."

"Wow." I've rarely seen Suzy stumped for words—it might actually be the first time.

"You're the expert on middle-aged women's hormones… what the fuck is going on with me?"

"It's really not that hard." She grins at me—that notoriously charming Ireland grin that both her famous sister and former-playboy brother possess. "You're in love."

"Yeah." I nod slowly, as though the thought hadn't occurred to me yet, while it's clear as day that I'm totally infatuated with Estelle. "Oh, god, Suze… she's so lovely, I can't even begin to tell you. So understanding and eloquent and kind. I was such a mess when she arrived last night. Any other woman would have run a mile, but she stayed and… I wanted her so much." My voice breaks a little, but Suzy is nothing if not understanding too. "And then…" I run out of words because my emotions are too strong for words. "It's like she cracked me wide open somehow. Just like that."

"Oh, Cassie." Suzy rubs her palm along my arm. "You really are in love."

"I'm an emotional wreck and I love it," I exclaim.

"Enjoy it, babe," Suzy says.

"There you are." Bobby saunters into the living room. "What are you two whispering about?" He studies my face. "Are you all right, Mama Cass? Because you've won the big prize, no doubt about it. Estelle is simply magnificent."

"I'm fine. It's just a bit much for a woman in menopause." Bobby's not like Hunter and the M-word doesn't shut him up so easily—nothing does.

"Oh, come here." He opens his arms to me. "Come and get your Bobby hug so you know that everything will be okay." Bobby is loud and brash but he's also the sweetest friend you can wish for. I step into his strong embrace. "You deserve her, and she deserves you," he whispers in my ear.

When I walk back out, I'm so drawn to Estelle, I head straight toward her and, a little possessively perhaps, put my hands on her shoulders.

She looks up at me. "Everything okay?"

"Yeah." It's hard to tear my gaze away from hers. I'm in two minds to get over myself and ask Bobby for that lube regardless of his reaction and whisk Estelle back to my place, but I'm also afraid my body might not be able to react like it did last night again. "You? With this rowdy lot?"

"Us? Rowdy?" Hunter pretends to be offended. "You were there when Sadie's surfer ladies joined us at The Bay the other week. That was rowdy. Compared to that, this is very demure."

"So rowdy that Hunter had to take his leave." Sadie slaps him on the shoulder. "Because he can't hold his own among a group of mature ladies."

"I'll be there tomorrow, and I'll stay for post-surf drinks," Hunter says.

"Good boy," Sadie says condescendingly—but Hunter deserves it sometimes. "Are you joining us again, Estelle?"

"Definitely." She gives my hand a squeeze. "We have to give Hunter a show."

I squeeze back, then return to my chair next to Estelle's, hoping with all my heart that Sadie's not going to use Estelle to try and get me on a surfboard as well.

But Devon says something about Finn and the subject changes and I look around this group of my close friends amongst whom I've sat as a single person for so long, it's hard to believe I'm here with Estelle now—gorgeous and inevitable Estelle.

Everything about this weekend is hard to fathom, apart from my night sweats on Friday—those were completely in character. My meltdown in front of Estelle was embarrassing and uncalled for but, somehow, from inside my skin, completely unpreventable. What followed is the most shocking plot twist of my life. I'd ironed a pair of pajamas, for heaven's sake. Although, as I was laying them out, that was when my head started spinning out of control. I used to be so good at just going with the flow, rolling with the punches and just seeing what happens. But my hormones no longer allow for carefree dating—or carefree anything.

I got so worked up about the shape of my body, as though I could somehow think it into a different, slimmer shape—into something more appealing for Estelle, a woman who doesn't experience sexual attraction. The whole thing was just such a mind fuck, I can be kind to myself about losing it as soon as she arrived—kind like Estelle. Because, in the end, it was nothing but her enormous kindness, her lovely, slow way with me that got me to surrender. How she got me to show myself to her as though it was a given—how she got me to do the opposite of what I thought I wanted. If I'd clung to my fear, if she hadn't gently coaxed me out of my clothes, amping up the sensual tension with every inch of my skin she revealed, I'd still be convinced that orgasms were no longer in the cards for me. I'd be utterly, completely, totally certain—and I wouldn't even care.

I just wanted a chaste sleepover—and to sneak a peek or two, perhaps. Instead, I got the climax of my life. The memory of her tongue—how insistent it was, as though no orgasm was simply not an option—on me makes me blush. As always, when my skin flushes instantly, I fear the worst, but it's not a hot flash. Maybe—who knows?—that obliterating climax rearranged my hormones in a way that keeps me free of hot flashes for a while. *Yeah right.* I can't be that lucky to have found Estelle and be spared one of the most embarrassing and annoying symptoms of the menopause all at once.

"Cassie's got it bad," I hear Bobby say.

"Sorry. What?"

"You were miles away but we don't blame you."

"Brain fog," I say, although my brain has never been clearer.

Estelle slides her hand along the back of my neck and, instinctively, I lean into it.

"Sure," Bobby says.

Despite this life-phase I'm going through, with all its discomforts, I haven't been this ludicrously happy since long before menopause. Estelle's hand on my neck. My friends teasing me about being smitten. And the memory of that insane climax strong in my body and my mind.

CHAPTER 26
ESTELLE

It's very different taking to the water with Cass's gaze on me. She, Suzy, Hunter, and Bobby are leisurely sipping wine on the deck of The Bay, no doubt talking about me and of course I'm curious about what they're saying. But I can't focus on them. The waves don't let me. Surfing is such an in-the-moment activity, demanding full-body control, that you can't think about the woman you're falling for. You can't sneak backward glances while balancing on a surfboard. I tried earlier and paid the price —a complete wipeout, to Linda's exuberant cheers.

But I know that Cass bought some lube today and that she'll be keen to use it later. While it was glorious to have her come like that, it's a delicate balance. Already, I feel I need to manage expectations. Already, there's a complexity creeping into our feelings toward each other that can so easily cause a bunch of problems.

"Estelle, come on," Sadie admonishes me. "Focus or you'll drown."

"That's a bit dramatic."

"The ocean does not reward half-heartedness." She

flashes her TV smile. "Although I get why you're distracted." She paddles closer toward me. "Cass is for later. You have all night together. This is now, okay?"

"Yes, boss." Maybe this is exactly what I need. Something to take me out of my head because, when you're like me, overthinking a situation becomes second nature. Sometimes, it even leads to thinking something to death before it has the chance to become something beautiful, and I don't want that to happen with Cass. So I do as Sadie says. I obey the natural command she has when we're in the ocean, trying to catch a wave. I block everything out, all the doubts, all the reasons for the many scars on my heart, all the papers I've yet to go through in my father's house, all the different ways I've tried to approach the problem he set me and failed—and all the ways things can go wrong between me and Cass.

I'm not very good at surfing yet, but there's a hint of promise when I try to catch a small wave and don't topple off my board immediately. More than promise though, there's a freedom to surfing that I seem to crave right now. A freedom from everything that has happened and has brought me here—even though it brought me to Cass.

On the board, you have to surrender. Your mind must go blank and you need to rely on instinct and muscle memory. To ride a wave, this gift from the ocean, is exhilarating and therapeutic at the same time. It's exactly what I need right now.

"Don't wait until next week to surf again," Sadie says while we paddle back to shore. "The more you practice, the more fun you'll have." I catch her gaze. "There's always a chance you'll catch Devon and me in the water and we're always willing to give you some tips."

"I'll take a private lesson from Sadie Ireland," Linda hollers.

Cass will be busy with the restaurant when it opens again tomorrow. I promise myself to spend more time in the ocean instead of poring over my father's papers which, I'm beginning to think, might be a waste of time. But to get rid of them is to say my final goodbye and I'm not ready for that yet, either.

"So." Cass's warm hand in mine feels right as we walk to her house. "What's your friends' verdict on me?" I ask.

"As I told you yesterday, they are all deeply and madly in love with you."

"Even Suzy?" It's a little naughty, but the words are out of my mouth before I can stop them.

"Maybe not Suzy, although she likes you very much." Our steps slow. "Knowing her, she'll want a one-on-one with you sooner rather than later."

"Really?" I ask.

"Just to get to know you."

"Not to question my motives?"

"That, too, I suppose." Cass emits a small chuckle. "Hunter thinks you're too good to be true, which is probably shallow gay for you being too hot for me, but it's not politically correct to say that."

"Jesus. Is he still in high school?" My reaction is sharp because I've been accused of 'being too good to be true' before.

"Sometimes, you'd think so."

"What did you reply when he said that?" In the end, Cass's opinion is the only one that matters.

She slides her hands up my arm and holds on to me. "That you're perfect," is all she says.

"Argh, you really are smitten." So am I, but it's different for me. We are not equals in this and that makes it difficult. I try to get my mind back into the zen-like state it needs for surfing, but I'm on dry land and experiencing some feelings of inadequacy that I don't know how to express.

"Fuck, yes," Cass says.

As always, at this early, hopeful stage, I don't know whether to warn her or to practice blissful ignorance. Although I think I communicate clearly about what I want and don't want, actions speak loudly, and we had sex. Of course, Cass looks at me differently since we slept together. Of course, she will want things that I won't be able to give.

"Me too," I say, instead of starting a preemptive conversation—because it's just a hell of a lot easier.

"Hey, um..." Our pace picks up, as though her next sentence needs momentum to get out. "I know my hormones are raging out of control and I've been getting a little carried away sending you pictures of my new most prized possession." That bottle of lube is all over our message thread. "But just as you told me that I set the pace... You set the pace, too. We set it together. I want you, but I'm aware it's different for you. I don't want you to feel pressured into anything."

My hopeful heart beats a little faster.

"Especially," Cass continues, "because of what I brought to the table before this weekend, you know, explicitly claiming that I didn't want sex... well, things have changed quickly."

"It's a little confusing for both of us, but that's as much

me as it is you." Communication is important, even more so when it comes to the parts of our personality we're least proud of. "When you told me about your body no longer being able to experience pleasure like before, I took it as a personal challenge. I wanted to make you come so badly."

"I noticed." I can't see her face, but there's nothing but glee in Cass's voice.

"I was not completely clear in my intentions about that, even though I know it can be such a slippery slope."

"Meaning?" Cass asks.

"We had sex, each for our own reasons. I wanted to make you come. You… wanted me."

"Yeah," Cass says on a sigh.

"But I'm afraid that…" For the life of me, I can't push the words past my lips. I don't want to put ideas in her head that may never show up of their own accord. Maybe Cass is deliciously uncomplicated and just wants orgasms by my hand—and tongue—for the rest of her life. Maybe she's the kind of person who is perfectly okay with what I have to offer. Maybe I'm the one with the massive chip on my shoulder and I should just shut up and enjoy the buzz of falling in love with this poised, intelligent and very talented woman.

"What are you afraid of?" Cass's voice dips into that low, careful register. "Because I'm afraid, too. I think it's pretty normal when you're at the start of something new with someone. And at a stage of your life when, every single day, it feels like the rug is pulled out from under your feet."

"Yeah." I'm afraid of all those things too, of course. On top of the one unshakable fear I carry into every new relationship, but that's for me to deal with.

"All I was trying to say." Cass comes to a stop and

turns fully toward me. "Is that we don't have to use the lube today."

"Let's see how frisky you are when we get home." Personally, I can't wait to look at her when my fingers slip inside her.

"You do look criminally hot in a wetsuit." Cass shoots me a grin. "And that tumble you made into the water halfway into the lesson was just… well, I'd say panty-soaking but my panty-soaking days are well and truly over, hence the disproportional excitement over a bottle of lube."

"You like to see me fall." I grin along with her. "I'm not sure what to make of that."

"I don't know what to make of myself any longer, so…" Cass slants toward me and kisses me on the lips. "And it's all your fault," she whispers in my ear before taking me home.

CHAPTER 27
CASS

As it turns out, I'm very frisky. I also have no more qualms about taking off my clothes in front of Estelle. Maybe that's why I took a tiny bit of pleasure in watching her topple off her surfboard, because it was an illustration of her own physical imperfection. She's not that perfect that she can hop on a surfboard after years without practice and casually ride some waves. Even Estelle Raymond can't do that.

The honest truth is I couldn't take my eyes off her, whether she was on or off her surfboard. That I couldn't wait to get her home. And of course we can just sleep together, I meant what I said earlier, but I wouldn't mind if we did more than spooning.

"Show me." Estelle sits on my bed in her familiar boy shorts and tank top, both stark white tonight and making her look even more sexy, although I don't know how that is even possible.

"Show you what?" I play coy. I'd like for her to show me what's underneath that tank top again. We've showered together so I've seen her fully naked but these are very different circumstances.

"Your new best friend. Better than Hunter for sure, since he would have mocked you for asking him for it."

"It's right there." I point at the nightstand.

"Ah, there you are." Estelle picks up the sizable bottle of lube. "You've been much talked about." She pretends to study the bottle in great detail. "Time to see whether you stack up."

My heart leaps all the way into my throat, although that doesn't stop the blood from rushing to my clit.

"Are you sure?" Clearly, she is. She's holding the bottle. But I still feel like I have to ask.

"Come here." She extends her legs and pats her lap, as though I would even fit there.

Fully naked, I climb onto the bed, swat the pillows out of the way, and sit with my back against the headboard. "You straddle me. Surely you don't mind, what with being such a top."

She looks at me with an expression I can't decipher. I can't read Estelle the same way I could past lovers.

She puts the lube to the side and crawls over. She plants her knees on either side of me. The moment is hot and full of promise, my clit raging in the tightness between my closed legs, and all I can think of is how much I want her naked on top of me—maybe even more than her using that by-now-infamous lube on me.

"This to your liking?" Her silky voice snaps me out of my secret desire and what I get in real-life is so overwhelmingly powerful, I instantly forget what I wanted a mere second ago.

Her hair cascades onto my shoulders, her lips are a fraction away from mine, her breath is warm on my lips.

She's like a tsunami of hotness from which there is no possible escape.

She waits for me to reply before kissing me. I look up into her dark eyes and curl my arms around her waist.

"Very much," I whisper.

When her lips touch down, goose bumps cover the entire expanse of my skin. Inadvertently, my hands slide underneath her tank top. She doesn't flinch. Still, I need to ask.

With great difficulty, I pull back from our kiss.

"Can I touch you here?" My voice is ragged with lust. My hands rest on the small of her back.

"Yes." Her lips pull into a smirk. "Hold on," she says, before pulling her tank top over her head. "Anything that's not covered, you can touch."

Oh, fuck. I'm getting way more than I bargained for. As if they have a life of their own, my hands move toward her breasts, my lips toward her nipples. One of my most fervent wishes has already been granted.

I wrap my mouth around her hard nipple, swipe my tongue gently along its tip, and my clit is completely beside itself. It's so damn easy to lose control of myself when I touch her like this. Because, almost instantly, I want more. But I also know I have to stop myself from wanting more. Still, there's a little voice in my head saying that this is only the beginning and when we first met, when we first had that conversation about her being ace, I most certainly wasn't expecting this. And look at me now. Lips hot around her nipple, hand cupped around her breast.

I glance up at her, try to look at her face, hoping to glimpse some sort of bliss, but it's not what I see, because this is only for my benefit. I'm the one who has to rearrange something in my brain. I'm the one who has to adapt to this, because she's already giving me all this. Most certainly not against her will—thank goodness she made that very clear—but our joy in this is not matched, and, truth be told, it's a bit of a bitter pill to swallow. Because I want nothing more than to give her pleasure, than to give her the same pleasure she gave me. It's the most logical equation possible. Yet it's not. So I let go of her breasts, even though everything about them is moreish, but I'm not someone who's in the habit of taking more than she's allowed—or thinks she's allowed.

Estelle must sense my hesitation. Surely she can't read minds, but I imagine she's been in this kind of situation a few times before.

"Hey," she says, as she maneuvers off me. "Whatever you're feeling is perfectly normal, but…" How can she still be so understanding and sensitive with all those scars on her heart she admitted to having accumulated? "We have that lube." Her voice has dropped into that low sexy place again and it connects directly to my clit.

Then, she's all over me, erasing any doubts from my mind again—she's unnervingly good at that. Because she's an expert at reading my body, at sensing what it needs, at processing, at lightning speed, what I like, what turns me on—her lips on my neck, her fingertips slowly trailing between my legs.

My body's all revved up, my cheeks hot and my core burning, when she finds my gaze, looks straight into my eyes, and asks with that silky-smooth voice of hers, "I'm going to fuck you now."

I should tell her that, between my legs, things have changed considerably the past few years. That I'm extra-sensitive and the softest touch can sometimes even be too much. I should communicate, but my throat is closed up with a lust so profound it has drowned all my words.

I'll have to trust that she will know—and I do. Estelle is so easy to trust it should be scary. I should be more careful, with my body and my heart, but look at where she has me again.

I spread my legs wider for her. I watch her, heart pounding furiously in my chest, as she grabs the lube and squirts a generous handful into her palm. Her fingers glisten and it's one of the hottest things I've ever seen. Slowly, she brings her hand between my legs and transfers some of the lube to me—to my throbbing lips.

She takes her time, as I trusted she would. While she plays with me, escalating my arousal, she lies down next to me, fixing her gaze to mine. I'm completely at her mercy. I'm totally enthralled by her, controlled by her gaze and her divine fingers.

She opens me up with a fingertip and, already, my breath stalls in my throat. She looks at me, as though she can read from my face what my body needs—what her fingers should do next.

Gently, she slides in farther and I feel it everywhere. Again, I don't know how this is possible. Again, she must have magic powers—although it could also be the lube. Because the past couple of years my vagina has no longer been a great ally. First, there was the dryness. Then, the pain, not obliterating but dull and as if wanting to spread the message that the good times were over now. That I should close my legs, and my private parts, for business. And I did. It was only Estelle who made me want to touch myself. And it's only Estelle who can now slide her finger, slowly and gently and stealing more of my breath the deeper she goes, high inside of me.

There's nothing but tenderness in how she gradually moves her finger inside me. Her gestures are so minute and perfectly matched to my sensitivity. There's not a hint of pain. It's all pleasure and surrender and I want to look into her eyes like this forever. She unravels me with the subtlest movement, tugging at a seam that's held me together in all the wrong ways.

I start moaning, my voice now also with a life of its own, to the rise and fall of the waves starting to lap inside me. I can't even remember a time when I was able to climax with just a finger inside of me. But everything is different now, and Estelle seems to know all about it. She must know, how else can she manipulate my body like this? How else does she know that adding a second finger would be too much and moving even a fraction faster would pull me out of this trance she's got me in?

But she does it just right, just the way I need it—the way I didn't even know myself I like it. Or maybe my body adapts to her. I don't know. All I know is that I feel connected to her in the most delicious manner, to her finger deep inside of me, coaxing ever louder moans from my throat.

"Come for me, Cass," she whispers, drawing out the 's' at the end of my name, like some sort of hypnotic hiss, and my body responds to it as though it was made to do so. Because I want to come for her. Because I can. It doesn't happen straight away, but I can feel it taking me over steadily. It builds from my core like a flame licking the inside of my skin and spreads through my muscles, and all because of her gloriously glistening finger inside me.

This climax is different than the first one she gave me. It seems to come from a different place inside of me. From somewhere I need to heal, someplace I've neglected because it was too painful to go to. It takes all the doubts I've had about myself the past couple of years, the pain from my break-up and the insecurities of my changing body, and drowns them in a sea of pure pleasure. Maybe Estelle had to be inside of me for this to happen. For this climax to wash over me and leave me slightly altered in its wake.

I come at her fingertip, my muscles convulsing, the walls of my pussy clinging to her. This time, I don't cry. I unambiguously enjoy the incredible sense of satisfaction, of deep pleasure, that only she could give me—that doesn't exist outside this bedroom, without her in it.

CHAPTER 28
ESTELLE

I've just thrown away a huge stack of my father's papers when the doorbell rings. It's Thursday afternoon and Cass must be preparing for dinner service, yet I hope it's her. I always hope it's her. We've been seeing each other for a few weeks now and although we both have things to deal with, it's been magnificent to get to know her better, to simply spend time with her—and August—at her house on the cliff.

Wiping my hands, I head to the front door, my heart doing its silly I'm-so-in-love pitter-patter.

When I open the door, Suzy stands in front of me.

"Hi." She holds up a box of something. "Red velvet cupcakes. Homemade by moi," she says.

"Suzy. Hi." I'm a little taken aback. Apart from a few of my dad's old neighbors, I haven't had a lot of visitors, expected or unexpected. Cass and I have gotten into the habit of meeting up at hers, simply because it's a lot more pleasant—and clean. "Come in. Ignore the mess."

"I hope you don't mind my impromptu visit."

"It's a welcome distraction," I admit. I'm starting to get

sick of my father's endless piles of formulas and calculations. Sometimes, I fear I may burn out all over again just from looking through them.

"I can hook you up with some guys who will take care of this place in no time," Suzy says matter-of-factly. "Although I get that a lot of emotions must be tied up in it for you."

"It's something I have to do myself, but I might change my mind soon." I usher her into the kitchen, which I keep the tidiest because I have to prepare a minimum of food for myself. "Would you like some coffee or tea?"

"Coffee. Black," Suzy says. I should remember her better from high school, but it's all such a blur. After my mother died, my dad and I sank into our bubble of comfort and grief and my memories from before the accident are strangely clouded. Either way, Suzy Ireland and I didn't travel in the same social circles at school. She was the quintessential popular girl, and I was the cliché math nerd.

"Can I offer you a cupcake?" I ask, pointing at the box Suzy brought.

"Yes, please," she says. "I used to work in a bakery. Picked up a few tricks."

"That's a long way from being a menopause consultant." I grab some plates and put a dark red cupcake on each. The people in this town sure love to feed me.

"I'm a jill-of-all-trades, but with Devon, I've really found a professional home. If my sister wasn't married to her and I wasn't aromantic, I would tie her down like nobody's business." She bursts into raucous laughter. "I'm also a too-much-information-too-quickly kind of girl. You'll get used to it."

We sit in the rickety chairs at my father's old kitchen table with our coffee and cupcakes.

"Cass is like a different person since she met you. Well, in some respects." Suzy is also not a beat about the bush kind of girl. Cass did say Suzy had expressed an explicit wish to grill me on my intentions. I guess this is it.

"So am I." I give her my best smile.

"It's pretty obvious why she has the hots for you. You're drop dead gorgeous. A math professor, no less. The gays are crazy about you." She holds up her hands. "I can totally see it. I like you too, Estelle."

"But?" I should be flattered by what she just said, yet I'm getting a slightly hostile vibe.

"No, no. Sorry. No buts." She raises one shoulder. "This is just my personality." A wide grin spreads across her face. "I'd like to get to know you better and, if you're willing to share, ask what your plans are?" She looks around the kitchen. "Are you staying? Are you going back to work?"

"I honestly don't know." In order to take a beat, I bite a chunk out of my cupcake. It's deliciously moist and just the right amount of sweet. Suzy really did pick up some tricks.

Time to find out how good she is at her new professional calling. As a menopause consultant and former life coach, I expect her to display a good deal of sensitivity and have a smooth way of handling a potentially difficult conversation—although, as far as I'm concerned, our little chitchat doesn't have to be difficult at all.

"Hm," I moan. "So good."

"Thanks." Her smile is just as dazzling as her sister's TV smile.

"I no longer have a job, so I can stay in Clearwater Bay as long as I want."

"You don't need to work?" Suzy asks.

"Turns out Daddy Raymond had a lot of money stashed away." By the end of his life, he probably didn't even remember—maybe that's why he never told me. "My inheritance was sizable."

"It's good that you don't have to rush back into work. That you can take your time to grieve and deal with all the practicalities no one ever warns you about."

"And learn how to surf with Sadie and Devon." I tried to catch some waves earlier today, but neither Sadie nor Devon was there, and it wasn't as much fun on my own—it seemed almost impossible to stay on my board without their encouragement.

"If that's your thing." She smirks. "I've been the black sheep of the Ireland family ever since I stopped surfing in my teens. But just because I grew up by the ocean, doesn't automatically make me a water person, you know? I like to walk. I like to feel the ground beneath my feet."

"Sure." A smile tugs at my lips. "Just like Cass. She's very adamant about not surfing." I remember what Devon told me about how beneficial it could be, mentally and physically, for women in the menopause. I'm sure Suzy has a different opinion on that.

"Yeah, me, Hunter and Cass are all land rats. We like to sit on the deck of The Bay and watch the surfers, but don't put a board under our arm, thank you very much."

"Nothing wrong with that." I sip from my coffee. Suzy hasn't touched her cupcake. "I'm not very good at it yet, but I love the weightlessness of it when I do manage to catch a wave and how I have to forget about everything else in order to stay on my board."

"I get it. My dad, bless him, still surfs every single day for that very reason."

"Good for him."

"Can I ask you a personal question out of professional curiosity, please?" Suzy asks.

"Sure."

"We're the same age and I've been on hormone therapy for three years now. Where are you in your journey?"

"Nowhere, I think."

"No symptoms? No mood swings? Hot flashes? Irregular periods?"

"No. I guess I'm a late bloomer."

"Good for you, really. Maybe you are one of the lucky few women who breeze through it like it's nothing, but it's not like that for the majority of us… Cass, in particular, has had a rough time of it."

I nod. "I know." It's hard to forget her meltdown prior to our first sleepover.

"And she refuses any medical help. She can be rather stubborn," Suzy says.

"Yeah, she told me why."

"Her mother's cancer was not hormone-sensitive. Cass knows this, but it's emotional for her. She can't break the promise she made to her mother. She'd rather suffer." Suzy sighs. "We've had so many conversations about it. I've sent her so many links to studies refuting what she believes. I've told her over and over again that she doesn't have to be in pain because she's a woman, but I might as well be talking to a brick wall. She refuses to hear me."

"It's her choice. If she has all the information, she decides."

"True enough. I just hate to see her so distressed. So unlike she used to be." She tilts her head as though asking, what about you? I don't reply because I'm not Cass, although, obviously, I don't enjoy seeing her go through yet another hot flash—but Cass is old and wise enough to make her own decisions.

"One thing did surprise me, though." Suzy narrows her eyes.

"What's that?" I wish I didn't because it makes me more defensive, but I have developed a sixth sense about this so I know what's coming.

"Please know that I'm not judging. I'm not in the business of judging. I'm aro, which is not the same, but it does mean I'm far from ignorant… Still, I was really surprised when Cass told me about the best sex of her life… in the menopause… with an asexual partner."

"You could just be happy for her." My voice is surprisingly steady.

"Oh, I am. I really am." She pins her gaze on me. "And for you, of course. Cass is a wonderful person."

"Again, agreed." What's with the subtext of this conversation? Is she trying to tell me something? Or is it just me who's got my hackles up because of the topic? "What is it you're trying to tell me?" I ask, meeting her gaze.

"I'm not sure." She brings a hand to her chest, as though she's guilty of something. "I'm very protective of Cass. The past couple of years have not been kind to her and I just… I'd hate to see her hurt."

"You think I'm going to hurt her because I'm ace?" In my experience, it's usually the other way around.

"God, no. I'm sorry, Estelle. We're getting off on the wrong foot and it's completely my fault." She shakes her head. "My friends are very important to me and…" She emits a dry chuckle. "I'm sorry. Now I'm just making excuses for my poor behavior. How appalling."

"You care about Cass and that's great." For a moment, I wonder if Suzy has feelings for Cass, but she's aromantic. "Can I ask *you* a personal question?"

"Please, do." She relaxes her shoulders.

"You never fall in love?" I know it's offensive to ask, but she hasn't been the most tactful either. And maybe I just want to know what her secret is. Sometimes, I wish my own heart could be a little smarter.

"I wouldn't put it like that exactly, but a romantic relationship is simply not for me. I've tried, of course. But the being in love part was always over in a flash and then, after that first haze of mind-altering chemicals, of being smitten, lifts, I always wonder what the hell I'm doing trying to accommodate another person. I have a great life. A loving family and the best friends I can wish for, but I prefer to be alone. I've never had that need to share my life with someone. I share my life with me. I do what I want, when I want it. I'm an aunt, a sister, a daughter, and, yes, also an annoyingly overbearing friend." She holds up her hands as if to say, what are you going to do? "But I'm nobody's partner. That's not me."

"And sex?" I might as well ask.

She points her thumb at her chest. "Mainly with myself." She shrugs. "One-night stands are just so... pffhhhh." She huffs out a loud, exasperated sigh that makes me chuckle. "Honestly, I can't be bothered."

When she's not grilling me, I do like Suzy. I like her directness and also that she's not like everyone else—that she's like me.

"I'm not going to hurt Cass," I say. "Not if I can help it. I'm crazy about her." If anything, I'm afraid she'll hurt me.

Suzy just nods, her gaze drifting to the untouched cupcake. "And she makes the best grilled cheese sandwich," she says matter-of-factly.

"And burger," I add.

"She's very good at what she does. It's a blessing to have a job that suits you so much." She picks up the cupcake and finally takes a bite, as though giving in not just to the sugar but to me, to the possibility that I might be good for her friend after all. We sit in silence as she chews. "What about you? Have you thought about a career after mathematics?" That must be the life coach in her rearing its head.

"No, not yet." I pick a crumb off my plate. "Math will always be a part of my life. It's like Cass and cooking. It's a part of us, but… I don't know. I'm taking the time I need to figure it out."

"And fall in love in the meantime." Suzy winks at me.

"Oh, yes," I say, my stomach fluttering at the thought of Cass.

CHAPTER 29
CASS

On the one-month anniversary of our unforgettable burgers-at-The-Bay date, I make Estelle a cake and put one candle in her piece.

She purses her lips and looks as though she's thinking hard. "I'm sorry," she says. "But I don't know what it's for. I hope that doesn't make me a bad girlfriend." It's the first time she refers to herself as my girlfriend and I'm dizzy with happiness—although the dizziness could also be the aftermath of the atrociously bad night's sleep I had.

"You're the best girlfriend ever," I say, not caring one bit how teenager-like that sounds. "Exactly one month and two days ago we went on our date to The Bay. Remember, when I said sex was off the table and you proceeded to seduce me with how ridiculously sensually you devoured that burger?"

Estelle chuckles. "I will never forget."

"I waited to make you the cake until we could properly celebrate." I've never been happier with my choice of running a slow restaurant, because it means I have plenty of time to date. To get to know Estelle better day by glorious day. Sex is certainly on the table, but not all the time—not like when Sarah and I just got together.

"I'm sorry I forgot." Estelle makes a spectacle of blowing out the candle.

"Oh, I know that mathematicians are notoriously bad with numbers."

"Numbers are not dates," Estelle says, her voice too damn sexy again. "But come here." She pushes her chair away from the table. "Let me make it up to you."

I clumsily straddle her on the chair—falling in love hasn't miraculously transformed my body into a slight, petite shape—and kiss her. God, I kiss her. I can't get enough of kissing Estelle. Sometimes it turns into more, sometimes it doesn't. Usually, I let her take the lead. My libido might have come roaring back to life, but I'm still a fifty-three-year-old woman with hot flashes and a restaurant to run. No matter how sexy Estelle is, I don't want to jump her bones all the time. But, from time to time, I do ache for how she can make me feel—like a hot-blooded woman she can't keep her hands off.

It's Saturday evening and I definitely want her to stay —and more.

We kiss more, until my half-sitting half-hovering position becomes too uncomfortable. I rise and hold out my hand. She takes it and I let her guide me into my bedroom.

We undress—me fully, Estelle keeping her shorts on— and roll onto bed and tonight she treats me to a special combination of tongue, fingers and lube and the orgasm is so obliterating it zaps all of my brain power.

I lie panting in her arms and, not for the first time, I can only think of one thing. I want her. I want to make her feel like this. Something feels incomplete—bordering on inadequateness on my part, even though I know it's not me. But there's a gap between knowing something intellectually and feeling something in your gut, especially when the intellectual part of your brain has been incapacitated by a mind-numbing climax.

I turn on my side and look into her eyes. I curl my arm around her waist, making sure my fingers don't dip too low.

"I want you so much, Estelle," I whisper. "You have no idea."

"You just had me." She smiles that ridiculously sexy smile of hers and it's almost enough.

"I want *you*."

"Cass. No," she says, her voice soft, almost pleading.

My fingertips dig into her waist a fraction. "God, I want to touch you."

She doesn't reply, just stares at me in silence, then swallows something out of her throat. "I need you to stop," she says, after a while. "You know why." Her voice is much sharper, snapping me out of my stupor.

"Oh, fuck." I pull back my hand, as though I shouldn't be touching her anywhere any longer. "I'm sorry. That was… not okay."

"I get it." There's a distinct note of sadness in her voice. "I really do, but I need you to get used to this, because I can never give you that."

"I know. God, I know. I was in…"

"It's okay." She brings her palm to my cheek. "It happens. It's only human for you to, um, want me like that, but…"

It might be human, but it makes me feel like a bad person nonetheless. On top of that, I might have spoken in the heat of the moment, but now that I'm having sex again, I really miss the giving part. I miss making my partner come. I miss being inside them. I miss what it takes for the other person to open themselves up to me like that. The mutual trust that leads to that kind of vulnerability.

"How did your former partners deal with this?" I ask, feeling as silly as I feel naive.

Estelle scoffs. "They didn't, hence the fact that they are my former partners." Her hand goes rigid against my cheek.

I cover her hand with mine. "Hey, I'm not them, okay? I'm me. And yes, I need time and I need to adjust, but…" But what? I'll get used to it? I probably will. "I still think you're too good to be true," I say, hoping my voice carries enough weight to make her believe me. Because this might be awkward for me, but I have no idea how it feels for her.

"I'm so fucking not." Her hand relaxes. "I'm a challenge, I know that."

"I like a challenge." I chuckle at my own lameness. "And I like you. A lot." I thread my fingers through hers. "And thank you for that orgasm. No wonder it took me a while to come back to my senses."

"I'm very good at taking the blame for a woman losing her mind." She sinks her teeth into her pillowy bottom lip.

"You shouldn't be." I shake my head. "Hey, I don't want to lose you, okay? You're the best thing that has happened to me in a very long time."

Estelle expels some air, then shuffles closer and wraps me tightly in her arms. "Oh, Cass," is all she says.

Even though it's Monday and we could be gawking at Sadie's surfer ladies—Estelle included—I've asked Suzy if I could speak to her in the privacy of her home.

It only takes a few sips of wine for me to blurt out what I've come to say. "It drives me absolutely crazy sometimes that I can't touch her."

"Figures," Suzy replies drily. "You want what you can't have."

"Please don't say it only makes me human. I know I'm a human and I know what I want." And I also know what I can't have.

"Sure, but, Cass, your only option is to accept Estelle as she is."

"I know, but… argh." I put my hands on my temples. "I don't know how."

"Talk to her," Suzy offers.

I shake my head. "We talk, but I can't tell her how much I want her. I don't want to make her feel like she's not enough for me."

"You're going to have to find a way to make her be enough for you." Suzy is full of wisdom tonight. "Estelle can't change."

"But I can? Is that what you're saying?"

"If you don't want to lose her." I was expecting a touch more compassion from one of my best friends.

"Of course I don't want to lose her, but… I can't shake this feeling that I'm missing something vital in our relationship. The way she is with me. How she brought me out of my shell. Brought me back to life, in a sense. How she makes me feel… It just all feels so one-sided sometimes."

"Because you can't make her come?" Suzy may be a bit sharp, but she sure hits the nail on the head.

"Yeah."

Suzy looks me in the eye. "You have to talk to Estelle about this. You can't keep this to yourself and grow increasingly frustrated by it as time goes on. She will understand, okay? She's been through this before, I assure you." Suzy's dealt with her fair share of preconceived notions in her own life. "Prepare her a meal. Make it cozy. Make the situation non-threatening and just tell her how you feel."

"But what difference does it even make if I tell her or not?"

"Communication. It's the only way it's going to work." Suzy smiles gently. "Don't wait until you're in bed and can't keep your hands off her, because that might be too much for her. Talk to her in a calm setting. Give it time. And don't forget to count your blessings."

Suzy's right about one thing, I have a lot of blessings to count—I may need a mathematician to help me add them all up. But I'm less convinced about talking this through with Estelle. It's not an easy thing to talk about and from what she's told me, most of her relationships have ended because of the very thing I want to talk to her about. I guess I'll just have to see what happens.

CHAPTER 30
ESTELLE

Days fly by in a haze of Cass, sorting through my father's stuff, more Cass, surfing with Sadie and the other women, Cass cooking for me, August jumping into my lap as soon as I sit down, and before I know it, another month has gone by. It's the two-month anniversary of our burger-date and while things are going great with Cass, I have noticed a slight change in her behavior. Sex seems to have slipped off the table as swiftly—and as unexpectedly—as it found its way on there.

I have no issue with this, but I can't shake the feeling that Cass might. So, one night, I sit her down for an important conversation I don't want to have.

It's Monday and she's had a few glasses of wine with Suzy and Hunter at The Bay, which, I hope, will make talking easier.

"Come here," I say, patting my lap, like I'm calling for her cat to join me instead of her. "I want to kiss you. Profusely."

"Did surfing make you frisky?" Cass is definitely tipsy,

otherwise she wouldn't say that. But I see it as a good thing tonight.

"Well, you know, Sadie Ireland is no slouch on a surfboard and she paid me a lot of special attention today."

Cass pretends to be highly offended. She gasps and, theatrically, brings a hand to her chest. "I can't compete with a former TV-star who's not even in perimenopause yet."

"Lucky for you, there's no competition." I beckon her over again, with my eyes as well my hands. "I only want to kiss *you*."

Cass sits next to me, her body angled toward me. She even seems less keen to kiss me, which worries me. Although, when I look into her eyes, there's no mistaking her desire for me. It's so plainly—and confusingly—on display, I can't help but worry.

I stroke her cheek with my finger. I want her to come to me, to bridge the distance between us.

Tonight, she does. There's nothing hesitant about her kiss. Her hands are all over the back of my neck and my hair until—also not for the first time—she pulls away abruptly.

"What's up with that?" I ask.

"With what?" She tucks a strand of hair behind her ear, her gaze skittering away.

"You've had enough of my kisses already?"

"No," she says on a sigh. "God, no, Estelle."

"Is it your hormones? Are they going haywire again?" It's a definite possibility and even though it's highly unpleasant for Cass, I can only hope that's the reason.

"Babe, I, um, I—"

"It's okay, Cassie." I slip my hand in hers. "You can tell me anything, but talk to me, please. Don't shut me out."

"I'm working through something." Cass shifts her body so she no longer has to look at me.

"Do you want to talk about it?"

"I know that we have to talk, but it's hard. I've never had a conversation like this. I never thought I would have a conversation about this…"

"Try. For me." My heart's already shrinking in my chest, like it can somehow brace itself for what's coming.

"I'm trying to…" Cass swallows hard. "Figure out how to live with wanting you and not being able to act on it." She squeezes my hand.

Oh, fuck. Here we go again. I exhale a breath and try hard not to sigh. I've learned a few valuable lessons from similar conversations in the past. But it's still hard for me not to take this personally.

"Is that why you don't want to have sex anymore?" I ask.

"Oh, Estelle, I want to have sex, but I'm afraid… I don't trust myself. I'm afraid of what I might say or that my hand may wander and that I will cross your boundaries and…" She huffs out some air. "I'm sorry. I know that I have to accept this. I just don't know how to do it." Her shoulders sag. "Not having sex seemed like a good enough solution."

"You know I'm okay with that, but I'm not sure you are."

"I'm not." It sounds like a scoff. "I want you so fucking much. You're so… everything I want."

Once again, I, Estelle Raymond, don't stack up. I'm not enough. I probably never will be.

When Cass looks at me, her eyes are moist. "What is the solution to this?"

Did I do this? Did I go about it all wrong again? Probably. What with the impromptu kissing her and saying that I can have sex, but I can only give. I should have just said that sex was a total no-go for me. Why do I have to make it so hard? Have I learned nothing from all that scar tissue on my heart?

"I'm not going to change, Cass." I shake my head. "I would if I could." In a fucking heartbeat. "But I really can't. I've tried everything." My eyes fill with tears as well, because I can't offer a solution—not an easy one, at least. Not one that doesn't require my partner to do all the work, which is always, invariably, the issue as well as the breaking point.

"I'm so in love with you," she says on a sigh, as though she's cursed instead of in love.

"I'm in love with you too." Most of the time, in my experience, it's not enough.

"I know that… I… have to find a way," Cass says. "I will. I promise you, babe. Just bear with me. Can you do that?"

"Of course I can." I thread my fingers tightly through hers. "Can you?" Because that's the real question here.

"If I have to choose between a life with you where I can't touch you fully and a life without you at all, the choice is crystal clear." She wraps her fingers around mine. "I want to be with you. There's no doubt in my mind about that."

My muscles relax, but only a fraction. Because what if this is only the first tear in the fragile fabric we have woven between us?

"I just…" She wipes a dangling tear from her eyelashes. "I like to give, sometimes even more than receiving. And I need the reciprocity of sex. I have such a desire to see you surrender. I know we use the words give and receive, but when you 'give' me an orgasm, I also feel like I give you something back. I give you something from deep inside of me, something special that's not just for anyone to have, and I crave that from you. I'm sorry, but I do."

I nod. "I get it," is all I can say, however. Because I can't give her what she so craves.

"That's what I'm trying to figure out." She exhales deeply again. "Sex isn't just an orgasm to me. It's intimacy and closeness and shared vulnerability and..." She pauses. "I honestly didn't think it would be this hard. To want you this much but hold myself back. To yearn for that connection and know I can't have it the way I need to."

"I'm sorry." As a rule, I try not to apologize for who I am, for how I was born, but sometimes, in moments like this, an apology is all I have to offer.

"I'm sorry too," Cass says. "That I'm not better at this. At accepting you exactly as you are. I mean, you are magnificent. You make my life a million times more fun. You've made me come alive again at a time when I really wasn't expecting it and I should be nothing but grateful, but..." Her voice trails off.

"You want the one thing you can't have." I wish it didn't sound so trivial, so cliché, so like something that can easily be changed—or accepted.

"Yes, but I also want you." A small smile appears on her face. "I was so afraid to have this conversation." Her hold on my hand loosens. "I have been meaning to talk to you about this instead of, you know, avoiding certain situations, but this whole thing... I'm so worried I will say or do the wrong thing, which isn't usually how I am, but... I guess I'm most afraid of losing you."

"Whether you lose me is entirely up to you," I say,

because that's truly how I see it. "I'm not going anywhere and…" I smile back, because how can I not? "There is no wrong thing to say or do. Everything is fixable. I know you are respectful. I appreciate that."

She grins and I'm delighted by the sudden mischief in her eyes.

"I was just going to say something thoroughly disrespectful." Her body shudders with laughter and it's a balm to my soul to see her chuckle, to see her shake off the heaviness of this moment.

"You have to tell me now. It would be cruel not to."

"More cruel than being disrespectful?" She might be in the middle of menopause but when she's playful like this, I get a glimpse of what Cass must have been like in her twenties—all naughtiness and sparkle.

"Very much so."

"I was going to say that you're too hot for your own good, Professor Raymond." She scoots closer.

"Ain't that the story of my life," I joke. "Luckily, I've found someone extremely respectful."

We burst into joint laughter which turns into kissing until all my worries are, once again, erased. The question is for how long.

Because we're acquaintances-bordering-on-friends now, I have a private surfing date with Devon. But it's as though the minute we take to the water, the waves have other plans.

"This happens sometimes," Devon says. "The waves just die." She shakes her head. "I'm sorry. Either we go for a swim instead or a drink at The Bay." She grins at me in a way that makes it pretty obvious which option she prefers.

After we've maneuvered out of our wetsuits and stowed away our boards, we reconvene at The Bay, basking in the early afternoon sun.

"How's your dad's house?" she asks over a bottle of Surfer Juice IPA.

"Suzy has set me up with two guys who will remove most of his old furniture." I have found nothing of professional value in my dad's papers, although, on a personal level, even though it felt like too much at times, it has helped me say my final goodbye to him. To go through his stuff with a fine-toothed comb. I still haven't solved his last problem and I've come to accept that I never will—that it was his special way of saying a long goodbye.

"Are you going to live there?" Devon asks.

"Good question." I stare into my coffee. "To be honest, when she's not working, I spend most of my time at Cass's house." I've even stayed there a few times when she was in the restaurant downstairs, just August and me chilling on the couch.

"Wow. Have you booked the U-Haul already?" The skin around her eyes crinkles as she smiles.

"Hardly."

"How's it going with you two?"

"Good," I say, and it's true, but it's not like it's all been smooth sailing. "Every new relationship has its challenges, I guess. What was it like when you and Sadie first got together?"

Devon chuckles. "I've known Sadie since we were kids." She nods, as though admitting to something. "But yes, of course we've had our challenges. Like her being straight, for starters."

"She doesn't look so straight now."

"She's bi and, well, she came to women later in life, as we like to say." Devon tips the bottle to her lips, her tattooed arms toned and gorgeous.

"Her sexuality is fluid, you mean?" Everyone knows Sadie Ireland was married to her male co-star on *King & Prince.*

"Yeah," is all Devon replies. She's so completely at ease with herself, I can't help but needle her a little.

"You're not afraid the fluidity can, um, flow back to where it came from?" I ask.

Devon chuckles. "Afraid? No." She shakes her head. "I know Sadie loves me but I can't control how she will feel in the future so it's not something I worry about." She twirls the neck of the bottle between her fingers. "We're solid. I know that much and it's more than enough."

"You look very happy together." My tone is suddenly wistful.

"Maybe you and Cass will be like Sadie and me in five years' time," she says, more a question than a statement. She might be needling me this time. Or going all life coach on me.

"I sure hope so, but…" I take the bait. There aren't many people I can talk to about this.

Devon just tilts her head and looks at me, giving me the time to find my words.

"I'm asexual and it's not that easy. For Cass, mostly."

"Oh." Devon's ginger eyebrows knit together. "Okay."

"I don't look it, but I'm a challenge," I joke, although it's also true.

"We're all a challenge in our own way."

"Some of us definitely more than others, but yeah…" I take a sip of beer. "I get that it's difficult. Imagine not being able to touch Sadie in the way that you want more than anything."

"Yeah, that's hard," Devon admits without hesitation. "But maybe it wouldn't be if it had always been like that. If I'd known from the start that's how it was going to be."

"I know that Cass is very fond of me—madly in love with me even—but I'm so scared that she won't be able to find a way to cope with that... very elemental desire. A desire I can't possibly hold against her." Even though the thought is harrowing, it's a relief to be able to express it out loud. "I'm afraid that she's going to leave me and my heart will be broken all over again and I just can't bear to pick up those pieces yet again..."

"You've had some experience with heartbreak?" Devon leans toward me.

"Too much and always for the same reason."

"It's normal to be scared," Devon says. "I'd be petrified if I was in your shoes, but it doesn't mean it's going to happen again."

"I don't know..."

"Are you talking about this with Cass?" she asks.

"Yeah, um, we try. These are not easy conversations to have and it's all been such a whirlwind."

Devon's expression tightens. "Do you think she might leave you over this?"

"Not right now, but... down the line. When she finds she can no longer deal with it. When she realizes she needs —she deserves—more than I can give her."

"Don't you give her a lot already?" Devon purses her lips. "Today's Cass is not the Cass from two months ago. She's like a different woman, all sass and confidence—all because of you."

"But still... for most women, it's not enough."

"Do you want me to talk to her?" Devon nods. "I'm pretty good at difficult conversations." She throws in a smile. "I want to help because I want things to work out with you and Cass. I really do."

"Thanks, but… right now, it's okay. We're figuring things out together, stumbling along. Finding our own unique way, I guess."

"I'm here if you need me," Devon says. "Any time."

"That's very kind of you." I give Devon my warmest smile. Everyone in this town has been so incredibly kind to me. I'm most definitely staying for the foreseeable future.

"That's what friends are for," she says, giving me a warm fuzzy feeling in my belly that I can't just ascribe to the beer. It also makes me think of my friends back in Berkeley, who were mostly colleagues, and whom I never had time for outside work because we were always so damn busy.

Look at me now, sipping beer while overlooking the ocean after my afternoon surf session that didn't happen. I've relaxed a lot, about most things, except the one thing about myself I can never change.

"Sometimes," I say, unsure whether this will make any sense to anyone who isn't me, "I'm afraid that my failure at relationships becomes a self-fulfilling prophecy. That I get so in my head about it, that I drive my partners to leave me in the end. That I give them no other choice because, ironically, I'm the one being difficult about it."

"It doesn't have to be that way with Cass." Devon nods as though she gets it.

"I hope not." I gesture at her empty beer bottle. "Can I get you another?"

"Why the hell not?" The smile she beams me lets me

know, among other things, that we're definitely friends now.

CHAPTER 31
CASS

It's Saturday morning, and I wake up on the couch, my back sore and a crick in my neck. I had to flee my bed, where Estelle was sleeping so peacefully, in the middle of the night because my body was burning up from the inside. I had to go outside, into the night air, to cool off sufficiently.

Before all that, at the restaurant, I fucked up someone's order during a brutal hot flash. A customer had to wait double the time for their entrée—inexcusable in my book.

When Estelle turns up in the living room, wearing nothing but a tank top and boxer shorts, the joy the mere sight of her usually awakes in me is very short lived. I'm crazy about her but I don't want her to see me like this, all wrinkles and sweaty clothes and just all-encompassing unattractiveness.

"Bad night?" she asks, stretching her arms above her head.

"Yeah," is all I say.

She just stands there, looking at me with her head tilted as though she's studying me for research purposes.

"Can I get you anything? A strong cup of coffee? A morning kiss? Both?"

I can't tell her that I can barely stand to have her—*her* of all people—in my house right now. I take a breath and try to say, in an even, mature voice, "Coffee would be great."

I can't have her kiss me right now. I need at least fifteen minutes under a cold shower, freshly laundered clothes and… I don't know, some miracle cure to feel better. To not feel this worn-out and ugly and like we are the oddest couple in the universe.

Look at her. She's breathtaking. And I'm not even allowed to touch her to make my—I stop my train of thought. I can't pretend it's not been a point of contention, that I haven't gone to war with myself over it too many times by now, but it's not Estelle's fault. I'm the one who, once again—just like with Sarah—falls short.

"Coming right up." Estelle reads my mood infuriatingly correctly and skips into the kitchen.

Gus jumps into my lap and no matter how awful I feel, I always have affection to spare for him. And he always makes me feel a little better. I can say to him whatever I want and he never takes offense—that only happens when I don't feed him on time.

I sink into the couch, my cat perched hotly on my thighs, my legs unable to move, not just because I'm held captive by August, but because they feel as though I ran a marathon last night—as if.

"Here you go." Estelle walks toward me with two mugs of steaming coffee. She hasn't read the room sufficiently right to make herself scarce—and why would she?

"Thanks," I barely manage to squeeze out of my throat.

"Hey, um, I was thinking…" She has that look of possibility on her face that I'm so not in the mood for this morning. Although, to be honest, I'm not in the mood for anything. "How about, after you've woken up properly, obviously…" She throws in an irritating smile. How can she be so gorgeous and annoying at the same time? "We go down to the beach together and I give you a private surf lesson?"

"Excuse me?" Estelle has really taken to surfing, spending time in the ocean almost every day. Good for her, of course, but I fail to see what that has to do with me.

"Surfing has helped me with so much and I've been thinking that, even though you're not into it, maybe, if I'm the one teaching you, you could benefit from it as well."

I can't believe this. She knows I hate surfing. Most of all because I wouldn't be caught dead in a wetsuit. But also because a body like mine doesn't find balance on some flimsy wooden board. That's just an illusion she must have dreamed up during that wonderful night's sleep she had.

"Babe, please. No." I sip from my coffee and she has made it exactly the way I like it but her kindness only stokes my diabolical mood—it's like waving a red rag at a bull.

"Why not?" she has the audacity to ask. "I've been talking to Devon and she believes in surfing being a great therapeutic tool for women in the menopause. Especially women who don't take hormones. You have to do something to… I don't know, work through it all, I guess."

"I would like you to leave now." I put my cup down.

"What? Why?" She brings her hand to my knee and Gussie takes it as his cue to jump off—and avoid whatever's coming. "I know you had a bad night. I knew that as soon as I saw you weren't in bed this morning. It's okay."

"It's not fucking okay." I huff out some air. "Everything's always fucking okay with you. Well, I don't feel okay. Putting me on a surfboard is not going to magically change that." I shake my head in utter disbelief. "You know I don't surf. I don't understand why you are suggesting this now. This morning of all mornings."

"I'm just trying to help." Estelle's voice grows thinner. Nobody's patience is endless.

"Help me how? By trying to fix me somehow?" I hear myself, and I know my tone is too harsh, but it's as though I don't have the power to stop myself. "This is who I am. Okay? Take it or leave it." Stop now, I tell myself. But I'm in no state to listen to anyone, especially myself—I don't hold myself in high enough regard for that. "I have to accept you as you are, so…" I even look her in the eye for the next zinger. "Why don't you try doing the same for me? I know it's hard, excruciating even, but this is our situation." Estelle's about to say something, but I'm not done yet. "I can't sleep. I can't think straight. And I can't even touch you."

The silence that follows is deafening. I know I've gone too far, but, sadly, it's also the truth. A truth that can't be spoken, yet I just did that. Well, it wasn't really me, it was a hormonally raging version of myself, but I also know that this fight I picked isn't only due to a horrible night's sleep and yet another menopausal meltdown.

Estelle goes quiet. Her expression closes off as she rises and starts to get dressed.

"We can talk about this another time," she says. She moves as if to kiss me goodbye but catches the look on my face—and stops herself.

I should snap out of it—why haven't I? This would be the point in the argument where I have behaved so appallingly that pure shame brings me back to my senses.

Yet, it's not happening this morning. My brain is too foggy and my body simply too drained of energy for such a sudden turnaround.

"We're not going to continue this right now," Estelle says. "There's no point." *Argh.* Her level-headedness drives me even more up the wall. "Call me when you're ready to have a proper conversation." She heads to the hallway. "I truly only wanted to make you feel better," she says, her voice finally breaking.

Without saying another word, she heads to the door, her movements angular and sharp—a masterclass in wounded body language. All the while, my exhausted, old body remains glued to the goddamn couch.

It takes me a full twenty-four hours to get it together. Not only because of the vicious hangover of shame I, deservedly, suffer from, but also because it's not as simple as showing up at Estelle's house with a bunch of flowers. I even, very briefly, considered turning up in a wetsuit, but I own no such monstrosity, and I already look enough of a fool.

Still wordlessly, she lets me in. Her father's house is nearly empty now, save for a few pieces of essential furniture and some chairs that Bobby has loaned her from his workshop.

"Cass," she sighs, her elbows leaning on the kitchen counter.

"I'm sorry." Estelle is the one looking exhausted now. My behavior must have cost her a night of sleep. Maybe Suzy was downright incorrect when she predicted that a menopausal and an asexual woman were a match made in heaven. Maybe Estelle and I are too broken, too bruised by life, to forge a romantic connection. That's the sense of defeatism that hangs in the air as I look at her this morning. Probably because I know that I went too far—that I really screwed things up between us with my out of control midlife fury. "I'm so sorry." On the way over, I tried to put together a speech in my head, tried to find something to say that could make things better, but I came up empty.

"The thing is," Estelle says, still standing and not inviting me to sit. "I'm not sure what that ridiculous fight was actually about. Was it about you or was it about me?"

"It was me." I step closer, but there's a kitchen counter between us. "It was all me."

"You can say that, but I don't believe you." She doesn't sound combative, which worries me. "I'm almost fifty, Cass. I'm done defending myself."

"You don't have to defend yourself."

"Then why do I feel like I have to?"

This conversation is a minefield of potential misunderstandings. I don't want to make anything worse by not addressing the issue directly.

"I shouldn't have said that I can't touch you," I say, lowering my voice to a whisper. I can't say it was below the belt because we're nowhere near ready for lame jokes yet, an accurate indicator of the dire straits we find ourselves in. "I shouldn't have said any of the things I said. It wasn't me. It was…"

"The hormones?" Compared to mine, Estelle's voice is loud and clear.

I nod, even though it makes me sound like a broken record—but again, it doesn't make it any less true.

"But, Cass, there are ways to deal with that. The night

sweats. The hot flashes. Medical ways, I mean. Not learning how to surf."

"I'm aware, but I've made my choice regarding that." Tears prick behind my eyes. "I completely understand that you would, um, choose not to have that in your life."

"I'm not going to break up with you because you're in menopause. I can deal with that."

"But?" I ask.

"I can't deal with how you feel about me. Really feel, I mean. Underneath… all the drama and whatever."

"What do you mean?" Of course, I know what she means. I just brought it up. But fuck, this is so hard. Before midlife started chipping away at it, I always considered myself a reasonable woman with plenty of empathy, but I haven't yet been able to shake off the profoundly fundamental desire to touch her. It goes infinitely deeper than simply wanting to be inside her. Now, instead of it being a lack I might learn to deal with, it has become a barrier to a more intense connection between us—like we can't get past a certain point we need to reach in order for our relationship to progress.

"You said it for a reason. I know that." She pushes herself up. "It's always the same."

"Maybe, but we talked about this. I just need some time."

"Time for what? To compromise? To accept that you can never have what you so long for?"

Yes, I think, but I can't say that. And maybe that's the real issue. Maybe I should say it. How else are we going to get out of this if we can't be honest with each other?

"Yes," I say, out loud.

"I don't want to be your compromise," Estelle says, her voice flat, like all life was just squeezed out of it.

"We both have to compromise. This isn't some fairy-tale romance by the seaside. But I love you, Estelle. I want to be with you. I really, sincerely do."

Estelle shakes her head. "I can't do it."

"You… can't?" My hands tremble against the cold countertop.

"I can't have my heart broken all over again. It's barely hanging by a thread. I just can't do it again."

"No, no, no," I say. "No, we are not doing this, babe. We are not breaking up over this, just because my hormones were raging yesterday. That can't happen."

"That's not why we're breaking up."

"We're *not* breaking up." I swallow a lump out of my throat and walk to her side of the counter. "Not like this. Not over that." I look her in the eye. "Please."

"Cass, be honest, with me and with yourself."

"I can't let you go." It's as though my body shrinks a size. "No, please." Tears start streaming down my cheeks. What the fuck have I set in motion? "Let's give it a day. Twenty-four hours. Please, don't make a rash decision now. We're both emotional. We can't think straight. We haven't slept. I hurt you yesterday and I'm sorry." I wish I could say it wouldn't happen again but I can't fool myself into that kind of wishful thinking. "But, come on. We can talk our way through this."

"I've had twenty-four hours to think about it already," Estelle says.

I take another step closer, reach for her hands, but she pulls them away.

"But… you didn't really give me a chance," I say.

"I did."

"You didn't. It's not like *that*." I snap my fingers. "You can't just rock up, turn my life upside down, make me come like I'm twenty years old again, and simply expect me to be okay with not touching you. It doesn't work that way."

"Oh, I know that."

"What you want from me is unreasonable," I say.

Estelle replies with stony silence.

"I'm crazy about you. And yes, I want you. I just... need some time." I'm running out of steam. "We have time, don't we? We're in no rush."

"Cass," all warmth has drained from Estelle's voice—it sounds icy instead of sexy. "I've made up my mind. I have to protect myself. You don't know what this is like for me. You don't know how this makes me feel." A tear slowly glides down her cheek. "You may think all you need is more time. You may genuinely believe that, but I have been here so many times before, I know exactly where this is going."

"You're so convinced I'm going to hurt you," I start to say, but my argument feels void even before I make it because I have already hurt her. During that wretched half hour yesterday morning when all I did was lash out and hurt her.

"I don't think we're right for each other after all," Estelle says.

"Are you really doing this?" My legs go weak. "Are you really dumping me?" To be honest, when I looked in the mirror this morning, my eyes full of shame, all I saw was a woman ready to get dumped.

"I'm ending things..." Estelle's voice is barely audible. "For both our sakes."

"It's not for my sake," I say. "I don't want this."

Estelle takes a step backward, until her back is against the fridge.

I am respectful enough not to make her feel cornered by the volume of my body in the tiny space we're in, so I also take a step away from her. But it reminds me of how we recently defused a similar conversation of mounting tension with a dash of humor and a sprinkle of self-awareness. It doesn't seem to be an option today. There's nothing funny about this situation.

"Please, Estelle." I head to the other side of the counter. "I hope you change your mind. You know where to find me if you do." I bow my head. "Please." I leave the house.

She doesn't follow me.

CHAPTER 32
ESTELLE

The next few days go by in a different kind of haze. One of sadness, hurt and, most of all, abject loneliness.

I haven't been out much, not even to surf, because I'm afraid of running into Cass's friends. They're all over this town and I know that, if I want to stay, which is looking more and more unlikely because Cass was the biggest reason to stay, I'll have to confront them at some point.

I miss Cass in everything I do. The meals I manage to prepare, for a hunger I don't feel, are bleak and tasteless compared to a simple sandwich she spruces up with pickled onions and crumbled seaweed. I miss seeing her amble into a room, looking for something, but spotting me instead, and bursting into a joyous smile. Most of all, I miss observing her at the top of her game at Savor, where she is not only the chef, but the master of her skills. Where she is both an extraordinary cook and a gracious hostess, a combination I couldn't get enough of from the start.

It's Thursday afternoon and I'm about to tear another page out of my notebook—another one filled with useless scribbles and calculations going nowhere—when Devon knocks on the kitchen window, startling me.

I'm glad it's her. She's gentle and understanding and I can explain to her why I had to leave Cass without having to come out as asexual again.

"Turns out it's you I have to talk to," Devon says, her hands on her hips. "I just heard the news from Suzy and I came straight over. How are you?"

I just sigh as I usher her in.

We take our coffees into the backyard, but the weather isn't cooperating. Gray clouds have been hanging over the bay ever since I broke up with Cass, as though the weather wants to fit my mood. A cold wind accosts us, but Devon doesn't seem to mind.

"Looks like my self-fulfilling prophecy came true sooner than I thought." I wish it was a joke, but nothing is even remotely funny these days.

"Give me the broad strokes," Devon says.

"What did Suzy tell you?" I ask.

"Just that you broke up with Cass. And broke her heart in the process."

"I'm sorry. I never meant to break Cass's heart." My stomach coils into a knot.

"What happened?" Devon wraps her hands around her coffee mug as the wind whips up her hair.

"We had a stupid fight. She woke up super cranky on Saturday after a really bad night and I tried to help, but we got into it instead and there really was no talking to her and then, all of a sudden, she blurts out how much she hates that she can't touch me and, um, well, if ever there's something that pushes all my buttons all at once…"

Devon peers at me over the rim of her mug.

"And I know she wasn't herself and, honestly, it isn't

even her fault. It's me. I carry too much baggage and it just made me feel so utterly lonely and unlovable in that moment. I left, hoping I could shake it off, but it got hold of me instead and... Cass accused me of being unreasonable and she's probably right, but, um, I can't repeat all the same arguments I've had a thousand times in my life already. I'm certainly not blameless and I made mistakes with Cass, but still... For some reason, I thought it would be different with her. That the... expectation wouldn't loom so large between us."

"To have sex?" Devon asks.

"She wants to touch me and I can't let her. I don't want her to. And I get it, but the facts remain the same."

Devon shakes her head. "God, it's so sad. I'm so sorry for you both." She pins her gaze on me. "Sadie said you didn't come to surf club on Monday. That's why?"

I nod. I haven't done much since the break-up.

"Will you come next Monday? I really think you should. I'll be there if you need me."

Devon's kindness is the first thing that makes me feel as though I'm not entirely made up of sorrow—and that my life doesn't have to be completely controlled by what I'm not.

"I assume Cass will be tactful enough not to gawk at us from The Bay." It hurts to say her name and even more so to think about her like someone I want to avoid.

"I'll talk to her. Don't worry about it."

"Our stupid fight was about surfing." I lean back in my chair, my body numb to the sharpness of the wind. "I suggested we try it together. Big mistake."

Devon chuckles. "Yeah, I can imagine."

"I know I have my issues but Cass is not without hers either and I'm not just talking about the menopause."

"We all have our shit to deal with, but…" Devon doesn't look as though she has to deal with a lot of stuff in her life, but then again, we're not that close yet—and we mostly talk about me. "You don't look too hot. Clearly, you're heartbroken as well, just like Cass. Would you consider talking to her? One more time?" She pulls up one shoulder. "It all just feels so sudden and abrupt and I get it, I do, but… you looked so genuinely happy together. Cass was thriving again. Obviously, I know her a lot better than I know you."

"Why would I talk to her if I know, in my heart of hearts, that I can't be with her?"

"Remember the reasons you did want to be with her. Remember why you fell in love with her. Remember how lovely it was to wake up next to her, to see her sitting at The Bay when you emerged from the water. Focus on that, not on what could possibly go wrong."

"Has anyone ever told you that you could have a great career in life coaching?" Finally, a hint of a joke.

"I know fear when I see it," Devon says. "Fear and anxiety are what I have to deal with the most in my line of work." She narrows her eyes but her gaze remains soft. "You're scared, so you retreat. It's a logical reaction, but what if you didn't? What if you did the opposite and something beautiful could come from it?" She half-smiles. "It's the irrefutable truth that you will never know unless you try."

"Wow, you've really come here to deploy the full extent of your powers on me."

"You deserve love too, Estelle," Devon says and it sounds irrefutable as well when she says it like that—so much so that tears fill my eyes. "You already love Cass and she loves you. It's pretty obvious to me." She gives me the full-wattage smile now. "Just talk to her one more time, with an open mind and an open heart and try not to be scared. I know it's easier said than done. If it weren't, I wouldn't have a job, but, honestly, I truly believe you owe it to yourself to not run away from this." She holds up her hand. "Don't say you'll think about it, because then you'll just think your way out of it again. Just say yes, then go to her."

"I appreciate everything you say, but you're coming on a little strong." A golden child like Devon—like she appears to be—has no clue what I've been through, despite her life coaching experience.

"I know, but I really need you to hear me."

"Either way, I don't want to disturb Cass until Savor is closed for the weekend." I can't believe I'm considering it already. "She must be exhausted." If I do go through with this crazy plan, I prefer not to have that conversation with overly tired, grouchy Cass.

"Tell you what." Devon's smile has transformed into a grin. "A friend of Sadie's is visiting this weekend. We're having a little get-together with the boys on Sunday. Come to lunch at our place for some light relief and relaxation, then you and I can talk some more if needed, and then I'll send you on your way to Cass, who will have had plenty of time to rest. How does that sound?"

"It sounds as though you've got it all worked out already."

"I am usually a woman with a plan." Devon finishes her coffee. "Do you have some more of this?"

"Sure." I head into the kitchen, to that dreadful spot where I banished Cass from my life, and think that, maybe, sometimes it can't hurt to take a friend's advice.

CHAPTER 33
CASS

It's my first full weekend without Estelle and I don't know what to do with myself. On Friday, I scoured the bookings, looking for reservations for one, hoping that she might have booked for the evening under an alias to not scare me off, but what's become Estelle's regular table was occupied by a couple in their twenties disgustingly in love, holding hands throughout their meal in a way that I would have thought lovely if Estelle hadn't smashed my heart to smithereens—although I'm very much to blame as well.

I can hardly say our break-up was mutual, but I sure played my part in it. I'm not innocent and it makes it easier to accept because I know I fell short, but I miss her. So, on Saturday night, instead of sulking at home, staring at her favorite spot on the couch—now painfully empty—where she liked to curl up with her notebook and Gussie, I meet Hunter and Bobby for too many bottles of wine at The Bay.

They can be two nosy loudmouths but tonight they're just excellent friends, giving me their shoulder to cry on, and drinking too much with me.

Once we've finished our second bottle, I want to order margaritas, but Hunter puts his foot down.

"I have to be up early tomorrow for Finn," he says. Bobby lost the power of speech a while ago. For such a big man, he's a real lightweight. He doesn't have the same wine drinking practice Hunter and I have developed over the years.

"Shall we walk you home?" Hunter offers.

But I don't want to go home. Only August misses me now and I love my cat dearly, but all I have to look forward to in my bed tonight is, most likely, another bout of night sweats. Excessive alcohol consumption hardly helps matters, I'm well aware, but it's the only thing that works against the gnawing pain in my soul.

I hug them goodbye and order a margarita for myself. The bartender also refills my water glass.

I'm halfway down my margarita when a woman I've never seen before sits on the stool next to mine.

"You look like you're drowning your sorrows," she says. Her voice is high-pitched but still smooth and she's so petite, I'm probably twice her size.

"Fuck yeah," I say. We're two strangers in a bar close to midnight so there's no need for decorum.

She orders two more margaritas, one for her and one for me. Then introduces herself as Bijou from Los Angeles.

"Do you want to talk about it?" she asks.

"Nah, it's just a broken heart. It will mend, won't it?"

"That's what hearts always do," Bijou says. "Guaranteed."

"I'll drink to that." I take in her face more thoroughly. She looks very sweet and girly and, in many ways, the very opposite of Estelle. Her hair is pulled back tightly and her eyes are pale blue. Her smile is warm and friendly. My friends have left and I can do with some more warmth and friendliness.

She lifts her glass to mine carefully so as not to spill any of the liquid, then, with her eyes on me, she takes a sip.

"Excellent tartness," Bijou says, sliding her elbows a little closer toward me.

"What are you doing in Clearwater Bay?" I ask, happy for the distraction of small talk.

"Visiting a friend."

"Where's your friend?"

"At her house. Dinner ran long. I wanted to stretch my legs before bed and saw this cute place on the beach. I couldn't resist."

I take another sip. "Is it awful to ask how old you are, Bijou?" What kind of name is Bijou, anyway? But I'm too tipsy to question it further.

She shakes her head as though women in LA are extremely forthcoming about how old they really are. "I'm forty-one."

"Good age. Hold on to that."

"Why do you ask?"

"Because I'm fifty-three and it royally sucks ass."

"Good to know," she says, a smile in her voice. "I'll keep that in mind for in a decade or so."

"Look at me," I say, barely noticing that the self-pity phase of drunkenness has well and truly set in. "I'm a menopausal mess. No wonder she left me."

"She?" Bijou nods. "I can work with that."

"What do you mean?"

"Nothing." She puts her hand on my arm. "There's nothing wrong with you. You're just a little tipsy, that's all."

"You don't know me."

"True enough. That's usually how I like it."

"Like what?" I'm so far gone, I can barely still decode what she's saying.

"I saw you sitting all by yourself at the bar and I came to sit next to you," Bijou says. "What does that tell you?"

My foggy brain considers her question. "That you wanted some company."

"Sure, but not just anyone's company. A beautiful woman's company."

She's lucky I didn't just take a sip or I would have sprayed margarita all over her. I look around me ostentatiously, because either this is some scam I'm too drunk to see through or she's actually talking about someone else.

"Yeah. Okay. Goodnight." I turn away from her. As far as I know, no one has ever been punked at The Bay at midnight, but there's a first time for everything.

"You're very alluring." Bijou's voice is so smooth and sweet, I almost want to believe her. But I have a mirror and I see with my own eyes every day that I'm neither beautiful nor alluring.

"What is this?" I pivot toward her again. All I see is that kind, sultry smile on her face.

"I'm doing a really bad job of flirting with you." Bijou looks me straight in the eye.

"Flirting? With me?" I know that Estelle didn't break up with me because I'm overweight and sweaty most of the time and I wouldn't be caught dead in a wetsuit, but still, in my muddled drunken brain, she might as well have.

"Yes, ma'am," Bijou says and the whole thing—her words and the situation—is so weird I burst out laughing.

"See," she says. "You're gorgeous when you laugh. I knew it."

I laugh some more and forget about this being a possible prank. I might as well enjoy it, even if it is some sort of twisted delusion.

"You're very pretty." If ever there was a lame attempt at flirting back.

"Thanks." She does this trick with her legs to shuffle her stool closer to mine. "See how easy it is to accept a compliment."

"I don't understand why you're flirting with me but I'm in no state to reject you." I shake my head. "Sorry, that came out wrong, as though I don't want you to flirt with me anymore."

"You want me to flirt with you now?" Her smile turns devilish and I can't stop staring at her lips.

"I do." I have absolutely nothing to lose. Although I might have something to gain. "Before this goes any further." I'm so tipsy, I just come out and ask it as though it's the most logical question in the world. "Can I touch you?"

Bijou tilts her head and narrows her eyes.

"I don't want to end up in bed with someone I can't touch." I shake my head. "I'm not doing that."

"I feel like we skipped a few steps." Bijou puts her hand on my arm again. "And, also, what the hell are you talking about?" She runs a fingertip over my bare skin. "Why would I flirt with you if I don't want you to touch me?"

"You'd be surprised." I drain the last of my margarita, as though I'm suddenly on a mission. "I live above the restaurant on the cliff. Would you like to come over for a nightcap?"

“I would like that very much.” Bijou empties her glass and slips off her stool.

I take her home and we drink water instead of more alcohol and we stumble into my bedroom. I’m drunk and therefore blissfully free of my usual hang-ups about my body, about getting naked with someone else, and, to be honest, there’s only one thing on my mind: I want to make Bijou come.

And I do. Many times.

CHAPTER 34
ESTELLE

Hunter looks a bit worse for wear. Bobby hugs me as though I'm his long-lost sister.

"How's Cass?" I ask him. "Have you seen her?"

"We got wasted with her at The Bay last night. She's not doing well," Bobby says. "Is there really nothing we can do to fix this?"

"We're working on it." Devon shoots me an encouraging smile.

Perhaps I'm most surprised that I'm here, with Cass's friends, while she's not.

"Where's your guest of honor?" Hunter asks.

"She texted last night that she wouldn't make it home and that I shouldn't worry," Sadie chimes in. "With Bijou, you never know."

"She's still not home? And she knew we were coming?" Bobby nods purposefully. "I know what that means."

We all sit down. Drinks are poured and it reminds me so much of that brunch a few weeks ago, when Cass and I were still full of potential. My stomach twists, not just because of the pain of breaking up, but because of what I promised Devon I would do after lunch. Because I'm going to see Cass.

A few minutes later, the gate swings open. A tiny woman, her hair still wet from the shower, walks toward us with her hands held up in apology.

"I'm so incredibly sorry."

"Walk of shame, girl," Bobby shouts.

"Calling it a walk of shame is so incredibly misogynistic," the woman, who must be Bijou, says. "But I won't get into that right now because, frankly, I'm too tired after the night I had." She fans her face theatrically.

"My husband sincerely apologizes," Hunter interjects.

"Where did you even meet someone in Clearwater Bay?" Bobby asks.

"Well…" It's as though Bijou only now clocks me. "Hi." She walks toward me. "I'm Bijou. I was Sadie's makeup artist on *King & Prince* for many amazing years." She extends her hand.

"Nice to meet you, Bijou." I shake her hand.

She slides into the empty chair between Sadie and me.

Devon pours her a drink while Bobby raps his knuckles on the table and says, "Spill, spill, spill."

"I ended up at this bar by the beach and there was this woman. All alone. Nursing a broken heart."

My stomach clenches.

"We got talking and hit it off and, oh my god!" Bijou tilts her head back. "She had some stuff to work through and she worked it all out on me, in the best way possible."

"Um, Bijou," Bobby says. "What was her name?"

Please don't say it, I think. Please don't say her name.

"Cass." Bijou's voice is rich with unbearable smugness. "She owns the restaurant on the cliff."

Something inside me collapses, probably that last tendril of hope Devon wanted me to hold onto.

"I'm—um." I rise and my chair tips backward onto the floor. "I'm not feeling well. I'm sorry. I can't stay for lunch."

Devon is quick to stand. "Come with me," she instructs but it's as though I've already used up all my remaining energy just by getting out of that chair. Sadie rises as well and gently leads me into the house.

"Was it something I said?" I hear Bijou ask outside.

"I'm so sorry about this," Sadie says.

"I understand you can't stay. I'll walk you home," Devon holds me by the elbow, as though I might topple over like that chair. "Fucking Bijou," she mutters under her breath.

But this is hardly Bijou's fault. Although her words will be etched in my brain for a long time to come: *She had some stuff to work through and she worked it all out on me.*

"Are you okay to walk?" Devon asks. "I can drive you. Big emotions like that can really hit you in the knees."

"I need to walk," I say. And I need to get the fuck out of here.

"Okay. Let's go." Devon and Sadie exchange the kind of glance I will never exchange with anyone—least of all Cass.

"Cass is free to do whatever she wants," I mumble.

Devon hooks her arm through mine. "You shouldn't have had to hear that. Maybe it's nobody's fault, but it was still cruel. I'm sorry for that."

"I can't go to her now." My voice is as wobbly as my knees.

"No, I get that." We walk in silence, because what's left to say after this? After life so adequately showed me why

Cass and I can't be together. At least she got what she wanted.

"I should probably tell Cass that you heard. We're all friends and I'd like to keep it that way." Devon curls her fingers around my arm. "Cass is hurting, too. You both are."

"Do whatever you need to do." Tears gather in the corners of my eyes.

"And you're coming to surf club tomorrow. I'll drop by and pick you up myself."

"I don't know, Dev." I'm not sure about a lot of things. Or maybe I am. Maybe it's time to make a decision. Maybe it's time to move on.

"I'll drop by regardless." When I leave, I'll probably miss Devon the most. And Sadie's surf lessons. And Bobby's hugs. And Hunter's bigheartedness. Suzy's delicious directness. And Cass… she would be the main reason to leave.

"I can stay a while," Devon offers when we've arrived at my dad's house.

"Thanks, but I'd rather be alone right now."

"Hey." Devon's gaze finds mine. "This isn't on you. You are who you are and there's nothing wrong with that." She sends me a smile. "I think you're wonderful and I hope to see you tomorrow."

The next afternoon, I go to Cass's house. Not to have that open-minded, openhearted conversation Devon and I discussed, but to tell Cass in person something she deserves to hear from me.

I'm not angry at her because we're incompatible. That

would be like being angry at August because he's a cat that wants breakfast first thing in the morning. I'm angry at myself for fooling myself into believing she and I could be something—that things could be different. Which only resulted in an extra scar on my heart.

When she lets me in, her eyes are red-rimmed and her cheeks blotchy. She doesn't look surprised to see me.

"I'm sorry," she says, as we walk into the kitchen. August rubs himself against my shin instantly. "Devon told me about what Bijou said. I'm so sorry. Obviously, I never meant for that to happen."

"It's okay." I wave off her comment because I don't want our conversation to go in that direction. I'd prefer to forget about Bijou altogether as soon as possible. Not because I'm jealous, although, strangely, I am. But because she could give Cass what I couldn't and that stings.

"It's not okay." Cass shakes her head. "It's mortifying."

"Why?"

"Why?" Cass repeats back to me. "Because…" She huffs out some air instead of giving me a reason.

"It's just how things are." It's so painful to stand across from her. Awkward doesn't even begin to describe it.

"Can we talk, please?" Cass takes two glasses from the cupboard. "Is water okay or do you want something stronger?"

"Water's fine."

Even when she's just pouring water into a glass, the kitchen is Cass's domain to such an extent she does it with enviable aplomb—with an assuredness she sometimes lacks outside of her comfort zone.

"Come." She walks us into the living room and I choose the chair that has become my favorite.

"I've come to tell you something," I start as soon as we

sit down, because I don't want her getting any ideas in her head. "I'm leaving town."

"You are?" Her eyes widen, and there's a hint of panic in her voice.

"It's too painful to stay now," I say.

"Because of me?"

I nod. "The Bijou incident made two things clear to me." I take a sip of water. "First, that I can't give you what you need, which I already knew, but I guess it's good to have confirmation."

"Estelle, no—" Cass starts to say, but I hold up my hand to cut her off.

"And that it really fucking hurts to hear about you being with someone else, even though, obviously, you are free to do whatever you want with whomever you want. I just don't want to hear about it. I can't."

Cass rubs her hands over her face, leaving her cheeks even redder than before. "I don't even know how it happened. The guys left and I was drunk and then, out of the blue, there she was. I just…" She shrugs as though she genuinely can't fathom it. "I don't just sleep with people like that."

"It doesn't matter, Cass." I rub my palms on my jeans. "I just wanted to tell you in person that I'm leaving."

"Are you going back to Berkeley?" she asks.

"To start with."

"Back to work?"

"I don't know." Clearwater Bay has been such a safe haven for me in the aftermath of my father's death and my burnout. "Probably not for a while."

"But, ba—" Cass misspeaks and the tension in the room goes up another notch. "You don't have to leave on my account. I thought you loved it here. You've made friends."

"*Your* friends," I interject.

"We can be civil with each other. We're adults."

"Seeing you all the time would just remind me of… what I can't have."

"For the record, you can have *me*." Is that a joke? I'm unsure and in no mood to chuckle.

"You know what I mean. This is your town and…" The first tears stir behind my eyes.

"Estelle, please, listen to me." Cass leans her elbows on her knees, tilting toward me. "I know I was a hormonal rage monster last weekend and I shouldn't have said what I said. It's obviously a massive trigger for you and I understand, but… I wasn't myself. Surely, you could see that."

"I heard what I heard and I saw what I saw." Time to rebuild that wall around my heart. But, damn those tears leaking from my eyes.

"Why won't you just… yield a little bit on this? Why can't we talk this through?"

This is exactly what I wanted to avoid. Another discussion about this. "Because, when it comes down to it, you can't really accept me for who I am."

"Says who?" She brings a finger to her chest. "I've never said that." Cass actually rolls her eyes.

"You don't have to say it for me to know."

"No way." She scoffs. "I'm not letting you get away with this." She takes a breath then lifts her gaze to meet mine. "I want you. I'm in love with you. And I choose you, no matter what."

"No, you don't." The tears in my eyes have all but dried up. "First chance you got, you jumped into bed with someone else."

"After you dumped me, so that's hardly fair."

"I can't un-hear what she said—"

"Estelle." Cass's voice is sharp like a knife. "You are using me as an excuse not to deal with your own fear."

"Maybe, but..." I push myself out of my chair. This is definitely not what I came here for. "I still can't do it."

"I'm glad you can at least admit to that." Cass gazes up at me. "That you're the one who can't do it." She looks away. "At least we're clear on that," she mumbles.

August zigzags between my legs, stopping me from rushing out the door. I know Cass is kind of right, but it doesn't change anything.

"Bye, Cass," I say before I stumble into the hallway.

"I might be menopausal, but at least I'm not a coward," Cass shouts behind me. It's just her voice, though. There's no sign of her as I walk out of the door.

CHAPTER 35
CASS

"I went by her dad's house earlier," I say to Suzy as we sit on her back patio, the sky dimming into evening, "but she's already gone."

"Like a thief in the night," Suzy replies. "Like she was ashamed of something."

"Have you seen her? Heard from her?" Another Friday evening service has gone by without Estelle at her favorite table.

"Nope." Suzy sounds a little offended, as she has every right to be. "We weren't super close, but a goodbye would have been nice." She refills my wine glass.

"You know how I thought after we first started dating that she was too good to be true." My stomach still folds in on itself when I talk about her, despite my nagging anger at Estelle for just upping and leaving like that. "Turns out that she was."

"I can see why she swept you off your feet, though." Suzy grins at me.

"Fuck, yeah. She really did, but..." That very first climax Estelle gave me, against all expectations, is still a huge deal to me. "For someone who claimed that communication was the key to a successful relationship, she sure sucked at it when it came to her being ace." I reach for my wine glass. "It was all such a mind fuck."

The back door of Suzy's house opens and shuts. Hunter walks into the living room.

"Hello, meno-bitches," he says, a big smirk on his face. "How are the estrogen levels today?" He's come to see me every single day since Estelle and I broke up, even if only for five minutes during service prep, just to check on me.

Hunter hugs us, then settles in a chair with a glass of wine. He pulls his phone out of his pocket. "Guess who texted?"

"Estelle?" Despite my ambivalence, I'd like to know she's doing okay.

"The one and only." He dangles his phone in front of me like it's a carrot and I'm a rabbit.

"What did she say?" I ask.

"Just that she's back at her house in Berkeley and misses us."

"Us?"

"The message was sent in the group chat Bobby and I have with her, so I assume she's referring to me and my lovely husband, but I'm just a simple gay man, and with you women folk, you just never know."

"She probably needs a breather from all the turmoil she's been through." Suzy sounds suddenly mild. "Her dad died. She quit her job. She met *and* lost you." Suzy looks at me. "It's a lot."

"Yeah," I concur.

"How are you holding up?" Hunter scoots over and pats my knee.

"When the restaurant's open, I do okay, but on closing days… It's tough."

"No more one-night stands with visiting makeup artists?" He gives my knee one final pat.

"Oh, god…" I lean my head backward.

"What was it like?" Suzy asks. "I'm just curious. You know how I feel about one-night stands."

"It was…" I wish I didn't remember, but I do. I was drunk and ravenous for Bijou but all I could think of, the entire time, was how much I wanted her to be Estelle. "Messy and good in ways it could never be with Estelle but also sad because it wasn't Bijou I wanted to be with."

"Even after your night with Bijou, you still want Estelle?" Suzy asks.

"I'm in love with Estelle and even though it was more complicated than I liked, we could have made it work." Although, in hindsight, it's easy enough to say. Now that I don't actually have to make it work, words are undemanding. I can also see Estelle's point of view. I can even understand her fear. And her complete unwillingness to go through all of that with me, at this stage of my life, by her side. "Anyway, it's over now, so." I drink to swallow a lump out of my throat.

"Bobby and I were talking about meeting up with her in San Fran," Hunter says. "First, would that be okay with you? And, second, if so, do you want me to talk to her?"

"There's no point. She has made up her mind. She's done with me." No wonder Estelle has so many scars on her heart. Sometimes, it was almost as though she wore them like a badge of honor for all the suffering she'd been through. I wonder if she loved me long enough for our break-up to add another one. "I think she was right all along. She's not relationship material." I sigh deeply. "The best I can do is try to get over her as quickly as possible."

"Rebound?" Hunter tries to sound excited, but we're all too old for that now. To plan a wild weekend away and go out all night, drink too much, and do things we regret in the morning.

"I already had my rebound sex," I say sheepishly.

A silence falls until Suzy breaks it the way only Suzy can. "Let's talk about my birthday then. About the big event in three short weeks."

"Remind me, do you want a male or a female stripper?" Hunter jokes.

"Everything's arranged," I say. "There's nothing for you to worry your almost-fifty-year-old pretty little head about."

"Thank you." Suzy smiles. "Can we talk about my present, then?"

"I thought us organizing the party was the present?" Hunter pretends to be offended, although Bobby is making Suzy an engraved rocking chair for her porch, where she loves to sit and strike up a conversation with anyone who walks by.

"Yes, and I'm very grateful, but…" She looks me straight in the eye. "Now that you're no longer so busy falling in love, I'd like for you to finally join my support group. It's not like you'd have to go far."

Being with Estelle has, at the very least, opened my eyes to how my menopause affects others, so I don't immediately dismiss Suzy's idea. The only reason I was horrible to her was because my hormones were in disarray. She was nothing but incredibly kind and empathetic throughout.

"Do it for your fifty-year-old friend, please?" Suzy bats

her lashes. "I wouldn't ask if I didn't think it could really help. Especially now."

"Okay," I agree, because I have to fill up the emptiness Estelle has left. The hours of free time I perfectly knew what to do with before I met her, but have now become a wasteland of loneliness and longing. Because we might both have acted unreasonably, it didn't make the love I have for her magically disappear.

I sit with my arms crossed, sipping the peppermint tea Suzy passed around earlier.

Savor has been transformed for the occasion. The tables have been pushed aside, a few candles flicker along the bar, and the chairs are arranged in a circle.

"All right, ladies," Suzy says. "Welcome to *Hot Flash Hour*. Which, you must admit, sounds better than *Dry Vagina Diaries*." She grins at us.

A round of chuckles bubbles up, even from me. If I had known it would be Suzy Ireland's comedy hour, I might have shown my face sooner.

"Let's do a quick check-in," Suzy continues. "Mood, symptom, craving."

"Mood: irritable," says Linda. "Symptom: joint pain. Craving: murder."

"For anyone in particular?" Suzy deadpans.

"My husband," Linda says without missing a beat. "If he tells me to 'just take a nap' one more time, I might 'just take a knife.'"

"I'll arrange to bake one especially for you into my next batch of brownies," Suzy replies. "Next!"

"Honestly?" says another woman. "Mood: hopeless. Symptom: night sweats. Craving: a different life."

The questions go around the circle. When it gets to me, all heads swivel.

I sigh. "Mood: raw. Symptom: missing Estelle. Craving…" I shrug. "Not peppermint tea."

A few murmurs of sympathy ripple through the group. I don't usually open up in front of strangers, but here we are.

"At least you're honest," Suzy says, giving me a warm smile. "That's is what we're here for. Honesty. Solidarity. Shared hormone-fueled rage."

"I miss wine," someone says.

"We all miss wine," Suzy answers. "But wine makes the night sweats worse." As far as I know—and I do—Suzy doesn't follow her own 'no wine' rule whatsoever.

"I don't care," Linda says. "Let me sweat with a cabernet in hand."

There's a burst of laughter, which feels surprisingly good in my chest.

Suzy leans forward, ignoring our calls for booze. "Tonight's topic is: What's changed about you that you didn't expect?"

There's a brief pause, then Linda speaks again. "My tolerance for bullshit. It's gone. Utterly vanished."

"I used to be the peacekeeper," another woman chimes in. "Now I just say, 'Nope, not today,' and walk away."

"I cry during commercials now," I add. I've cried while watching TV three times this week.

"That's hormones *and* heartbreak," Suzy says gently. "Give yourself a break."

"I don't recognize myself sometimes," someone whispers.

"You're not alone," Suzy says. "Our bodies are changing. Our minds are changing. And sometimes we mourn the version of ourselves that felt more... in control. But she's still in there. Just with better boundaries and a worse memory."

"Worse everything," someone mutters.

Suzy laughs. "Perhaps, but there's also the better perspective. More compassion. Deeper friendships. And—this one's important—finally being done giving a shit about what anyone thinks of us."

"Except ourselves," I say. The words escape me before I can think them through.

Suzy tilts her head at me. "Maybe that's our next topic, then. Forgiving ourselves for not being who we used to be—and learning to love who we are now."

A silence settles in the room.

"Okay," Suzy says after a beat. "Now someone please say something inappropriate so we can continue on a bright note."

"I shaved my mustache for this," a woman I haven't met before remarks drily.

And just like that, we're laughing again. Maybe Suzy was right and this group will actually help me—especially now that Estelle has gone.

CHAPTER 36
ESTELLE

One of the things I miss the most, apart from the lovely people, is surfing in Clearwater Bay. I can surf in Berkeley, but I have a half-hour drive to get to a beach with waves I feel comfortable with as a novice, and it's simply not the same.

There's no Devon with encouraging words in the water. There's no middle-aged ladies surf club with Sadie Ireland. There are no raucous drinks at The Bay afterward, followed by only a short stroll home.

It's hard to believe how deep the place has sunk into my bones after only a few months. The place *and* the people.

Picking up my life in Berkeley is easier said than done because ninety percent of it revolved around the university I no longer work for. My friends are as busy as I used to be, running from classes to meetings to office hours to more meetings while life just passes them by.

I've been texting with Hunter and Bobby, trying to set up a weekend in San Francisco, but they always have something going on.

Every time I go to a restaurant, I think of Savor and I think of Cass even more than usual. Her final words are like an echo in my brain and I've had to ask myself whether I really am a coward. Whether I should have given us another chance—something I was open to before she slept with Sadie's former makeup artist. Before she made it clear what she really wanted.

I've been back almost three weeks and every day I'm hit with the disconcerting sensation that this town, where I spent most of my life, no longer feels like home. I miss Clearwater Bay—the people, the place, the surf—so much more than I thought I would. Turns out, moving on didn't just equal moving back here.

My phone chimes with a message from Bobby, who texts me almost every day.

It's a picture of a rocking chair he made with the message:

What do you think? Suitable for Suzy's fiftieth?

With a much-needed smile on my face—messages from Bobby always have this effect on me—I text back that it's stunning, just like its maker.

He texts back almost immediately with a picture of himself in full party get-up: a hot pink tuxedo with satin lapels, sheer shirt underneath, and enough sparkle to make RuPaul weep.

The big do is this Saturday at Savor. Do I look the part or do I look the part?

I message back that I'm speechless and we go back and forth for a while and all I can think of is how much I'd like to be at Suzy's birthday party. How much fun it would be to see them all in their glad rags, chattering away, being merry, drinking too much. To see Suzy in her element as the belle of the ball. To see Cass…

But I'm no longer invited to the party.

I keep staring at Bobby's messages, as though if I look at them long enough, I'll miraculously be invited again. Or that he'll send me another message that says: *Estelle, please come. We miss you. Cass misses you.* But life's not like that. I know that much.

I toss my phone on the couch. The silence in my apartment is too loud. I haven't played music in days because every song seems to remind me of Cass somehow. Even the instrumental playlist I used to swear by while cooking —in order to focus on the food and not be distracted by too absorbing lyrics—somehow conjures up the image of her in the Savor kitchen, sleeves rolled up, chef's hat tall on her head, joy written all over her face as she taste-tested something off a spoon and asked me, "Tell me honestly, babe. Does it need more sass or just a little more Cass?"

How I miss her.

And not just her. I miss Suzy's unfiltered honesty. Hunter's one-liners. Bobby's outrageous commentary. How Sadie, just with her presence, made balancing on a board in the water so much easier.

In Berkeley, everything feels flat. Like I'm living in a paused scene, and someone forgot to hit play again. I'm so tired of pausing.

Maybe that's what cowardice really is—letting yourself linger in safe, familiar stillness instead of taking a leap into the messy unknown. Maybe Cass was right, after all.

I pick my phone back up. I open Bobby's message again and stare at the words:

The big do is this Saturday at Savor.

No one explicitly uninvited me, nor told me to stay away. Maybe the only person keeping me from going… is me.

I scroll through our old group messages—pictures from The Bay, from Devon and Sadie's backyard, from impromptu dinners at Cass's where the wine flowed too freely and we always ended up talking over each other.

I can already hear Suzy's loud cackle if I show up unannounced. She'll either hug me senseless or show me the door.

I open my calendar app. Saturday is blank—hardly a surprise. Should I take a leap and just go?

I sit back and let the idea settle. Because sometimes you don't need an explicit invitation. Sometimes, you just need to show up.

I drive to Clearwater Bay on Saturday morning. I've been awake since five o'clock, eager to get going. I contemplated texting Bobby and Hunter that I was coming, but I didn't want them to either make a big song and dance about it or, worse, convince me to stay away.

As I pass the town limits, my heart fills with something I've been missing in Berkeley. The feeling of home. Maybe it's because I grew up here. Or because my dad moved back after his retirement and spending time in his house cracked me open a little. Or maybe it's because as soon as I hit the main road, I see the ocean through the gaps between the houses and, at the far end, the restaurant on the cliff.

I can't blame myself for leaving, nor for coming back. I pull up to my dad's house and take a breath. I study it from the outside and it certainly needs some TLC. Not long before I left, Bobby came over and shared his ideas for the place and got very excited about its potential.

For the first time, I can see myself living here. I could walk to the beach for a daily surf, something Sadie and Devon swear by—according to them, a day not surfed is a day not lived. I can walk to Bobby and Hunter's for gay gossip. I can walk to The Bay for burgers… Burgers at The Bay will always remind me of Cass. But I hurt her and she hurt me. And we both have our hang-ups. Maybe she has forgotten about me already. She has a restaurant to run and a party to plan and friends to hang out with—and probably hot flashes and night sweats to suffer through.

I make my way inside and instead of seeing the dusty old interior, I see it the way Bobby described it to me. The way it could be. An accent wall here. Some glossy wallpaper there. A new kitchen turned this way, with a reading nook by the window.

Before I make a final decision, I owe Cass a conversation. Maybe Clearwater Bay is big enough for the two of us—although I may no longer be welcome at the best restaurant in town.

I do some much-needed cleaning, then put on my party outfit—nowhere near as audacious as Bobby's—and, my heart beating in my throat all the way there, head to Savor.

CHAPTER 37
CASS

Savor looks different again. We've removed most of the tables so there's room for a dance floor spacious enough for Bobby's exacting demands. There's a disco ball—obviously—and colorful spotlights, and if anyone was under the impression this was going to be a subdued fiftieth birthday party they would be very wrong. It's going to be a wild one, loud and boisterous, like its guest of honor.

My staff, who all love Suzy, are in charge of catering, and Sadie and Sam have hired plenty of wait staff to keep everyone topped up. It's been a joint effort to put this party together—and also a welcome distraction.

Bobby, in a hot-pink suit that only he can pull off, sidles up to me and says, "We did well, Mama Cass. Our Queen Suzy will be very pleased."

"She'd better be," I joke, although there isn't anything I wouldn't do for my best friend, who has, once again, been there for me every step of the way through this break-up.

There's no more time for contemplation because Sadie and Sam arrive with their sister in tow. Suzy marvels at what we've set up for her and it warms my sad, old broken heart to see my friend so happy.

The restaurant fills with people. Delicious food is served and champagne flows freely.

I'm in a quiet corner, chatting to Suzy's father Jack, when I wonder if I'm hallucinating. It can't be, yet I'm not so tipsy as to start conjuring images of people who aren't here. I squint and tilt my head. Obviously, I don't know all Suzy's friends, but she would have told me if one of her acquaintances was an Estelle lookalike. The hair. That gait. I only see her from the back, yet I know it's her.

"Excuse me, Jack." I make my way through the room, trying to find Hunter or Bobby, who have been in touch with her, so I can ask if they know anything about this.

But Estelle is already wrapped in Bobby's hot-pink arms and Hunter is grinning from ear to ear next to them. What is going on here?

Pulse racing, I head over. She looks gorgeous again and the corners of my mouth pull upwards as though they have a life of their own. It's possible that a subconscious part of me is happy to see her, even though the last three weeks have been blue and lonely and tinged with that gnawing feeling of a missed chance at something beautiful.

Estelle's gaze finds mine. "Hey." Her voice is still as sexy as ever.

"What a surprise," Bobby coos.

"Let's give them a minute, babe." Hunter pulls his husband away.

"I hope it's not too bad a surprise," Estelle says. "I haven't come to ruin your evening. I promise."

"I—um… I need a moment to process that you're here."

"Maybe we should talk in private for a few minutes?" Estelle suggests.

My heart doesn't know what to do with itself. This would also be the perfect moment for another well-timed hot flash to make its appearance.

"Let's go upstairs," I say.

I ignore the looks we get as we weave through the crowd to a side door into the hallway. Going up the stairs, the party noise isn't nearly loud enough to drown out my heart beating in my ears. I'm not sure if I'm excited or scared—maybe a bit of both.

August is appalled by the racket downstairs. He flicks his tail once and refuses to budge from his perch by the window.

"Are you still angry with me?" Estelle asks.

"I'm not angry, I'm just..." I thought she was angry with me for sleeping with Bijou and by doing so sending her some sort of secret message that only she could understand: that I no longer wanted her. But that's how it goes with your thoughts after a break-up. They swirl together into a jumble of all the things that went wrong until you can no longer make heads or tails of it. Or maybe I'm just terribly confused because she's standing in my living room right now. "Why are you here?"

"So many reasons."

Not just for me, then. Good to know. But still.

"I missed... everything." Her voice is so quiet, I can barely make it out over the noise from the party. "Most of all you, but, um, I know this is not the time or place for that conversation." She blows out some air. "It's hard to explain, but I just really wanted to be here. I can't find my groove in Berkeley and I just wanted to come back."

No big love declaration either. No big speech full of regret for how things turned out.

"Okay. Sure." I don't really know how to react.

"I don't usually do this," Estelle says. "I don't usually come back."

"Meaning?" My palms are sweaty.

"I know I hurt you and I'm truly sorry," she says. "I really miss you, but I haven't changed… or maybe I have, because why else am I here?"

She doesn't sound as though she has thought this through very much, but sometimes, that's how you make the best decisions.

"You did hurt me," I say. "By leaving. By cutting me off."

"I know." She pushes a strand of hair away from her face. "It's what I do. I see that now."

"I'm glad you're here." All my foolish heart needs is the tiniest glimmer of hope. And if nothing else, at least we can have one last epic party together.

"So am I," Estelle says. Her divine lips curve into a smile and I have to use all the restraint my body can muster to not bridge the distance between us, to not throw my arms around her and kiss her, but that's not what this is. From the start, we've been cautious, each for our own reasons, and that's also not going to change now. "I'd like to stay for a while, if that's okay with you."

"I don't have a problem with that." It figures that Estelle is not a grand gesture kind of person. But small gestures can have impact too.

"You should go back to the party," she says.

"Let's go back together." I do take a step toward her now.

"Yeah?" Her voice is soft as butter and her dreamy eyes pull me right back in.

"Yeah." I reach for her hand. "Let's party," I say. Like we never broke each other's hearts into a thousand pieces. We'll figure out the rest later.

The party is in full swing. Suzy's being twirled around by Sam to a nineties anthem from our youth that has everyone going wild. Bobby is vogueing solo under a spotlight, because of course he is.

Estelle and I slip into the crowd. Our fingers no longer touch but her presence is all I'm aware of.

Despite the vogueing, Bobby spots us first, his eyebrows nearly launching off his face. He beams like it's his own birthday and not Suzy's, who, when our gazes cross, gives me a look that says 'we'll talk later'.

The music changes to "Show Me Love" and it's as if a switch gets flipped to the next level of dance floor mayhem. Ah, the power of a good tune from when we were young and foolish and didn't know a thing about life —and couldn't care less about any of it.

Estelle turns to me and her expression is clear—must dance now. I let the music transport me for a few minutes, so the tension in my muscles can dissolve. I try not to stare at the way Estelle moves—effortless and unencumbered, like she's dancing only for herself. She's wearing a pair of jeans that cling in all the right places, and an emerald silk blouse that shimmers every time she turns under the lights. Her sleeves are rolled just high enough to show the sculpted line of her forearms.

There's a looseness to her shoulders, like she's finally

exhaled after holding her breath for weeks. She laughs at something Hunter says and tosses her head back, and that small motion—the flash of her throat, the sheen of her skin in the light—makes it impossible for me not to stare at her.

She's not putting on a show. That's not her style. She's just gorgeous, maddening Estelle and I'm trying my best to not come undone by her being here.

We dance with the group, with our friends, and for the length of the song, I forget the past three weeks. Then the beat changes. The tempo drops. The lights dim. Suzy's not going to like this because she hates them with a vengeance, but it's time for a slow dance to a romantic song.

Estelle catches my gaze. She steps toward me and, just like that, we move toward each other. As if our bodies can't possibly imagine doing anything else, her arms curl around my shoulders and mine around her waist. We sway and my cheek brushes the side of her face. Her body fits perfectly against mine—like we're both exactly where we belong.

We move slowly, the air between us thick with unspoken things. Her hand rests lightly at the back of my neck, her fingertips barely brushing my skin, but I feel them everywhere. I close my eyes and the scent of her pulls me under again. Because I've missed her so much.

Not just the shape of her body against mine or how she always knew how to handle me. I've missed *her*. The calm she brought. How she let me feel whatever I needed to, even when it was ugly—especially then. Her patience. Her stubborn and at times incomprehensible kindness. How she took me in her arms with all the love in the world, even when I was drenched in sweat after a hot flash. How could I have let her go? But it wasn't up to me.

I keep one arm around her waist, the other slides slowly down until our hands meet at our sides. Her fingers curl into mine without hesitation, and it's the gentlest touch I've felt in weeks.

I don't look at her face. I can't. If I do, I might very well burst into tears. So I keep my cheek resting against hers and try to memorize this moment: her breath at my temple, the steadiness with which she holds me like nothing ever happened, like we didn't fall apart.

She squeezes my hand softly. And I realize that no one's ever made me feel more at ease when I didn't have it together. No one's ever held my mess with such grace. I press my palm flat against her back and pull her just a little closer—like I never want to let her go again.

CHAPTER 38
ESTELLE

I never want this dance to end, because I have no idea what comes after. Cass might be appalled by what her body made her do—push herself so close to me. She might remember how I cast her aside—how my fear cast her aside—and say, "thanks, but no thanks, I've had enough of that."

Before our breakup, the loneliness, the anxiety, and the too familiar feeling of being misunderstood all combined to put me on the defensive. I shouldn't have got my hackles up; I should have waited to see where Cass and I might go, because all of my anger and loneliness was nothing compared to how I felt in Berkeley. Far away from her.

My brain spun it into me missing Clearwater Bay and all that came with it—the friendship and the surf and that warm feeling of being home—but what I really missed was Cass. What I really missed was this. My arms around her, our fingers interlocked, and that dizzy sensation in my belly when I'm with her without worrying.

The music stops abruptly and someone taps a microphone. Reluctantly, I let go of Cass. She looks at me sheepishly but there's no time for an emotional aftermath of our dance, because Suzy's brother, Sam, wants to make a speech.

"Sorry about that tender moment, Sis," Sam says. "I promise it won't happen again." Everyone laughs while Suzy pulls a horrified face.

Sam speaks for a few minutes, then hands the mic to Sadie, whom I've seen more in a wetsuit than in regular clothes. I can't wait for surf club on Monday.

I'm an only child so I'll never know what it feels like to have siblings speak about you the way Sam and Sadie speak of their sister. Suzy is positively beaming when it's her turn.

I glance at Cass as she watches her friend address the crowd. She's gorgeous with that huge smile on her face and her eyes all lit up like that. She looks like someone I don't want to run away from ever again. Even though what I told her earlier is true. I've always been a done-is-done kind of person. Life has made me so. I never go back for a second helping of hurt, for more of not being good enough. But I came back for her.

I can only hope she'll have me.

To no one's surprise, Suzy's speech is funny and ambling and long, but you only turn fifty once and it makes me think of my own fiftieth birthday later this year. All I want for that birthday is to be able to spend it with Cass. To make it that far with her. I have a long way to go, because we've only danced together so far. I haven't won her back yet, but I will try my utmost to make it happen.

We all give Suzy the generous applause she deserves. And of course I think about that time she came to see me, worried that I might hurt her friend. And I did hurt Cass. But I'm here to undo that.

"Hey, girl." Bobby grins at me. "Give it up for Bobby, please." He holds up his hand for a high five.

Confused, I slap my palm against his.

"I sent you that message for a reason," he says. "I was so subtle about the whole thing, I can barely believe it myself, but you're here. You came. All it took was one picture of me." He winks at me.

I chuckle, more than happy to give him credit for what he did. He's right. If he hadn't texted me about the party, the thought might not even have occurred to me to come.

"That was some next-level nudging," I admit.

Bobby leans toward me, all divine pink campness, and whispers in my ear, "Now go get your girl, damn it." He follows up with the kind of Bobby-hug I could grow accustomed to.

I glance around for Cass but she's chatting with the guest of honor. I have time to get my girl. I'm not going anywhere.

"Hey, stranger." Devon only needs a crisp white shirt to look dazzling. "Welcome back." She opens her arms to me and I gladly step into her embrace. As she holds me, I think that, even in the best possible scenario, I could not have dreamed of such a warm welcome.

"I saw you dancing with Cass earlier," Devon says. "From where I was standing, it looked as though you were both very much into it."

"I know what I feel, but I don't know what Cass is feeling." If anyone can give me some solid advice, it's Devon.

"How do you feel?" she asks, instead of giving me a few words of wisdom. "What's different?"

It's a fair enough question. "I guess I needed some

distance to really see what I was letting go of, what I was missing. I couldn't see it when I was still here, when I was in the middle of it."

"You had to go away in order to come back?" Devon asks.

"Something like that."

"I hope you can work it out." She smiles gently. "I really do."

I nod. "Me too."

The DJ turns up the music and it's like the entire surface of Savor instantly turns into a dance floor. Devon and I get swallowed up by a mass of writhing bodies and I can only hope that, somewhere in this sea of dancers, I will soon find Cass again.

I do find Cass and we dance together, with her friends—*our* friends—until the early hours. It's not a night for talking and I'm glad for it. It's good that we can have these euphoric moments together before we actually have a conversation.

When I check my watch for the first time, it's nearly three in the morning. I'm exhausted from the dancing, which my body is not used to, and the emotions, and the long day I had.

Cass is chatting to someone I don't know. The crowd has thinned but there are a few die-hards left on the dance floor.

"People our age don't go out dancing nowhere near enough," a familiar voice shouts into my ear.

"Our age?" I arch up my eyebrows as I look at Sadie. "You're five years younger than Suzy and me."

"As if that makes a difference." Sadie slings her arm around my shoulders. "I'm glad you're back. Surf club's not the same without you." She lets go and smiles wistfully. "Do you know that Dev and I reconnected at my fortieth? Birthday parties in Clearwater Bay seem to have some sort of special romantic power. Use it to your advantage."

"I was about to head home," I say.

"Find your second wind. Trust me. It will be worth it." Sadie grins at me, then shuffles onto the dance floor again. As soon as she clocks her, Devon wraps her arms around Sadie and they fall into a kiss that has Bobby ostentatiously fanning his face.

I'm not sure I have a second wind, but I only have to look at Cass in order to stay a little longer. I wait patiently until her chat ends, then walk up to her.

"You throw a great party," I say.

"My feet are fucking killing me," she sighs. "Shall we sit for a minute?"

I follow her to an area by the window—the same window I had my regular Friday night table at—where some chairs are set up.

"I'm exhausted and I'm drunk," she says, "and I'm also over the moon that you're here."

"Thank goodness." A smile spreads on my lips.

"I still like you so much…" She extends her hand, and I take it in mine. "I still think you're so special."

My tipsy brain is already beside itself. "Ditto," I say. "Can we talk. Properly. Soon."

"I'd like that." She sucks her bottom lip between her teeth. "Although all of tomorrow is booked for the worst hangover ever." She grins at me. "You might want to stay away from me for that."

"I've seen you in... various states." I'm pretty sure I can deal with hungover Cass.

She chuckles and gestures at me. "How come you still look so good?" She shakes her head. "I don't understand that about you." She points all her fingers at herself. "Look at me. I'm a disheveled, drunk mess while you look like you've just arrived."

"You must be wearing a very flattering pair of invisible glasses if that's how you see me."

"You're so fucking gorgeous." It almost sounds like an insult. "I know I've reacted to that in ways that weren't always very nice. I'm sorry about that. I can hardly hold your beauty against you. And how you don't suffer from the menopause. And how you pick up a surfboard and just get into the water with the likes of Sadie and Devon. And look damn good in a wetsuit while doing so."

It's unsure whether Cass is complimenting me or disparaging herself—maybe a little of both.

I slant toward her. "I'm not you and you're not me."

"I've had some time to think..." Her tipsiness is making her extra frank. "And it's possible that we are incompatible, but not for the reason you're so convinced we are."

"Okay." I guess we are already having the conversation.

"Bijou," she says on a sigh. "That was nothing, but you never gave me the chance to explain that to you. Yes, I slept with her. And yes—" She nods decisively. "I touched her in ways I can't touch you, but... it was an empty touch. It was soulless. I was so fucking drunk, anyway. It's not that I don't remember, but it was not memorable, you know? Not like every single time with you." Cass expels some air. "When you walked away, it made me see something I hadn't before. I could touch a hundred women and none of them would make me feel what I feel just being in the same room with you."

"But what about the reciprocity? The intimate vulnerability you miss with me?" I might as well ask her now that she's so forthcoming.

"Well, yeah, that's not there, but there are so many other things… It's no secret that I think you're too hot for me, too kind, too smart, too everything…"

"That's only because of how you feel about yourself at this particular time in your life," I reply.

"Maybe, but… I don't know." She chuckles. "You came back."

"I came back," I repeat, while slipping her hand in mine. "For you."

"I called you a coward." She pitches her body toward me.

"I was a coward."

"You were just hurt." Her face is less than an inch removed from mine. "I shouldn't have called you a coward."

"I hurt you too," I say.

"At least we're compatible when it comes to that." Her lips scrunch up. "That doesn't make any sense, does it?"

"It doesn't matter." I lean in. "None of it matters right now."

Cass's gaze flicks to my mouth and lingers there. Her breath brushes against my lips and the whole world stops. The music from the dance floor becomes distant and irrelevant. It's just us here in this secluded corner of Savor—in the exact spot where we first met.

I tilt my head just slightly, still unsure whether I should kiss her, although I can't see how I can possibly stop now.

Then, she bridges the final distance between us. Ever so slowly, as though she's making sure I can still change my mind. But this is all I want.

When her lips touch against mine I feel like I've truly come home. My fingers tighten around hers. Our kiss deepens. Her hand cups my cheek, her thumb caressing my jaw. Her lips taste of champagne and recklessness and the kind of hunger that only comes from waiting too long.

I lean into her more, into all of it. The rush and the ache. The impossible tenderness of what we're doing—because it is kind of impossible.

When we part, it's only because we need air.

"You really did come back for me," she whispers.

"I'm here for you *and* for your hangover tomorrow," I say.

"That doesn't surprise me about you one bit." Her voice falters. "It's exactly who you are and I fucking love you for it." She pulls me close and kisses me again.

CHAPTER 39
CASS

The morning after the party, I wake up with a splitting headache and a body that feels eighty-three instead of fifty-three—but none of it matters. I kissed Estelle. It was late—or early—and I was pretty tipsy but I remember every second of it. I remember my elation when I first spotted her. Our sensual slow dance. And, finally, that kiss. It's the best hangover cure ever, it would appear, because I feed August with a spring in my step and I brew a strong pot of coffee with nothing but possibilities on my mind.

I can't wait to see her so I text her—because I can.

An hour later, she turns up at my door with a box of cinnamon rolls from the bakery in town.

"There you are," I say, as I open the door to her. I take the box, put it on the sideboard, and pull Estelle into a long, warm hug—an even better hangover cure.

She grins at me when we break from our embrace. "I was worried you'd be more apprehensive."

"Fuck apprehensive," I say. Obviously, my brain is not running at full capacity, but maybe it's better that way.

"I like the sound of that," she says.

We settle in the kitchen with coffee and the pastries and all I want to do, when I sit across from her, is touch her—which brings us right to the crux of the matter.

"May I start?" Estelle asks.

I look into her eyes and nod.

"I want a relationship so bad, it always tends to backfire," she says. "And it's entirely possible that I'm not relationship material. That's what all the evidence points to, but… I'm still so in love with you, Cass." She rubs a fingertip against her temple. "My hangover really isn't helping my speech, but I hope I'm getting my point across, which is that I fucked up and I'm sorry and I hope you will give me another chance, even though I ran away the minute things got tricky."

"But you came back."

"I couldn't stay away," she says. "My life is different now. I can't bury myself in work in order not to have to deal with my feelings. All I have is time and time has taught me a thing or two."

"Such as?"

"If I want a relationship to have a chance, I have to let go of certain preconceived notions—like that I will never be good enough for one. Notions I very much like to make the other party feel responsible for." She casts her gaze down. "I do realize that, but… at least I can see it now."

"You're more than good enough for me," I say.

"I have to believe that. I have to believe *you*… it's not easy and it's not going to happen just like that, but as you said that day I ended things, we have time, and I'd like to take that time. With you. If you'll have me."

"If I'll have you?" I know what it's like to act a certain way because of how you feel about yourself deep down—

and to be completely unable to stop, even when you know why you're doing it. I don't feel good enough for her either, albeit for different reasons. So I try not to say something self-deprecating and, instead, I reply, "I don't know how any of this will play out, but I do know one thing for sure." I pause. "My life is so much better with you in it."

Estelle beams a wide smile, but then she becomes serious again. "For the longest time," she says, "I tried to make myself believe that the desire for a relationship would just go away. That if I kept busy enough, filled every moment with something useful, or loud enough to drown it out, it would fade. That the need for closeness would disappear—the longing for someone who stays. Someone with whom I could feel safe. Someone who truly sees me, and still wants to be there. I thought it would simply wither if I starved it of my attention." She lets out a trembling breath. "But that need didn't go away. So I pushed it down, deep into that place where I keep all the things I don't know how to deal with. And then I built something over it. Something hard and solid. I laid concrete all over it. Reinforced. With iron bars, just to be sure my silly, impossible desire wouldn't rise up again when I wasn't paying attention." Her eyes meet mine again. "But then I met you. And I didn't want it buried anymore. I wanted you, instead." She pauses. "That scared the hell out of me. That's really why I ran away." She looks me straight in the eye. "Because an open heart makes a hell of an easy target."

There are so many things I want to say. I want to respond in kind to her beautiful display of vulnerability—and here I was accusing her of being incapable of that, as though it's only possible fully naked in bed—but I have to let her continue.

Estelle inhales deeply, then slowly exhales, as though she's been waiting a very long time to speak the next words.

"Today," she says, "I'm giving you the demolition permit." Her gaze stays on mine. "You're the only one I trust with it. The only one I want holding the jackhammer." It's almost too much when she looks me straight in the eye—like I'm the one with intimacy issues now. "We've already cracked the surface. You've already broken through that first layer, turning it into rubble, piece by piece." A tiny smile reaches her lips. "Now I'm bringing you the rest. These leftover chunks of reinforced concrete I've been living under. I want them gone."

I don't say anything—I don't think I could if I tried.

"I will admit." Her smile widens. "With big demolition works like that, things might get messy."

"You're here for my mess, I'm here for yours."

"Let's talk about you." Her voice is soft and everything about her is inviting and completely unguarded.

"Thank you for sharing that with me." What Estelle just told me is so much more emotionally satisfying than a night of sex with a stranger can ever be.

Her smile transforms into a grin. "I'm considering renovating my dad's house, hence the building metaphor."

"Building?" I arch up my eyebrows. "Sounds more like destruction to me." I reach my hands across the table. "Lucky I'm in possession of a jackhammer now." I slip my fingers between hers. "Thank goodness this gorgeous woman from Berkeley just gave me one."

We both chuckle, and it truly feels like we can just take it from here. That, somehow, we've arrived at a place where we're both comfortable and can be honest and can build something strong enough to withstand the inevitable hot flashes and further conversations about all the reasons we don't feel good enough.

"What about you?" Estelle asks, our fingers still firmly interlocked. "What do you want? Are there any power tools you'd like to give me?"

I grin at her and maybe it's the hangover or the vulnerability she has just shown me, or the memory of how she danced last night, before she kissed me again, but I only want one thing.

"No, but, um, I'm trying to be less of a giver these days, anyway." I wait to see how my quip lands.

"Not even a kiss?" She flicks her tongue over her lips.

"I'm still in training, so a kiss is most certainly still on offer." I get up and walk over to her. By the time I reach her side of the table, she has pushed her chair back, and I straddle her, a little awkwardly but unable to care about how it looks, because I only care about one thing. Her lips on mine—and what comes after.

We kiss and there's nothing tentative about it. It's not like last night when we were still uncertain about each other's reaction. Still, I break from it and trace a path to her ear.

"I'd really like for you to fuck me now," I whisper, and I don't think it's inappropriate in the least. Not anymore. In fact, it feels like something I should say right now.

She did ask me what I wanted.

"I like looking at you like this," Estelle says. Her voice has that husky quality that makes my body temperature rise to dangerous heights.

Her hands are careful but unflinching as she undoes

the buttons of my shirt, her gaze trailing over every inch of skin she reveals. Because she's the only one doing the touching, it's deliberate and focused.

"Part of me still can't believe you're really here again," I whisper, and it's true. After all that's happened, this feels impossible.

She leans in and brushes her lips against the skin of my throat. "It's truly the only place I want to be."

My shirt falls to the floor, and I don't feel self-conscious about my fifty-three-year-old body. Not with her—not anymore. Her hands glide up my arms, her thumbs circling just under my collarbones, and I could come undone from that alone.

With Estelle, nothing's ever rushed. It's all slow intention and I'm deliciously drowning in it. Her mouth finds the hollow at the base of my neck, lingering there, and I close my eyes.

By the time she's got me laid back, stripped down to nothing but longing and goose bumps, I'm already breathless.

She's taken off as much of her clothing as she ever will, and she straddles me. She's all over me again and, today, I actually love that she's not asking for anything but is giving me everything.

"I want to make you feel good," she whispers—and who doesn't want to hear that?

I nod, not trusting my voice. When her tongue flicks over my nipple and her hand traces lower, I feel like I'm being put back together somehow. Like she's found all my broken pieces and is assembling them carefully, without instruction.

And then she licks me. Her tongue is firm and slow, right against the center of everything I am. Her hands rest on my hips, anchoring me gently. Her tongue works in lazy circles at first, then quickens, responding to the rhythm my body dictates.

When I come, it's a full-body unraveling. It's the grief I've held in my muscles and the want I never thought I'd feel again. It's Estelle's name in my throat. It's not just release. It's surrender. To her. To us. To something I didn't think I'd get to feel again.

CHAPTER 40
ESTELLE

I lie next to Cass, our legs tangled, my body still, but thrumming underneath. It's not a high. It's definitely not arousal. It's not even pride. It's something gentler and more grounded.

Cass is silent beside me. Her fingers draw slow, meandering lines on my arm. I don't want her to stop. But this is always the most precarious part—after. When I'm wide open in ways others don't always understand.

I don't feel desire the way she does. Not physically. But I feel something else. A pull in my chest so strong it threatens to tear me in two. I want to give this to her. Not to prove something, but because I'm in love with her. Because as far as love and romance are concerned, we are very much alike.

She turns toward me, her eyes a little glassy. "Are you okay?" she whispers.

I nod. "Absolutely fine." I close my eyes for a few moments, because I don't feel the need to look for signs of what she wants and I can't give. Not today, and hopefully not ever again—although that's the kind of wishful thinking only a hungover, lazy brain can truly believe in.

But it's different today. Her unspoken excitement doesn't radiate off her any longer.

Cass tucks a piece of hair behind my ear. "Thank you for that," she says, grinning from ear to ear.

"My pleasure." I turn fully toward her so I can see her gorgeous face.

"Can I ask you one of my annoying questions?"

"I told you," I say with a smile in my voice. "There's no such thing as an annoying question when it comes to this." Because I know what the subject of her question will be. I always know and it's okay.

"Wait until I've asked it." She traces the edge of my ear.

"Be my guest." I've never had an issue talking about being ace, only with dealing with other people's expectations.

"What it's like for you when you, um, lick me. When you make me come. What do you feel?"

"It makes me feel connected to you," I say.

"But physically," she asks. "There's nothing?"

"No," I say truthfully—a dangerous admission, but if I can't say it now, our reunion won't stand much chance.

Her face doesn't change, but I've learned not to guess what the other person's thinking. I continue before her thoughts can run away with her.

"I used to think I had to fake it," I say. "That no one would stay with me if I didn't act all lustful in return and let them touch me."

"That's terrible," Cass says.

"I went off that pretty quickly, because it *is* terrible and, for me, not doable, although I'm sure a lot of women—asexual or not—do it often enough."

"Promise me you'll never fake anything for me."

"You have my word because it's impossible." I manage a grin, but it's not as though all my insecurities have miraculously dissolved. "Can I ask you an annoying question?"

"Always." Her hand glides to my shoulder and settles there.

"You said that it didn't mean anything with Bijou. That it was soulless and I get that, but… what did it feel like in your body? To touch her like that?"

Cass makes a sound halfway between a sigh and a scoff "You're right. That *is* a very annoying question."

"You never have to sugarcoat for me, babe."

"It's not a matter of sugarcoating anything." Is that a hint of exasperation in her voice? She did say my question was annoying—and it is. "I'm just not a hundred percent sure of what you're asking me with that question. What it is you really want to know."

"Is it something that you think you'll want again? To be with another woman in that way?"

"What?" Cass shakes her head. "Babe, you're doing it again."

"Yeah. I am." Fuck. I know I am. I'm projecting my insecurities onto her again.

"Okay. Look." Cass takes a breath. "To answer your question painfully honestly." She's regained her calm and speaks softly. "Yes. I will want that again, but that's okay. I don't need to have every single thing I want. For instance, I'd very much like to be able to lose weight from eating burgers at The Bay. Can I have that? No, I can't. I can have the burger, but I can't lose weight by eating it. I know that and it's perfectly fine." She slides her hand down and grabs mine. "I can have you which is, just to be clear, a million times better than having a burger at The Bay…" She pauses. "Although watching you eat one truly is a feast and does make me feel like I'm getting everything I've ever wanted in life." She throws in a chuckle. "But I'm getting off track."

"You really are." I hold on tightly to her fingers. "What were we talking about again? Did you just pull off the greatest distraction of all time?"

"And I didn't even have to cook you a meal for it." She catches my leg between hers. "By the way, I'm making you the best grilled cheese of your life later."

"Are you sure you don't want to get a burger at The Bay instead?" I ask.

"How dare you prefer someone else's food over mine." Her eyes narrow. I still have no idea what she's thinking and that, too, is something I have to accept.

"Are we good?" I ask, my voice much more serious than what our conversation evolved into, because my question isn't about burgers or grilled cheese sandwiches anymore.

Cass smiles, then her expression softens. "Before you left, I kept saying I'd get used to it, like I could will myself into being okay with it all. But I was still looking for a loophole. Now I'm just here. With you. No workarounds. No pretending." Her smile turns into a grin. "So, yes, I think we're very good." She tilts her head. "Although I can only speak for myself, but you've been back for almost twenty-four hours and I haven't had a hot flash yet."

"Only an orgasm," I joke, but inside, I'm smiling—because of what she just said.

"I'm sure that somewhere among the countless scientific studies on menopause, someone has investigated the effect of orgasms on hot flashes and concluded they provide significant relief, so..."

"So?" This is how I know for sure we're good. Cass doesn't tiptoe around me being asexual. It doesn't stop her from asking what she wants—and from referencing a joke we shared at the beginning of our relationship.

"So, how about we conduct our very own case study on the impact of two orgasms within the span of an hour on the frequency of hot flashes in a fifty-three-year-old woman over the next twenty-four hours?" Cass continues.

"That's an awfully complicated way for you to ask me to fuck you again."

"Just doing my bit for science," Cass says, but she can't keep a smile from lighting up her face.

"Where do you keep your lube again?" I reply. "We're going to need it this time around."

CHAPTER 41
CASS
TWO MONTHS LATER

Hunter, Suzy, and I are sitting on the deck of The Bay. I'm wearing a sweater against the early autumn chill in the air, but Sadie's surfer ladies don't seem to care about the cold.

"Estelle's getting really good," Hunter says. "Not bad for a woman her age." He's simply unable to give a compliment without tacking on a backhanded remark. I've always known this about him—and while I accept it, I still give him grief for it every chance I get.

"At least she's out there," Suzy says, surprising me. "Unlike you."

"We're the land rats," Hunter says. "You'd tear me to pieces with your sharp land rat's teeth if I only tried on a wetsuit."

"Excuses. Excuses," Suzy says.

Estelle hasn't tried getting me on a surfboard again. She surfs almost every day now and she talks about how it benefits her often, but as we've established many times, I'm not her and she's not me.

Hunter's phone rings, and I take the opportunity to gawk at Estelle, much like I did in this same spot when I first became aware of her. Things couldn't be more different now. We're together and even though our journey has had its bumps in the road—still has from time to time—we're solid.

"Bobby's joining us soon," Hunter says, putting down his phone. "He says that if his boss lady can be out surfing with her menopausal friends, he can stop busting his mighty fine ass in her father's house."

"It's only you who calls surf club menopausal," Suzy says. "Bobby's evolved enough to not use language like that."

"That's only because he has a massive woman crush on Estelle," Hunter says.

At first, I was a little apprehensive when Estelle and Bobby started hatching plans to renovate her dad's house together. Bobby makes furniture and Estelle's a mathematician—what could possibly go wrong? But apart from being excellent with numbers, Estelle's also very good with her hands—something I can most certainly attest to. And they get on so well, they finish each other's sentences now when they talk about the house.

Estelle has a project she can put her energy into and she's working with a friend. Bobby adores her and enjoys rising to the challenge of making Daddy Raymond's dusty old dwelling into a gorgeous abode—his words. And I get to have Estelle live with me during the renovations and, if all goes well, hopefully have her stay afterward. We're those lesbians now.

But it's pure heaven when I go upstairs after a long service and she's waiting for me, cozily curled up in a chair with August in her lap. It's not something I believed was still in the cards for me after Sarah left, but here we are. All it took was a stubborn, brilliant, asexual woman to waltz into town and sweep me off my feet.

I still refuse to take hormone therapy and I have regular hot flashes and night sweats and I have to pluck my chin every other day, but I also attend Suzy's weekly support group at Savor and—surprise, surprise—it's really helpful to simply talk about the discomforts of the menopause but also about the unexpected joys. Upon most attendees' suggestion, we've swapped the tea for wine and we have a good laugh every single week. It helps with the mood swings and the hormonal outbursts the rest of the time.

My gaze is drawn to Estelle again, as it always is when she's around—I shouldn't even think this, but between all the surfing and tearing down walls in her father's house, she's gotten even hotter—and a smile tugs at my lips.

Even though I'll never get to touch her the way she touches me—which can be damn hard at times—it's something I can live with because what I get in return for simply being with Estelle—for the huge privilege of being her partner—is beyond measure. It's not a matter of tolerating her asexuality—a thought, she has admitted, terrifies her at times—but simply of recognizing that, just like me, she's human. She has her hangups and her quirks and things she doesn't do no matter what, and so do I. I don't surf. I barely swim, although, a few weeks ago, on one of those utterly gorgeous Clearwater Bay late summer days, she dragged me to the cove beneath the cliff Savor is perched on and the two of us swam naked in the Pacific Ocean—a thrill I won't soon forget because Estelle took off all her clothes for me.

It was more foreplay than anything, because I'm a sexual person again. I still think my body is too big and it doesn't comply with what I want it to do more often than not, but her presence, and how she treats me with respect and patience and—always—endless kindness, makes it so I don't hate my body like I used to any longer. How can I when it gives me such unexpected and profound pleasure?

I no longer think of myself as a failure at romantic relationships. The other day, I saw Sarah and her wife strutting along the boardwalk. Sarah was very pregnant and both of them were beaming with the happiness I couldn't give Sarah. Instead of stinging, it made me genuinely happy, too.

"I'm not joking," Hunter says. "For once." He sends me a smirk. "If we were all twenty years younger, Bobby would want to have a baby with Estelle like I had one with Devon." He shakes his head. "And to be perfectly honest, I'm not sure he'd want to turkey baste the whole thing, if you know what I mean."

"I'm so glad you're not joking," I say.

"You know me," Hunter says drily. "I'm the serious one of the group."

"Speak of the devil," Suzy says.

"Hello, ladies." Bobby sags into a chair. "What are we talking about?"

"Your woman crush on Estelle." Hunter blows his husband a kiss.

"I'm so happy she came back." Bobby finds my gaze. "Thank you, Cassie."

I blow him a kiss as well because there's no telling what would have happened if Bobby hadn't coaxed Estelle to Suzy's party, although I'd like to believe she would have come back regardless. Because we belong together.

CHAPTER 42
ESTELLE
THREE MONTHS LATER

I got exactly what I wanted. How, I still don't know, but I'm celebrating my fiftieth birthday with Cass, and our friends, in Clearwater Bay.

It's not a huge bacchanal like Suzy had for her fiftieth, but it's more than I could ever have dreamed of. Cass has made us a delicious dinner at our home. A few of my friends from Berkeley have made the trip and every single one of them has complimented me on how relaxed and wholesome I look.

"You're positively glowing," my former colleague Diane says, wine glass in hand. "Whatever they're putting in the water here, I need to bottle it and take it back to Berkeley."

"It's not the water," I say, feeling Cass's eyes on me from across the room. "It's the company."

"And the surfing," Sadie chimes in, raising her glass. "Our student has become the master."

"Hardly," I laugh. "I still wipeout at least once per session."

"But you get back up," Devon adds. "That's what counts."

Surfing life completely agrees with me, although with winter approaching, I spend much more time indoors with Cass and Gussie.

Despite some inevitable snafus, Bobby and I are having a great time renovating my father's house. His taste in interior design is much more moderate than his taste in clothes and we always manage to meet somewhere in the middle of the bling and color he likes and the more demure tones—or as Bobby tends to call it: more beige-boring-beige—I prefer.

Working with him, taking everything one step at a time, slowly dismantling the house I grew up in, has been an extra blessing, on top of what being with Cass and surfing have done for me.

For all his grandstanding, Bobby likes to really think things through. We've tentatively started talking about going into business together, flipping houses, but we'll see. I had no idea this is where life would take me after my father died and I have no idea where it will take me next.

I do know that, if she'll have me—and I think she will—I want to stay with Cass. Beautiful, warm-hearted Cass. She has her good days and her bad days, but don't we all? The other night, during a night sweat, she yelled she was going to sleep in the walk-in freezer at the restaurant. I barely managed to talk her out of it.

My own periods have become increasingly irregular, but, to Cass's frustration, although I know she's secretly happy for me, I don't seem to suffer much from peri-menopause. According to Suzy, I'm one of only a very lucky few—not an experience I'm used to in my life. Although I got more than lucky with Cass.

Whenever the opportunity arises, I take my seat at the table by the window at Savor, like I did when I first arrived here, and Cass woos me with her exquisite food all over again. It's one of the small-but-big pleasures of my life these days—so, yes, how lucky am I?

I glance around the table, filled with my friends, Cass beside me, and I do—in every fiber of my being—feel like I'm enough. I'm plenty for everyone here. For Sadie and Devon who are my teachers on the waves but, much more than that, who have become friends I can always confide in. For Suzy, who is such a great friend to Cass, she has, by some sort of special osmosis, also become mine. For Hunter and Bobby, the most hilarious gays in all of Northern California, who crack me up on a daily basis.

"To my gorgeous bestie Estelle!" Bobby raises his glass, his voice as loud as his bright yellow shirt. "Who proved, as the gifted mathematician she is, once and for all, that lesbian plus lesbian equals U-Haul!"

Everyone laughs, including me.

"We didn't move in that quickly," I protest, feeling my cheeks warm—because we kind of did.

Most of all, I'm enough for Cass. I know because she tells me every day. And, maybe, for the first time in my life, I'm enough for me. For years, I managed to convince my logical mind, with carefully constructed reasoning, that I was. But the mind alone isn't enough. My heart took its time, but it caught up eventually—because of Cass. Because of how she sees me, accepts me, and loves me exactly as I am.

My gaze wanders to the sideboard where the notebook with the problem my father left me gathers dust. I haven't picked it up in weeks because I've finally accepted that Richard Raymond played one last prank on me. I'll never know whether it was deliberate or not, but I can choose to believe my father set me an unsolvable problem to delight me and, perhaps, teach me one final lesson before he passed. That most things in life are not neat like a perfectly solvable math problem. That solutions are sometimes hard to come by, and that's okay. Not every problem needs to be solved. The world keeps on turning. Life keeps on going.

Tonight, my life includes a second slice of birthday cake, Bobby demanding a Madonna playlist, and Cass reaching for my hand under the table, like she always does when we sit next to each other.

And—this is a lesson I learned all by myself—it's all so much more fun with a wonderful woman by my side.

GET THREE E-BOOKS FOR FREE

Building a relationship with my readers is the very best thing about writing. I occasionally send newsletters with details on new releases, special offers and giveaways.

And if you sign up to my mailing list I'll send you all this free stuff:

1. An e-book of *Few Hearts Survive,* a Pink Bean Series novella that is ONLY available to my mailing list subscribers.
2. A free e-book of *Hired Help,* my very first (and therefore very special to me) lesbian erotic romance story.
3. A free e-book of my first 'longer' work, my highly romantic novella *Summer's End,* set on an exotic beach in Thailand.

You can get *Few Hearts Survive* (a Pink Bean Series novella), *Hired Help* (a spicy F/F novelette) and *Summer's End* (a deeply romantic lesfic novella) **for free** by signing up at www.harperbliss.com/freebook/ or scanning the QR code below

ABOUT THE AUTHOR

Harper Bliss is your go-to author for emotional and steamy sapphic romance, delivering stories that resonate with readers who crave love, passion, and a touch of drama.

Beloved series like French Kissing and Pink Bean have captivated fans around the globe with their unforgettable characters and heartfelt journeys.

Recently, Harper has been creating the BlissVerse—a universe of interconnected celebrity romance stories, all loosely set in the same world.

After years of adventure in Hong Kong and beyond, Harper now writes from Ghent, her favourite Belgian city, where she lives with her wife, Caroline, and their high-maintenance cat, Dolly Purrton.

Harper loves hearing from readers and you can reach her at the email address below.

www.harperbliss.com
harper@harperbliss.com

www.ingramcontent.com/pod-product-compliance
Ingram Content Group UK Ltd.
Pitfield, Milton Keynes, MK11 3LW, UK
UKHW040935270825
7595UKWH00015B/97

9 789464 339574